D0282498

# STRACHEY'S FOLLY

The Donald Strachey Mysteries
by Richard Stevenson

*Death Trick*

*On the Other Hand, Death*

*Ice Blues*

*Third Man Out*

*Shock to the System*

*Chain of Fools*

*Strachey's Folly*

Richard Stevenson

# STRACHEY'S FOLLY

*A Donald Strachey Mystery*

*St. Martin's Press ✦ New York*

 For information, address St. Martin's Press, 175 Fifth Avenue, New York, N.Y. 10010.

**Library of Congress Cataloging-in-Publication Data**

Stevenson, Richard

Strachey's folly : a Donald Strachey mystery / by Richard Stevenson. — 1st ed.

p. cm.

ISBN 0-312-18669-X

1. Strachey, Donald (Fictitious character)—Fiction. 2. Private investigators—New York (State)—Albany—Fiction. 3. Gay men—New York (State)—Albany—Fiction. I. Title

PS3569.T4567S76 1998

813'.54—dc21 98-5326

CIP

First Edition: July 1998

10 9 8 7 6 5 4 3 2 1

*To Bill and Jeannette Herrick*

The jist of the opening scene of this fictional story was suggested to me by Mike Learned, one of the estimable former Peace Corps volunteer gang, to whom I am grateful.

# 1

"This is screwy. This is nuts. This has to be some kind of pathetic, sick joke!" Maynard Sudbury unexpectedly blurted out.

Timothy Callahan and I stared at Maynard as he stared down with a look of shocked bewilderment at one particular panel in the AIDS Memorial Quilt.

"Jim Suter is not dead," Maynard said, gawking. "I don't think he's even sick. I saw him in Mexico not more than two weeks ago."

Maynard brushed away the shock of sandy-colored hair that had flopped across his ever-youthful Midwestern farmboy's face. It seemed as if he needed the clearest vision possible in order to take in and try to comprehend this shocking sight.

Just a few cottony clouds were strung out across a pale sky, and the sun was surprisingly warm for D.C. in October. At midday the Washington Monument cast a short shadow, none of it touching any of the forty thousand–plus panels of the Names Project quilt. The tens of thousands of visitors to the Columbus Day–weekend quilt display were silent or spoke to one another in low voices as loudspeakers broadcast a solemn recitation by grieving survivors of the names of the AIDS dead. Every two or three minutes a jet en route to National Airport screeched down an electronic flight path above the nearby Potomac, but no one seemed to mind the noise. Most of the people were too absorbed in remembering—lovers, pals, sisters, brothers, daughters, sons, parents—or too caught up in one or another of the life stories, depicted or sketched, of people cut down by the plague.

A tanned, middle-aged woman with a bandage across the bridge of her nose and two younger women who bore what looked like a family resemblance to each other and to the older woman turned and peered at Maynard. They saw a short, muscularly lean, fifty-year-old man with a thick head of unruly hair, an open, expressive face, and intense brown eyes that were now full of angry perplexity.

Again, Maynard said disgustedly, "This is just so screwy. I can't figure out what the heck this panel could possibly be doing here."

Timmy and I, along with the three nearby women, looked down at the panel and then back at Maynard, whose outburst was not just out of sync with the sweet melancholy of the occasion but out of character for Maynard, one of the most subdued and even-tempered men I had ever known. Timmy had been Maynard's friend since their Peace Corps days in India in the late sixties, and, during our twenty years together, Timmy had often spoken, when Peace Corps stories were told, of Maynard's famous sangfroid.

Maynard Sudbury was a man who had once talked a small mob, one man at a time, out of beating an Andhra Pradesh taxi driver to death after the driver had struck and badly injured a cow. Maynard had accomplished this feat while employing no fewer than three languages: English, Hindi, and Telugu. The regional Peace Corps director had later admonished Maynard, telling him he had been lucky the mob hadn't left him broken and bloody as well—or, if the mob hadn't, then the police.

Maynard, Timmy said, had displayed the same equanimity with the Peace Corps staff man that he had with the street mob. He explained that it was not his rationality that had saved the driver, and certainly not his Peace Corps training, but that it had been his naïveté. He had been living in rural India only a few weeks when the incident took place, he said, and—having spent his entire life up until then in small-town Southern Illinois—he had acted on impulse, and at the moment of Maynard's intervention the villagers had looked upon him as some kind of holy fool, and they let the driver go. Later, Maynard once told me, some of the same people came to regard him as an unholy fool, but that was another story.

"Maybe," Timmy said to Maynard tentatively, "this panel is for another Jim Suter, not the one you know. Who is Jim Suter, anyway?"

As the quiet throngs continued to circulate among the maze of quilt sections, the three nearby women stood and watched us, and a burly young man in a University of Tennessee T-shirt, who had paused by the Suter panel, seemed also to be interested in our small drama.

"Suter's a Washington freelance writer and conservative political operative," Maynard said. "Jim and I had a brief, torrid romance about fifteen years ago that didn't last. Jim was in his mid-twenties at the time and still in his caveman mode of spreading his sperm around. I was old enough by then to want to start nest-building, and anyway, we had some serious political differences. It was a real Carville-Matalin match, except there was no way this one was ever going to last."

The three women next to us walked on now, quietly murmuring to one another, and they were replaced by a young, whiffle-haired, apparently lesbian couple in huge farm overalls and with rings in their noses. The beefy Tennessean stayed on and gazed down at the Jim Suter quilt panel along with Maynard, Timmy, and me.

I said, "It does look, Maynard, as if this Jim Suter was a writer—like the one you knew."

*"Is* a writer," Maynard said flatly, "like the one I *know.* Jim sure wasn't dead when this panel was sewn into the quilt—the panel submission deadline for the main part of the display was last spring sometime. Jim wasn't dead two weeks ago, and I'll bet you he isn't dead now."

"And those look like his dates?" Timmy said. "Or date?"

"I think they are," Maynard said. "The birth date anyway."

The standard coffin-shaped, four-by-six-foot cloth panel with Jim Suter's name and the dates "1956–1996" on it was a plain black fabric with white Gothic lettering. Unlike so many of the colorful and even affectionately whimsical quilt panels spreading for acres around us, Suter's panel was stark and funereal except for a sketch of a typewriter, encased in clear plastic and sewn on, with typed pages streaming out of the typewriter and up toward Suter's name and dates.

Timmy got down on his hands and knees for a closer inspection and reported up to us, "These look like manuscript pages, but I don't recognize what they're from. What kind of writer was Jim Suter? *Is.*"

"He's a freelance, right-wing political hack," Maynard said, as if this were a standard inside-the-Beltway job classification.

Maynard got down beside Timmy—we were all wearing khakis and light sport shirts—and I joined them as they examined the manuscript pages stitched to the panel and appearing to fly out of the picture of a typewriter. At the top of each page was the slug "Suter/Krumfutz" and a page number.

"This looks like Jim's campaign bio of Betty Krumfutz," Maynard said. "Jeez, what a cruel thing to do to a writer. We've all written things for money that we'd rather forget about. But congressional campaign biographies commissioned by a candidate represent about as low a form of literary endeavor as exists in the English-speaking world. Dead or alive, I don't think Jim ever did anything bad enough to deserve to be remembered this way. Although I know from experience that Jim was what I would call ethically challenged in some areas of life, and I know there are people around Washington, mostly gay men, whose opinion of Jim is rather low, mainly for personal reasons."

Maynard sprang back upright, and Timmy and I climbed back to our feet with more effort. He was the fittest of the three of us, although Maynard had joked the night before, when he met our train from Albany, that he maintained his youthful, lean physique with the aid of the intestinal parasites he picked up while writing the sixteen travel pieces that had been collected in *Around the World by Yak and Kayak.* Maynard had been doing more conventional, less adventurous travel writing over the past year, but he'd been unable to shake the bugs he'd picked up in—he thought—Zambia, Burkina Faso, or possibly Kyrgyzstan. He said he'd gladly learn to live with a nice set of love handles if he could rid himself of a persistent queasiness and regain his appetite for food that was spicier than New England boiled dinners or Congolese *fufu*.

Timmy said, "I suppose it would have been okay to be doing Republican campaign bios for, say, Abraham Lincoln or Teddy Roosevelt. But having worked for Betty Krumfutz certainly isn't what you'd want in your hometown obituary. I mean, if you were actually dead. Which you say Jim Suter isn't."

"Are the Krumfutzes behind bars yet?" I asked. Betty Krumfutz had been a Pennsylvania Republican congresswoman who had run on a "pro-family, pro-gun" platform in 1992, and even as Bill Clinton carried the state, she had easily replaced the retiring incumbent in her conservative upstate district. It came out, though, a year after her reelection in 1994 that both Mrs. Krumfutz's first- and second-term campaigns had been financed by illegal contributions from a Central Pennsylvania construction magnate, among others, and ineffectually laundered by the candidate's husband and campaign manager, Nelson—who had in any case, secreted half the five hundred and sixty thousand dollars in donations in an account he kept under his mistress's name, Tammy Pam Jameson, in a bank in Log Heaven, Pennsylvania, the Krumfutzes' hometown.

"Both Krumfutzes are out walking the streets right now," Maynard said. "Nelson was convicted in May but is free on bond while his conviction is appealed, and Betty was never charged with anything. She surprised everybody and resigned her congressional seat after she swore at a three-hour news conference last year that she'd been grievously wronged along with her constituents and she would never give up her seat. Then, when Betty quit abruptly, the speculation around town was that somebody had gotten the goods on her, too, and an indictment was imminent. None ever came, but people I know on the Hill are still waiting for the other Krumfutz shoe to drop. Nelson's a crook and Betty could well be. It's really an indication of how unprincipled Jim Suter could be—not just reactionary, but unprincipled—that he ever got mixed up with the god-awful Krumfutzes."

"But maybe he didn't know," Timmy said, "that they were crooks—or Nelson was—when he signed on with them. Didn't that all come out later?"

"Timothy, you're as charitable as ever," Maynard said. Then he went on gravely, "Jim didn't know the Krumfutzes were crooks, but he knew they had won an election partly by smearing the moderate-Republican fish-and-game official who ran against Betty in the 1992 spring primary. I ran into Jim in a bar right after he signed up with Betty and Nelson, and he said one of the tactics they'd used against this hapless fellow was, the guy had accepted a campaign donation from a Penn State gay group, and Betty and Nelson ran television ads showing two male officers of the group chastely kissing at the end of a gay-pride parade in Pittsburgh. The ad asked if this was what parents wanted taught to their children in local schools—as if Betty's opponent had come out for same-sex kissing instruction to be added to Pennsylvania's public school curricula. Jim *knew* the Krumfutzes had done this, and he still went to work for them."

Timmy said, "That does reflect poorly."

The crowds viewing the quilt continued to move by and around us. Some people stopped at quilt panels nearby and spoke quietly. Some pointed, some gazed with fierce concentration, some people hugged one another and wept. The two young lesbians beside us moved on, as did the man from Tennessee. The recitation of the thousands of names went on and on.

I asked Maynard, "If Jim Suter was such a creep, what attracted you to him fifteen years ago? Or was he less of a reprehensible character back then?"

Maynard blushed faintly. "The attraction was mainly physical. I mean, it wasn't *just* that. Jim is smart and knowledgeable and, despite a cynicism I eventually got pretty tired of, Jim can be fascinating on American political history and Washington history. He actually grew up here in the District. But I realize now that the attraction was mostly sexual. He had a great athlete's body—he'd been a wrestling star at Maryland—and he has a wonderful face, bright and handsome and with radiant skin, and with piles of blond ringlets all over his head, like a kind of sensual Harpo Marx. It's what's inside Jim's big, gorgeous head that sooner or later turns a lot of people off. It did me, anyway. And I've run into a couple of other people—or maybe it's a couple of hundred—whose experience with Jim was similar, or worse."

"When you saw Jim in Mexico recently," I asked, "what was he doing down there?"

"I only wish I knew," Maynard said, and pondered the question. "Here's what happened. I'd gone down to the Yucatán for a quick go-round for a piece I did for the *L.A. Times* on touring some of the lesser-known Mayan ruins. None of it was terribly exotic, but I hadn't been to the Yucatán for several years, so I went down mainly to update the hotel, restaurant, and other nuts-and-bolts stuff. I was in Mérida walking across the zocalo one day when all of a sudden here comes Jim Suter, of all people, walking towards me. I said, 'Hey, Jim!' and I stopped. And what does he do? He pretends not to see me, and he walks right by me, eyes straight ahead. I stood there flabbergasted and watched him walk away, and he never looked back.

"I thought about running after him," Maynard said, "but it was obvious he recognized me—or that he'd been aware that *somebody* had called his name—and he had been careful not to look my way and to hurry away from there as fast as he could without breaking into a full trot. I had an appointment to keep with a hotel marketing director a few minutes later, so there was no time for me to go chasing after somebody who—it soon occurred to me—probably didn't want me to know he was in Mexico.

"Anyway, I couldn't think of any other explanation for Jim's behavior. When we broke up after our three-week fling back in '81 or '82, we'd parted on basically friendly terms, and we always talked and caught up with each other whenever our paths crossed—which in gay Washington happens fairly often, especially if you're both writers. Washington, this supposed great world capital, is more like Moline in that regard—very small-towny. Or so it seems, anyway, to gay New Yorkers who live here and tend to talk as if they've been exiled to Ouagadougou. As for me, the only other city I'd ever spent much time in was Vijayawada, so Washington has always seemed to me to be a pretty exciting place."

A sturdy-looking woman in a trench coat, shades, and a golf-cart-motif silk scarf tied tightly around her head had stopped in front of the quilt panel with Jim Suter's name and was looking down at it.

Timmy said, "Maynard, how can you be sure the guy you saw in Mérida was actually Jim Suter? Couldn't it have been some other gorgeous, beringleted, blond North American?"

"Timmy," Maynard said, sounding faintly irritated in the casual and familiar way old friends can sound with each other without suffering any huffy consequences, "this is a very beautiful man whose very beautiful face I slurped on and chewed at rapturously nearly every night for three weeks. This was not an experience I repeated frequently in my life, it pains me to have to remind you. Do you think I might fail to recognize such a face if I saw it again?"

Timmy said, "You put it so vividly, Maynard, I can't fail to see what you mean."

"Anyway," Maynard said, "it was plain that the man I called out to in the zocalo was determined not to acknowledge my presence. All he wanted was to get out of there as fast as he could. And if it wasn't Jim Suter, then why would he? And, of course, if it *was* Jim—which I'm positive it was—why would *he* want to run away from me?"

We all puzzled over Maynard's question, but none of us had an answer to it.

The woman in the trench coat and golf-cart scarf had gone down on her hands and knees and had been examining the manuscript pages on the Jim Suter quilt panel. She quickly got to her feet now and moved toward us as Maynard pronounced Jim Suter's name aloud. We were unable to see her eyes behind the shades, but the woman's round mouth was open and her face frozen, as if in fear.

The woman stared hard at us for a brief moment. Then suddenly she turned and moved quickly away, running almost. She jostled one knot of five or six middle-aged men in jeans and plaid shirts who were spread across the walkway between the quilt sections twelve or fifteen feet from Maynard, Timmy, and me.

Maynard said, "Hey, what the heck was she doing here!"

"The woman in the trench coat?" Timmy said.

"Yes. Jeez."

"Who was she?"

Maynard said, "I've never actually met the woman, but a friend pointed her out to me in the lobby of the Rayburn building one time. And I'm reasonably certain that that rattled woman who looked like she was scared to death by Jim Suter's quilt panel, or by something on it, was the unindicted former congresswoman from Pennsylvania, Betty Krumfutz."

# 2

Maynard had bought a small brick town house on the one hundred block of E Street, Southeast, back in the mid-seventies before the Reagan boom drove Capitol Hill real estate prices beyond the reach of mere adventure-travel writers. The rows of late-nineteenth-century houses on Maynard's side of the street had been built as servants' quarters for the burghers, pols, and lobbyists in the grander houses opposite Maynard's humble row. Maynard's house, like the next-door neighbors', was a simple, two-story box with bay windows, tiny patches of flowering shrubs, and a black wrought-iron front stoop. While the E Street houses' small rooms might have been considered claustrophobic in, say, St. Louis, on Capitol Hill, with its lingering emanations of life during the Van Buren administration, the little houses, now full of urban professionals instead of black cooks and Irish maids, just felt cozy.

Maynard had stuffed his home with folk art he had toted home from six continents, and in his ten-by-twelve-foot, fenced-in backyard, Maynard had built a rock fish pond surrounded on three sides by a garden he described as "Japanese-slash-Italian-slash-Camerooni." The Camerooni part was a big clay pot out of which climbed a restless, meandering yam plant, now defunct for the winter.

We arrived back at the house just after ten. Maynard drove us from Washington's Adams-Morgan section in his little Chevy Sprint. This followed a leisurely Ethiopian dinner—Maynard stuck with the relatively mild vegetable dishes—and several cups of a type of Abyssinian coffee Maynard said would be sure to keep us awake for eight to ten days. We said that didn't sound like much fun, but the coffee, black as lava and nearly as thick, was ripe with cloves and other unidentifiable spices. It was so alluringly strange that we kept drinking it, thinking the next small cup would seem suddenly familiar. None ever did, and now, back at Maynard's house, we were wired.

Timmy was watching the ten-o'clock news on the little TV set on a shelf in Maynard's dining room, I was browsing in that morning's *Post,* and Maynard was sorting through the mail that had arrived after we left the house that morning.

"Will you look at this!" Maynard said. "It's a letter from—guess who? Jim Suter."

"Is it from Mexico?" Timmy asked.

"Yep, it is. The postmark is blurred, and I can't make out the date, and there's no return address. But I know Jim's handwriting, and this is from Jim, for sure," Maynard said, and ripped open the airmail envelope. I could see that the postage stamp pictured an Indian with a flat, sloped forehead in noble profile.

Before we'd left the quilt display earlier, Maynard had sought out a Names Project official. The woman had been disturbed when Maynard insisted that a panel for a living person had found its way into the quilt. The official explained that records on panel submissions were kept back in San Francisco, and she would attempt to track down the source of the Jim Suter panel when she returned to California on Monday. She and Maynard exchanged phone numbers and each agreed to try to sort out this weird development.

"Holy cow, Jim's in some kind of bad trouble," Maynard said to Timmy and me, his wire reading specs perched on his sunburned nose. "He's in trouble and—jeez, that's not all. This is awful." Maynard was holding what looked like a single page of dense script handwritten on one side of some crinkly, thin paper. He finished reading and said, "This is entirely amazing."

Maynard passed the letter to Timmy, who read it aloud. It was dated Monday, September 30, twelve days earlier.

" 'Dear Maynard,' " Timmy read. " 'No, you weren't hallucinating. That was yours truly you saw on Saturday in Mérida. I'm guessing you were in the Yucatán for a travel quickie and you'll be back in D.C. by the time this letter makes its way through the Mexican postal system and lands at Dulles. (I once asked a postal clerk in Mérida, 'Who do you have to fuck in order to get a letter out of this country in less than a month?' and, I have to admit, his unusually forthright reply caught me off guard.)

" 'Hey, Manes, I do apologize for my rudeness on Saturday. Although, in fact, it was not mere bad manners at all, it was sheer panic. The thing of it is, I did not want anyone in D.C. to know where I was. And when I saw you, I just clutched. What I should have done was to simply, straightforwardly, ask you not to tell anybody, under any circumstances, that you saw me down here, and of course you would have agreed to that, sans explanations, which unhappily I am unable to provide. But you always trusted me, if I haven't misread our friendship, which has been based on the flesh and the soul, rather than the mind, what with my being a sensible chap of the center and your being to the left of Enver Hoxha, somewhere out around Ted Kennedy, etc., etc.

" 'Hey, Manes, am I being evasive? Cryptic? A tiresomely circumlocuting pain in the butt? Okay, then, friend, here's the actual deal. The actual deal is—hold on to your sombrero—somebody is trying to kill me. Did I write what I think I just wrote? A careful rereading of the text suggests I did. This extremely awkward state of affairs, Maynard, can be explained by the following: someone thinks I know something that could send quite a few rather large enchiladas to prison for muchos años. Comprende, Señor Sudbury?

" 'And—I guess this is the main reason I am writing you, Manes—if any of these people knew that you had seen me in Mérida, they might think that you know what they think I know, and they would want you out of what they perceive to be their hair, too. Sorry about this, but please do take it seriously. You've been around the world thirty-nine times—including bloody Africa, for chrissakes!—and you know as well as anybody that murder doesn't just happen in mall movies—and in malls—but that it can and does happen in real life.

" 'So please do not—DO NOT—mention to anyone that you saw me, here or anywhere. It's especially important that you tell no one on the Hill or with the D.C. Police Department that I'm down here or that you have seen me or spoken with me. Okay? Look, I'm sure your curiosity circuits are popping right about now. I know I'd be drooling down my bib with curiosity. All I can really say is, someday I'll explain all this, if I can—and if I can ever again show my still quite presentable face in D.C. Meanwhile, mum is definitely the word.

" 'Hey, Manes, if all this sounds just too, too ominous—well, believe me, it is.'

"Signed, 'Your friend Jim, still unlucky in love.' "

Timmy laid the letter on the dining room table and said, "Wow."

"Lurid, isn't it?" Maynard said, attempting jocularity, though he shifted in his seat like a man unnerved.

"Could Suter be making it all up?" Timmy asked. "You said he was unprincipled in a lot of ways. Maybe he's trying to manipulate you or manipulate events back here somehow."

"Jim's cynical," Maynard said, "about his own life and about the human race in general. But I've never heard of him jerking friends around in a devious way. If anything, he's known for his brutal honesty. That's why I guess I think I have to take what he's saying seriously."

Timmy said, "Nice guy, this Suter. By writing to you like this, now he's got you involved in whatever he's mixed up in. By warning you of the danger, he puts you in more danger. Now you've got this dangerous knowledge of some kind of plot. You don't know enough of the specifics to really protect yourself. This letter both helps you and increases your vulnerability. Suter sounds like an extremely complicated kind of friend to have."

Maynard blinked a couple of times, as if he didn't want to dwell on that. He said, "Maybe now we know why somebody put a panel for Jim in the quilt. It was meant as a threat or warning to him. Or," he went on, looking apprehensive, "maybe the panel was a threat or warning to other people who know Jim and who know what somebody thinks he knows, or who are thought to know what somebody thinks Jim knows."

"That part of the letter is murky," Timmy said. "About how somebody *thinks* Jim knows something that could send some big enchiladas to prison."

"What's murky about it?" Maynard asked. "It seems clear enough to me."

"But it sounds as if it's murky even to Jim," Timmy said. "If somebody thinks Jim knows something incriminating, why can't Jim simply tell these people he doesn't actually know what they think he knows?"

"Because," Maynard said, "maybe he doesn't know who 'they' are. 'They' are threatening and warning him—apparently they've made actual threats on his life—without ever identifying themselves."

"But if 'they' think Jim knows they did something criminal, then why would 'they' not identify themselves when they communicated their threats and warnings to Jim?"

I said, "Is the fatiguingly abstract tenor of this discussion typical of the conversations you guys had in the Peace Corps in India? It must have been exhausting. For you and for India."

"No," Maynard said, "our conversations back then tended to be more descriptive than analytical. We talked a lot about *(a)* poultry-debeaking techniques and *(b)* the peculiar qualities of our bowel movements."

"Of course, the latter is still true in your case," Timmy said, and he and Maynard both enjoyed a hearty guffaw over that.

One of the odder aspects of being the spouse—or "spouse-figure," as Timmy described me in his employment forms at the New York State Assembly—of a former Peace Corps volunteer was having to listen occasionally to these people converse not about the complexities of development in the third world—although they sometimes did that, too—but nearly as often, it sometimes seemed, about their memories of their exotic stools.

When JFK spoke of tens of thousands of Peace Corps men and women bringing back their relatively sophisticated views of Africa, Asia, and Latin America to enrich our nation, could this have been what he had in mind?

Timmy suddenly said, "Hey, look, it's the quilt," and reached over and turned up the volume on the television set.

There it was, this gorgeous, heart-swelling mosaic of lost lives—lost but well-remembered—spread across acre upon grassy acre of some of Washington's most historic open space. These were the lawns where the Bonus Army had encamped, the hunger marchers had been ignored by Herbert Hoover, Marian Anderson had sung, Martin Luther King had had a dream. The television coverage of the AIDS quilt opened with some voice-over statistics and a slow, panning shot from the air. Then a Names Project volunteer was interviewed, as were several men, women, and children who had come to see the panels they had sewn for people they loved and who were gone. Finally there were sound bites from some sympathetic strangers, people who simply found this great monument to loss beautiful and moving.

Back in the studio, the news anchor concluded the quilt report by saying, "Today's display was also marred by a mysterious act of vandalism. Late this afternoon, just before the quilt panels were folded up for overnight storage, two men ripped a section off of one panel. The men escaped before security personnel could intervene. Typed pages coming out of the picture of a typewriter were taken from a quilt panel memorializing Jim Suter, of Washington. Police would not speculate on a motive for the vandalism. But a Names Project official said that earlier in the day questions had been raised about the Suter panel and the display organizers planned to investigate." The news reader had been somber, but now he looked instantly delighted, as if he were deranged, and said, "Today's balmy weather should continue, according to Flavius, and after a short break . . ."

Timmy turned down the TV sound and we all looked at each other.

Maynard's brown eyes were shining and he said, "Betty Krumfutz!"

"If the only parts of the quilt that the vandals took were the typed pages from the Krumfutz campaign bio," I said, "there does seem to be a connection to Mrs. Krumfutz's hurried, discreet appearance at Suter's panel."

"Hurried, not to say panicked," Timmy said. "That woman was in a complete state."

I asked Maynard, "Did you read what was on the pages? They were slugged 'Suter/Krumfutz,' but are you sure that what was actually typed on them was Jim's Krumfutz campaign bio?"

"That's what it looked like. I saw some stuff there about Betty's antiabortion record in the Pennsylvania legislature. And another page had a paragraph on school prayer and getting patriotism back into history textbooks. I didn't read any of it with care. It just looked like standard religious-right boilerplate. But the pages I saw seemed to be exactly what the page slugs said they were, Jim's Krumfutz campaign bio."

"I'm surprised," I said, "that that stuff doesn't move directly from the printer to the recycling bins. But I guess it must have some effect, or politicians wouldn't spend their campaign millions on it."

"A small percentage of voters—usually the slower, more gullible folks—actually read campaign handouts as if they were as imperishable as Alexander Hamilton," Maynard said. "And often all it takes to swing an election is one or two percent of the vote. So it's not a waste of money when a candidate churns that stuff out."

"But," I said, "there must have been something on those sheets of typescript on the quilt panel that somebody badly wanted to keep out of public view. And when I looked at the pages, I saw what you both saw, and there was nothing remarkable about any of it on the surface. Maybe there was something revealing on the backs of the pages—although it's hard to imagine why anyone would be afraid of any words or pictures that weren't visible." I asked Maynard, "Did Jim Suter actually use a typewriter, and not a word processor or computer?"

"As a matter of fact, he did—does," Maynard said. "Jim is one of those writers who are sentimental about their old Underwoods and Smith-Coronas and are scared to death that if they throw over the machine they've always written on, they'll never write again. It's a karma thing, and I understand it. I compose on a Mac, but I keep a fresh ribbon in my IBM Selectric. I'm prepared for the day when I look into my video terminal and I can imagine nothing there besides *I Dream of Jeannie* reruns. And if the IBM quits—hey, I once lost my notebook in Eritrea and scratched out some notes with my Swiss army knife on a slab of sandstone. In fact, that's it right there on that shelf."

Maynard indicated a long, flat rock with scratches all over it. It sat next to a framed photograph of Maynard in the company of several slender Africans holding AK-47s, looking righteous and determined, and surrounding a Mobil Oil tanker truck. Next to this picture was one of Maynard and his lover of eleven years, Randy Greeley, who had been a Unicef field organizer and had died in a poorly aimed rocket-propelled-grenade attack by somebody—no one was sure who—in Somalia in 1993.

I said, "Maynard, it looks as if whoever designed the quilt panel for Jim knew him well enough to know he uses a typewriter instead of a computer."

"It does," Maynard agreed. "But of course that's a lot of people. Jim is among the more prolific hacks in the District. He's always been a writer who gets around, professionally and otherwise. Writer-slash-operator is a more apt description of what Jim docs."

Timmy said, "Do you think Betty Krumfutz saw something on Jim's panel today that freaked her out and she sent some goons over to rip those pages off the quilt?"

Maynard said, "Well, yeah, it does look as if she did," and then he shook his head, as if he was both baffled and apprehensive and had no idea what to make of any of the afternoon's peculiar events.

We sat silently for a minute, deep in thought, the television jabbering in the background.

"I'm wondering," Maynard finally said, "what—if anything—I ought to tell the Names Project. Or even the police. I guess I can't tell anyone that I heard from Jim, or where he is. Not if it might actually endanger his life—or mine." Maynard smiled nervously, and we smiled nervously back.

"No," Timmy said, "and you specifically are not to tell the D.C. police where he is. Or anybody on the Hill. I take it that means Capitol Hill the national legislative establishment, not Capitol Hill the neighborhood."

Maynard said, "It probably means both."

"Has Jim ever had problems with the law?" I asked. "Of a political nature or otherwise?"

Maynard looked doubtful. "Not that I've ever heard about. And if he'd been mixed up in the Krumfutz scandal, that would have come out in court. I'd guess no. His ethics are malleable, but Jim has plenty of lawyer friends, and my guess is he's been able to stay a centimeter or two on the nonindictable side of the law."

Timmy sat up straight. "Then that probably means that—jeez! It might well mean that the D.C. cops are actually involved in whatever the conspiracy is that Jim knows about!"

"Conspiracy?" I said. "What conspiracy?"

"Well, what would *you* call it?"

"Timothy," I said, "it seems to me unlikely that the entire District of Columbia Police Department would conspire to assassinate a political writer." I told Maynard, "Timothy, as you know, is overall a rational man. But when he was a boy in Poughkeepsie, the nuns told him stories about Masons plotting to snatch and devour little Catholic children, and to this day Timothy's imagination occasionally runs away with itself."

Timmy gave Maynard a look that said, "I've told you about how off-the-wall Don can be on the subject of my Catholic background, and now you've seen it for yourself." What he said out loud was, "Some cops are corrupt, and often dirty cops are dirty together. Word of this phenomenon has even reached some lapsed New Jersey Calvinists, I think."

Maynard, already unsettled by the letter from Jim Suter and the strange vandalism of the even stranger quilt panel, now looked alarmed over the possibility that his houseguests might be headed for a spat. He said, "Don, Jim did say explicitly that I shouldn't mention his whereabouts to the D.C. police, and he seemed to be saying not *any* D.C. cop."

"Right," Timmy piped up. "That was in the letter."

"I get the point," I said. "The point, it seems to me, is this: be careful of the D.C. cops because one or some of them may be connected to threats against Jim Suter or even attempts on his life. Let's just not become unduly paranoid, imagining some Oliver Stone–style plot against Jim Suter that everybody from the D.C. meter maids to the ghost of LBJ is a party to. Just for the moment, let's be cool—whatever that might turn out to mean in practical terms."

"But that's just it," Maynard said. "What do I do with what I know? I guess I'll have to do something. I told that woman from the Names Project that Jim Suter is alive, and then his panel was vandalized. So *she* might give the cops my name."

We pondered this dilemma. After a moment, Timmy said, "Why don't you call the Names Project woman—what's her name?"

"I left it in the car," Maynard said.

"And find out if she told the cops about you, and if she didn't, ask her not to. Tell her you have your own reasons for not wanting to get involved at this point, which is true. Ask her if she'd mind keeping your name out of it, at least for now, and then get in touch with her when you have a clearer idea of what this . . . this conspiracy is about, and how far it extends, and exactly what the dangers are to Jim and to you. I have to use the word *conspiracy,* based on the situation Jim described in his letter. In English, there just isn't any better word for it."

"Timothy," I said, "maybe it wasn't the nuns. Maybe it's all the years you've spent as an employee of the New York State legislature, an institution that makes a Medici court look like a Quaker meeting. Whatever the reason, your overstimulated sense of melodrama is getting the best of you—as I suspect Jim Suter's might be getting the best of him. Maynard, has Suter spent a lot of time in Mexico? Living among the cops there could certainly leave a man with a powerful sense that somebody might be out to get him."

"Jim's been taking vacations in the Yucatán for years," Maynard said, "and I think he has friends there. As for the Mexican police, they're an ugly fact of life down there that people have learned to live with when they must and avoid when they can, like the bacteria in the water supply. I doubt that Jim has been unhinged by them. He's a worldly guy. You know, I think I will call the woman from the Names Project and at least find out what she told the cops. Just so I'll know what to expect."

Timmy said, "I think you should."

Maynard crossed his living room full of primitive and modern art and artifacts—paintings, carved-wood fertility totems, village-life-narrative wall hangings in brilliant primary colors—and walked out the front door.

"I wonder," Timmy said, "whether Maynard should tell the quilt official that the pages ripped off Jim Suter's quilt panel were from Jim's Krumfutz campaign biography and that he saw the actual Betty Krumfutz down on her hands and knees at the quilt this afternoon. I really don't see, Don, how you can sneer at the possibility of a conspiracy when—"

From outside the open front door came three loud pops. Then we heard the revving engine of a car speeding away down E Street, followed by silence.

Seconds later, when we reached Maynard—sprawled on the brick sidewalk next to his car, his blood pumping out of his body—he was still breathing, but only faintly. Timmy knelt by Maynard and began to speak softly to him as he searched for the correct pressure points to push against, and I raced back into the house.

# 3

The George Washington University Hospital trauma center was where the Secret Service had rushed Ronald Reagan after John Hinckley Jr. shot him, along with James Brady, a Secret Service agent, and a D.C. policeman on the sidewalk alongside the Washington Hilton in 1981. Nancy Reagan later told reporters that as the Gipper was wheeled into the emergency room, he had cheerfully quoted W. C. Fields to the effect that, given a choice, he'd rather be in Philadelphia. But in fact, Reagan was lucky he had been shot in the District of Columbia, just blocks from GW. This hospital's emergency staff specialized in treating the thousands of gruesome gunshot wounds arriving each year from various points, mainly in the Northeast section, of one of the world's bloodiest capitals outside the Balkans.

Maynard was not jocular on his arrival at GW, he was unconscious. Timmy had been allowed to ride with him in the ambulance, and I followed soon in a cab. Maynard's wounds, one abdominal and one to the head, were so serious that he was quickly evaluated and moved directly to an operating room.

Timmy and I settled into a lounge outside the recovery unit where Maynard would end up if he lived. "He's in tough shape" was all we'd been told by an ER resident, and we both understood what that meant.

"It's just too ironic," Timmy said miserably. Even though we were both charged and alert from having drunk too much Ethiopian coffee, Timmy looked exhausted, haunted, suddenly older. It was an indication of how wounded he was that he seemed only dimly aware that his shirt and khakis were stained—caked in some places—with Maynard's blood. I had held Timmy's hand for some minutes but automatically let go when two elderly black women entered the waiting room and seated themselves.

"What's ironic?" I asked.

"You know."

"That Maynard survived Africa and Asia, but he might not survive Washington?"

Timmy grunted. Mounted on the wall across from us was a television set tuned to what looked like a self-esteem-industry infomercial. A muscular man rapturous with self-confidence was pumping up an audience whose faces were full of yearning for an end to self-doubt. The man's tapes, they wanted to believe, would bring clarity into their lives, and perhaps belief. The pitchman had a good thing going and he looked as if he knew it.

I said, "Maybe Maynard will make it. It's not over yet. You've been telling me for years how resilient he is."

Timmy sat slumped to one side of his chair, staring into space, his Irish eyes vacant and ringed, his ordinarily silky blond wave—he was the only man I knew with a kind of naturally art deco hairstyle—wet with sweat against his skull. He grunted again and shook his head hopelessly.

A gaunt, hollow-eyed man with both eyes and hair the color of lead and a sport coat of nearly the same shade entered the room and peered around. The two DC Metropolitan PD patrolmen who had responded to my 911 call had not asked many questions about the shooting, and something told me that this was the detective assigned to the case tracking us down. He walked over to Timmy and me.

"Are you the two that came in with Maynard T. Sudbury?" the man asked tonelessly.

"Yes," Timmy said. "How is he?"

"That I couldn't tell you." He continued to gaze at us with eyes that were cold and unrevealing.

"Are you a police officer?" I said.

The man produced his wallet, flipped it open and shut, put

it back in his jacket pocket, and said, "Ray Craig, Detective Lieutenant, MPD." He looked at me, then at Timmy, then back at me. He made no move to extend his hand, and unsure of how to react to Craig's chilliness, or just rudeness, neither of us offered ours.

Timmy said, "We're really worried about Maynard. The resident said he was in tough shape. 'Tough shape' were the words he used."

Ray Craig did not reply. He studied Timmy and me for a moment longer. Then he turned and dragged a molded-plastic chair up to us, its metal legs snagging bits of carpet as it moved, and seated himself in front of us, his knees nearly touching ours. He leaned forward, and now I was within range of his powerful odor, stale nicotine and tar. Had I once smelled like this? I knew I had.

"Which one of you is Callahan?" Craig said dully.

Timmy said, "I am."

Then Craig looked over at me and said, "You're Starch?"

"Starch? No."

Craig got out a small notepad and read, "S-T-A-R-C-H, Donald."

"It's Strachey. S-T-R-A-C-H-E-Y. As in Lytton."

"Lyndon?"

"Lytton. L-Y-T-T-O-N. Lytton Strachey, the brilliant English biographer and fey eccentric. There was a so-so flick about him and his sort-of wife last year called *Carrington*. Maybe you caught it."

I felt Timmy tense up beside me, but Craig just colored a little, which suited him. He stared at me appraisingly for several seconds. Then he said, "Tell me exactly what happened on E Street tonight." He leaned back a little—a mercy—and continued to look at me as if I were the one who needed airing out.

I explained to Craig that Timmy, Maynard, and I had dined at an Ethiopian restaurant in Adams-Morgan and that from around ten on we had been hanging around Maynard's house watching television news and talking. I said Maynard had left something in his car, he had gone out to get it, and seconds after he went out the front door, Timmy and I heard sounds that could have been gunshots. We also heard a car speed away. We ran outside and discovered Maynard bleeding and unconscious on the sidewalk alongside his car. I said I immediately went inside and telephoned the police while Timmy tried to stanch the flow of blood from Maynard's body.

Craig continued examining me in a way that felt both hostile and somehow prurient. I was not touching Timmy, but I was aware that his respiration had increased.

Craig said, "So, what'd Sudbury go out to his car to get?"

"Maynard went out to bring in a name written on a piece of paper," I said. "We had all gone to the AIDS quilt display during the afternoon. We ran into an acquaintance and wrote her phone number on a Names Project brochure Maynard was carrying. He had left the phone number in his car and had gone out to retrieve it when he was shot."

Craig seemed to roll this information around in his mind. Then he shifted, shot Timmy a surly look, and said, "What's your connection with Sudbury? You don't live around here. You live in New York State." His tone suggested that anybody residing outside the District of Columbia might be of a different species from those residing within the District and whose associations with Washingtonians went against nature.

Timmy croaked out, "Maynard and I are old Peace Corps friends. We were in the Peace Corps together in the sixties. Donald and I stay with Maynard whenever we come to Washington. We're—we're just old Peace Corps buddies."

Timmy might as well have announced to Craig that he and Maynard had been members of the corps de ballet of the 1965 Fonteyn-Nureyev *Giselle* tour. Craig sniffed once, then looked Timmy up and down in the way he had just looked at me. He said, "Talk to me about your . . . buddy." He gave *buddy* a pronunciation that was somewhere between a sneer and a leer. "Does Sudbury have enemies?" Craig asked. "If so, who?"

Timmy went through the motions of mulling this over. "I

can't think of any enemies Maynard has. He's generally well-liked. Of course, Maynard has been PNGed out of a number of countries. But I assume you mean domestic enemies. Personal."

Craig's eyes narrowed. "What's PNG?"

"Declared persona non grata. Maynard is a foreign reporter and travel writer. Some officials in some countries didn't like what he wrote about their governments. But I doubt any of them tracked him down to E Street in Washington and shot him."

"Skip the opinions," Craig snapped. "If I want your opinions, I'll ask for them. Just tell me what you know." He had his pen and notebook out but he wasn't writing any of this down. "Married?"

"Maynard?"

Craig's eyes flashed for a brief second. "Yes, Maynard. Maynard T. Sudbury. That's who we're talking about here, isn't it? Maynard T. Sudbury, the shooting victim."

"Not married," Timmy said, jaw clenched.

"Sudbury is gay," I added. "His lover died in 1993."

Craig's face tightened. "I'll bet you two are that way inclined also. Am I right?"

"Are we gay? You bet."

He snorted dismissively. He looked at me and at Timmy, then shook his head, as if our being gay was the most preposterous thing he had ever heard. "I want the names of family, friends, and associates. Start with family." Now his pen was poised.

Before I left for the hospital, I had grabbed Maynard's address book off his desk. If he died, I knew it was possible Timmy or I would have to notify his family. I had glanced through the address book quickly to make sure it included some Sudburys in Southern Illinois—it listed six—but I didn't take it out of my pocket for Craig. Timmy and I fumbled through our memories and named a number of people, in Illinois and in Washington, whom we thought the police would be duty-bound to notify and/or question. Neither of us mentioned Jim Suter.

A surgical intern walked into the lounge we were waiting in, and our eyes went immediately to him. But he did not approach Timmy and me. He went instead to the two elderly black women, looked down as they looked up, and shook his head sorrowfully. The women said nothing, just stood quickly and walked with the doctor out into the corridor as he spoke to them in a low voice.

Craig looked up from his notebook and said, "Did Sudbury have any recent arguments or disputes with any of these people?"

Timmy said, "Not that he mentioned to us."

"That's a no?"

"Yes, that's a no."

"What about you, Starchey?" Craig stared at me and didn't blink.

I said, "I had no argument with Maynard, no. It's Strachey. S-T-R-A-C-H-E-Y."

"You weren't the asshole who shot your buddy Sudbury?"

"No, I wasn't."

"What about you, Callahan?"

His face radiating heat, Timmy said, "Of course not."

Craig's eyes came briefly to life again, and he said, "Did you suck his dick?"

Neither of us answered. Craig's gaze flicked back and forth between us. Finally, I said, "Neither of us has a sexual relationship with Maynard. He's a friend. In New York State, friends don't normally suck each other's dicks. Maybe the customs are different south of the Mason-Dixon line, and that's why you asked the question. If so, I'm happy to be able to clear up any misconception about sexual customs in the North."

Craig's mouth tightened and he stared at me hard. One of his loafers had begun to jiggle at high speed. It was apparent that he was making mental notes, and he was looking at me as if he wanted me to know it. After a moment, Craig lifted his pen again and said, "Sudbury's a travel writer. Where's he been to recently?"

After seeming to consider this carefully, Timmy said, "Maynard has been to Swaziland, Botswana, and Zimbabwe in the past year, I know."

Craig noted this with no apparent interest and said, "Where else?"

"Mexico," I said, "within the last couple of months."

"Mexico?" Craig's nose twitched and a light went on in his eyes and stayed on in a way it had not stayed on before.

I said, "Maynard was in the Yucatán researching a travel piece for the *Los Angeles Times*. He talked about enjoying the trip and he didn't mention any incident there—or any incident anywhere else—that might have led to his being shot tonight on a Washington street."

"Uh-huh." Craig waited, and when no one spoke, he said, "Did Sudbury go to Mexico frequently?"

"Not frequently, no," Timmy said.

"I think you know," Craig said, "this shooting doesn't look anything like a robbery."

"I know," I said.

"The shooter never stopped. Sudbury's wallet wasn't taken."

"No."

"The perp apparently had no interest in robbery," Craig said. "Somebody drove by, popped Sudbury, and drove away. Drive-by shootings in the District are seldom random. Normally that's something gangs do to members of other gangs. That's drug gangs, to be specific. Do you have any reason to believe that Sudbury is part of a drug operation?"

Timmy flushed. "I think not."

Craig said, "Yeah, I think not, too. Not some street-punk operation anyway. So you don't know who might have wanted to shoot your buddy in the head and in the gut?"

His face purple with anger now, Timmy said, "No. I do not."

"When did you say Sudbury was in Mexico the last time?" Craig asked.

"Two weeks ago."

Now Craig gave me the beady eye. "You said Sudbury was

down in Mexico in the last couple of months. Which is it? Two weeks ago or the last couple of months?"

"Two weeks ago is within the last couple of months," I said. "Neither of us is telling you anything that's remotely contradictory to what the other is saying. So, what's the problem, Lieutenant?"

"The problem is that I think you two faggot assholes are telling me lie after lie after lie. The problem is, I think your buddy Maynard T. Sudbury doesn't just write about Mexico when he goes back and forth down there. And the problem is, I think when he goes down there, he may be involved in the type of illegal activities that can get a man shot in the gut on E Street when there's no other reason for that to happen. And the other problem is, I think you two pathetic queers know it."

Timmy shook his head in disgust.

I said, "That's a lot of problems you've got to contend with there, Lieutenant."

"That's what I say."

I said, "The biggest problem of all, as far as I can make out, Lieutenant, is you. With police work like this, in fact, it's no wonder Washington has one of the highest murder rates in North America. Up in Albany, New York, where we come from, police investigations aren't always handled as skillfully as a lot of us would like. But I've rarely encountered police presumption and speculation as wildly prejudiced and inaccurate and harmful to an investigation as I've witnessed tonight. This city obviously is not only the murder capital of the Eastern seaboard, it's also looking more and more like the capital of police fecklessness. You strike me as a blithering incompetent, Lieutenant, a disgrace to your department and to your profession."

This was not calculated, just sincere. It was reckless, too, although with hospital staff often passing by in the corridor, there seemed little chance an inflamed Craig would pistol-whip us or attempt to arrest us on a trumped-up charge. Craig did not, in fact, explode. He just colored again, looked at me dully, and said, "The murder rate in D.C. isn't all that high if you don't calculate in the niggers. The niggers distort the stats. It's easy to get a misleading impression. But Sudbury is no nigger. Even though it sounds to me like he sucks nigger dick."

I gazed at Craig and said nothing. Timmy was looking at his own lap and slowly shaking his head.

"So you two cocksuckers are sure you don't want to tell me about some trouble your buddy Sudbury said he was in? Some trouble down in Mexico?"

Timmy muttered, "There's nothing to tell."

Craig studied us with his dead eyes, then said, "Listen to what I say to you. Don't leave the District without checking with me. Have you got that straight?"

Neither of us had a copy of the Constitution to wave in Craig's face, but I knew it wouldn't have helped. For Craig stood up without another word, turned, and quickly walked out.

After a moment, Timmy said, "Is he just a rotten human being and one of the worst cops in the United States, or was there a lot more going on just now than was apparent on the surface? Why, for God's sake, did he keep harping on Mexico, for instance, over and over and over again?"

Before I could think about what might have been paranoid imaginings and what was well-founded fear, a doctor in OR gear walked into the lounge and came over to us. He didn't look happy, but he wasn't averting his eyes either.

# 4

Maynard's chances of surviving were better than even. The surgeon told us that the head wound was messy but superficial, and the much more serious abdominal injuries had required major replumbing—just short of a colostomy—and if Maynard lived through the next twelve hours, full recovery was a good possibility. The surgeon said Maynard's sturdy constitution and overall good health were a big help, but that infection was a danger and Maynard would have to be closely watched over the next day.

Timmy said, "He's already got a stomach infection."

"He does? What's that?" A small, soft-eyed man with a cleft chin, the surgeon looked interested in this.

Timmy explained how Maynard had apparently picked up a parasite that wouldn't let go in Zambia, Burkina Faso, or Kyrgyzstan. "He's had it for going on a year," Timmy said.

"That'll be the least of Mr. Sudbury's problems," the doctor said. "Infections like that are a month in the country compared to the kinds that urban North American hospitals have to worry about."

Timmy said he didn't find that reassuring, and the surgeon left us with instructions on how to attempt to pry information on Maynard's condition out of the hospital bureaucracy.

At just after 2 A.M., in a cab rolling south and east through Washington's nearly deserted early-Sunday-morning streets, I said to Timmy, "Ray Craig isn't the worst cop I've ever run into in my long career of running into law officers who'd have been equally comfortable on either side of the law, but he may be the second or third worst. He's so in thrall to his own insecurities and hatreds that he can survive professionally only in a place where most of the actual criminals fit his idea of a criminal stereotype—black or Hispanic or whatever. Bust enough black heads, and he's bound to catch an actual criminal sooner or later. It's cops like this that create juries like the one that acquitted O.J.

"But nasty as Craig is, Timothy, I didn't come away with any sense that he's aware of Jim Suter's letter to Maynard or Suter's alleged perilous situation, or the Suter quilt panel or Betty Krumfutz or any of that. He's not a party to a nefarious plot who was digging around to see what we know. Craig is just another unimaginative, mildly disturbed cop in love with the obvious who, when he hears about shootings and Mexico, he immediately figures drugs. But I wouldn't interpret his remarks to mean anything more extensive or more worrisome than that. Trust him with what we know about the Suter situation? No way—the guy's a flake and an incompetent. Clue him in at this point and he's liable to get Suter killed, and maybe us, too. But is Craig worse than a bigoted hack? I don't think so."

Timmy had been fidgeting restlessly as I spoke, and now, keeping his hands down low, he gestured urgently in the direction of the cabdriver and said, "Yes, I'm sure you're right. Maybe we should just forget about all that." Then, looking otherwise wild-eyed, he winked at me.

Now he thought the cabdriver was in on it? Whatever he thought "it" was? I leaned up and read the driver's name spelled out alongside his photograph on the cabbie's license mounted on the visor. He was a slim black man in a brown sport coat that gave him a dressed-up look, and his name was Getachew Tessemma. The man had been soft-spoken and polite when we'd climbed into his cab. I assumed the name was African, maybe Ethiopian; with his slender nose and dark, delicate eyelashes the size of marquees, Tessemma resembled the maître d' at the restaurant we'd eaten in six hours earlier.

Tessemma's had been the only cab parked outside the hospital when Timmy and I came out. I was aware that sweet, placid people could be treacherous—I had been deeply involved in the great Southeast Asian disaster arranged for the nation by Johnson, Nixon, Kissinger, and others. But was it remotely possible that this unprepossessing African who waited for fares outside a hospital in the middle of the night was somehow out to do us both in? I thought not.

I caught a glimpse of the street signs as we rode along Seventeenth Street, NW, the American Red Cross headquarters on our right, and then the old Pan American Union building. Timmy had gone to school in Georgetown and knew D.C. much better than I did, but I had visited the city often enough to know its basic layout. I said, "This is a good route to Maynard's house, isn't it? We're going to the Hill by way of the Tidal Basin and the Southwest freeway. We've been with Maynard when he's taken this route."

"It's one way of getting there," Timmy said, and glanced nervously left and right at the passing Washington scene.

We cruised past the Mall, where, just east of the Washington Monument, the AIDS quilt panels had been folded up and stowed away for the night. The exterior columns of the Lincoln Memorial, off to our right, were dark, but I caught a glimpse of the big, illuminated marble statue within the structure. The great man was seated stiffly in an armchair in a characteristically formal pose of the era. Today he'd be grinning in a designer polo shirt, maybe seated at the wheel of his and Mary's retirement RV.

We rolled past the Tidal Basin, where House Ways and Means Committee chairman Wilbur Mills had been nailed for DWI in 1974 and his companion, Argentine stripper Fanne Fox, had ended up splashing around zanily in the drink. In the American capital, history was everywhere.

Within minutes, we were off the freeway, onto the quiet residential streets behind the mausoleum-like House office buildings, and headed up E Street. At Maynard's house, midway up the block, yellow crime-scene tape was still stretched around his Chevy and tied to a street sign. But the cops were gone and the street deserted. We paid Tessemma, who did not shoot us in the back as we stepped out into the cool October night, and we walked up Maynard's front steps.

Maynard had left his keys on the dining room table before the shooting, and I had picked them up to lock up the house when I left for the hospital. Now I unlocked the wooden front door and stepped into the foyer, with Timmy close behind. Lights were on in the living room and dining room, as they had been when I left, but the rooms were otherwise not the same at all.

Drawers had been opened and their contents dumped on the African and Central American rugs. Books had been flung from shelves. Paintings and other artwork were largely undamaged, but many were hanging cockeyed, as if whoever had tossed the place had conducted a search so methodical that even the wall art had been carefully examined for—something.

Timmy said, "I've never seen this done before. It's nauseating."

I had seen it before and found it just as sickening this time as the last time and the time before that. I said, "Don't touch anything yet," and walked through the dining room and toward the kitchen in the rear of the house.

"Are you going to call the police?" Timmy said. "I don't know about that."

"I don't either. Although if we don't call the cops and it does turn out that some of them are involved in this, they may be inclined to think we know more than we actually know. It might be better for us—and for Maynard and maybe Jim Suter—if we look like a couple of uninvolved outsiders who are shocked and frightened by all of this, but ignorant of—whatever it is that's going on."

"Of course, that's exactly what we *are.*"

"You don't have to remind me."

The kitchen was bedlam. Every pot, pan, and plastic refrigerator box had been left out on the counter or on the floor. The cupboards had been emptied of food and dishes. Food was piled in the sink—spices, Wheat Chex, fruit, peanut butter, peanut oil, sorbet, half a thawing frozen chicken.

"There's where they came in," I said, and we looked over at the sizable section of the back door around the lock that had essentially been dismantled.

"I'm surprised," I said, "that nobody heard this happen and reported it."

"Maybe somebody did report it. And the police never came."

"Oh, sure. The 911 operator, the dispatchers—they're all in on this . . . thing. This conspiracy so vast it's got tentacles reaching into every level of law enforcement in the District of Columbia. Timothy, I'm not ready to go quite that far."

"How far are you ready to go?"

I tugged the broken door open and flipped on the switch for the backyard floodlight. The patio and fish tank seemed undisturbed. The back gate in the tall board fence was shut and locked. The intruder, or intruders, had apparently clambered over the fence both coming and going.

We made our way back to the dining room and up the half-open stairwell to the second floor. The mess upstairs was like the mess downstairs. Nothing seemed to have been purposely smashed; the chaos appeared to be the result of a methodical search that had been unsuccessful over a long time and across a lot of square footage.

I said to Timmy, "This job must have taken a couple of hours. I left for the hospital at about ten-forty. It's two thirty-five now. If the intruder was watching the house and waiting for us to leave, he could have jumped the fence early. But that would have involved a heavy risk of being overheard. If he'd waited for all the neighbors to go to sleep, after midnight, say—and on a Saturday night that would have been unpredictable—then he'd have run the risk of our coming back and catching him in the act."

"Unless, of course," Timmy said, "he or they were in touch with someone who could keep him or them informed about our location and movements. Then there'd be no risk at all of discovery."

"Uh-huh."

The middle bedroom, where Timmy and I were staying, had been ransacked just like Maynard's front bedroom. Our bags were open and our clothes strewn about.

"Jeez, I ironed that shirt myself," Timmy said. "Now look at it."

"You've had a rough night, Timothy. I just hope nobody went in the bathroom and sucked on your toothbrush."

"Look, you know what I mean."

I did. We went into Maynard's office in the small back room. File drawers had been yanked open and papers were everywhere. The disk boxes next to his computer were open and empty. Maynard's computer files were evidently gone. The telephone answering machine on the desk was not blinking. I checked for the tape; it had been taken, too.

Timmy said, "It's a good thing you picked up Maynard's address book before you came to the hospital. I'll bet they'd have taken it."

"Maybe."

Timmy suddenly looked up from the debris around Maynard's Mac and said, "The letter from Jim Suter! Do you think they took that? Where was it when we left the house?"

"It was right where it is now. In my pocket with the address book. I grabbed it just before the cab arrived."

"Good for you. Any particular reason you picked up the letter? Surely you didn't suppose for a second that Maynard's getting shot and that strange, turbulent letter with all the talk in it of murder and people on the Hill and death threats and the D.C. police—you didn't think all that suggested some kind of terrible conspiracy, did you?"

"No, I just did what I thought Maynard would have wanted me to do: keep that letter safe."

"Well, that's a good reason, too."

While Timmy changed out of his bloodstained clothes and went about straightening up the mess in the guest room, I walked down to the bathroom. The medicine cabinet had been opened and most of its contents dumped in the sink. The magazines stacked on the shelf next to the toilet—*The New Yorker, The New Republic, The Nation, Smithsonian, Blueboy*—looked as if they had been rifled; several lay open on the tile floor. I flipped through the *Blueboy,* then resumed examining the scene. The toilet paper had not been unrolled, a sign, perhaps, that the intruder whose job it had been to search the bathroom was essentially anal retentive, despite the nature of his assigned duties that night.

Downstairs, the doorbell rang. I stepped into the hallway. Timmy appeared in the guest room doorway and stood very still. There was an alertness in him that I knew was partly caffeine and partly fear. He said in a low voice, "Should we answer it?"

"I guess we should see who it is."

I started down the stairs as the bell rang again, and Timmy followed me.

In the living room, I pulled the curtains aside and looked out the bay window at the front stoop. A man stood there, but it was his car, double-parked alongside Maynard's Chevy, that drew my attention. It was a D.C. police patrol car, its flashers flashing.

"It's a cop," I told Timmy.

I went around and unlocked the door, opened it, and stood face-to-face with Ray Craig.

Craig said evenly, "Somebody in the neighborhood reported a disturbance in this house earlier. The officers who responded to the call were called to a robbery over on Half Street before they could investigate. I recognized the address on the report and thought I better come over and see what the problem was." He peered over my shoulder at Timmy, standing perfectly still, and at the wrecked interior of Maynard's house. His nicotine stench wafted into the room, and Craig said, "Looks like you had a break-in. Anything missing that you know of? It's been a real pisser of a night for you and your buddy Sudbury."

"It has," I said.

"We were just about to call the police," Timmy said.

Craig stared at him hard, his face still devoid of expression, but with something in the set of his head on his narrow shoulders that suggested suspicion mixed with contempt.

# 5

Our wake-up call at the Capitol Hill Hotel, three blocks from Maynard's house, came at eight. I immediately got an outside line and phoned GW to check on Maynard's condition. An ICU nurse said he was "stable."

Death is the stablest condition of all, but I knew she didn't mean that.

"He's alive," I told Timmy.

"Thank God."

Ray Craig had left us at 3:15 A.M. He had noted the damage and remarked on how no valuables appeared to have been taken. He said the break-in did not seem to have been a burglary, and again he asked if we knew of any enemies Maynard had, in Washington or in Mexico. He inquired about Maynard's Mexican "associations" half a dozen times. Again, we told Craig we didn't know of any enemies Maynard had in Mexico, which was true.

Craig also asked, "Did Sudbury bring men back here for sex?" This came just as Craig was about to leave. It was a reasonable question for an investigator to ask following an assault on an urban gay man in the nineties. But the faint trace of a leer on Craig's ordinarily blank face lent the question a quality that was both lubricious and gratuitous. Also, it seemed to come as an afterthought, a bow to investigatory convention.

Timmy had told Craig, "Maynard is a sexually alive adult male who dates from time to time. It wouldn't surprise me if some of his dates have spent the night with him. But Maynard is old-fashioned in some respects, and I think cautious. He wouldn't have invited anybody into his house whom he didn't know reasonably well."

Craig sniffed and said, "Yeah, sure."

I told him, "We were lucky you had a chance to stop over here tonight, Lieutenant. This must have taken you away from more important cases."

"This is important," he replied, but added nothing more. He told us it would be a good idea if we did not spend the rest of the night in Maynard's house. He said he'd ask a patrol car to check the front and rear of the house periodically. Craig recommended a hotel several blocks away on Pennsylvania Avenue, just east of the Capitol, and he offered us a ride. We declined the ride. We waited ten minutes after Craig had left, then hiked the three blocks up to the Capitol Hill Hotel on Second Street, SE. It was not the hotel Craig had recommended, just one we'd seen, while walking in the neighborhood, that looked quiet, comfortable, and, as Timmy had put it, "unthreatening."

In the morning, we'd slept but we did not sparkle. After I called GW, Timmy checked off the names of people in Maynard's address book who were friends Maynard had mentioned to Timmy, and while he showered, I made calls. It was an hour earlier in Southern Illinois on a Sunday morning, so I figured I'd phone Maynard's family last and let them know that he had been shot and badly wounded.

No actual human beings answered my first three calls, but I left messages explaining who and where I was and informed Maynard's friends of his misfortune. On the fourth and fifth calls, I reached a man and a woman respectively, and they turned out to be writers, too. The man was another freelancer, the woman, Dana Mosel, a reporter at the *Post*. I nearly asked Mosel how I could locate a D.C. police official of undisputed high integrity, someone I could confide in on a matter that law-enforcement higher-ups might refer to as "sensitive." But I decided that a more roundabout route to a clean cop was called for, so I let it go.

Both of Maynard's writer friends were shaken by the news of the shooting—which had taken place too late to make the

Sunday papers—and his friends said they would notify others and would visit Maynard at GW as soon as his condition allowed. Both asked, "Was it a robbery?" I said that that was still unclear.

I was about to make another call when Timmy came out of the bathroom. "I'd better talk to his parents," he said. "I've never met them, but Maynard might have mentioned me. You know the way Peace Corps people tell stories back home."

I said I knew. The eleven-year-old son of another of Timmy's old Peace Corps friends liked to refer to the tales of India that his father told as "Dad's twelve stories."

"Do you think Maynard is really safe even in the hospital?" Timmy said. Ray Craig had assured us that the hospital's security staff would keep constant watch over Maynard, and at GW he was in no danger of being attacked again by his E Street assailant.

I said, "Why? Are you afraid that whoever shot Maynard is going to sneak into the hospital, dress up in a surgical gown swiped from a closet, walk into Maynard's room carrying a clipboard, and stick a hypodermic needle in his ear? Timothy, I'm surprised your feverish imagination can't come up with something cleverer than that old TV PI-show cliché."

"As a matter of fact, my feverish imagination has. Jim Suter's letter talked about people who sounded as if they were powerful enough to place somebody inside the hospital."

"You mean to say 'deep' inside the hospital, don't you? That's the way it's usually phrased in the mall-movie trailers and doctor-show promos."

Timmy tugged his pants up around his slender waist and said sourly, "I really don't know what's going on with you, Donald. But you seem to be in total denial of the meaning of the events of the past eighteen hours. First, we discover a black, funereal AIDS quilt panel for Jim Suter, a man who apparently isn't dead. The panel has pages from Betty Krumfutz's campaign biography on it. Then Betty herself shows up, examines the panel, and flees in horror. A few hours later, the panel is vandalized and the pages stolen. Meanwhile, Maynard receives a letter from Jim Suter saying Suter's life is in danger because he knows something—or somebody *thinks* he knows something—that can put important people in prison."

I said, "The letter actually said 'muchos años'—'big enchiladas' being jailed for 'muchos años.' Maybe that means these people are Mexican."

"Possibly, yes. And then," Timmy went on, yanking a shirt over his head, "somebody shoots Maynard—*shoots* him! With a gun! Poor Maynard—Maynard, one of the sweetest, most decent . . ." His voice caught, and he shook his head in despair.

I reached out, took Timmy's hand, and pulled him onto the bed next to me. "And then," he continued in a tremulous voice, "this cop shows up who's some cold-blooded, suspicious, creep-show weirdo, asking all the wrong questions. And *then* Maynard's house is ransacked in an obvious search for something somebody desperately wants to get hold of—something incriminating, presumably. And then, and then, and then—you say I'm being *paranoid?"*

I kissed him lightly on his big, white, beautifully shaped ear and spoke into it. "Yes and no."

"Oh, I see. Yes, I'm being paranoid, and no, I'm not. Oh."

He flopped back on the bed. I lay down beside him and lit a mental cigarette. I said, "Look, I understand that a lot of these awful things that are going on must be interconnected. Betty Krumfutz and the quilt vandalism, the shooting and the search of the house, and probably the quilt panel and Jim Suter's letter—yes, some or all of those form part of something bigger and even worse than the sum of all those ugly parts. If I didn't believe that, I wouldn't have observed Jim Suter's wishes—and Maynard's—and feigned ignorance with that strange, obnoxious cop.

"I'm only suggesting, Timothy, that even actual conspiracies have limits that are nearly always narrow. Whole hospitals, whole police departments, whole taxi fleets, are not parts of plots, except in Orwell, or Kafka's imagination, or—what? Oliver Stone? Nixon's tapes? A Pat Robertson fund-raising letter?"

Timmy smiled weakly. Then quickly he grew somber again and said, "You're right, but . . . how are we supposed to know *which* cop, or *which* taxi driver, or *which* hospital employee is the one not to trust? That's the problem I'm having right now."

Skeptical as I was of conspiracy theories to explain evil in human affairs, it was plain enough that Timmy's fears were not groundless, just, it seemed to me, highly exaggerated. Even more important, his fear was interfering with his analytical powers and clouding his judgment—often far keener than mine—in a way I knew was not going to help. I believed that taking the first train home to Albany would have been the smartest thing for him to do until he regained his perspective. But I knew he wasn't about to do that: he wouldn't leave Maynard; he wouldn't leave me.

I said, "What we have to do, I think, Timothy, is find somebody in authority who we can trust absolutely—someone who is known and trusted by someone in Washington we know and trust—and then confide in that person and ask him or her to help. What we need first and foremost is an honest cop. Preferably a top-echelon honest cop."

"That makes sense," Timmy said. "But how would we ever be sure that the honest cop was an actual honest cop and not someone whose sole purpose in the police department wasn't to pose as an honest cop and gain the confidence of people like us and then—do something. Get rid of us or whatever."

"Boy, you *are* freaked out."

"I guess I am."

"Do you want to go home?"

"Of course not. I mean, I'd love to, but it's out of the question."

"I figured that. Would you like any help in getting through this? I mean beyond what I have to offer—kind words, back rubs, active and/or passive anal intercourse three point two times a week, et cetera?"

"No, what you have to offer sounds sufficient, Don. Why? What else did you have in mind?"

"I don't know. Pharmacological assistance perhaps, of a legal or illegal variety?"

"Nah."

"A priest?"

"No, as you just pointed out, I've got you for anal intercourse."

"How about a Jungian analyst? A little dream work might be just what the doctor ordered for a boy overcome with the heebie-jeebies. Or an orthodox Freudian perhaps. I've heard Washington is overrun with them. 'So zen, tell me, Mr. Callahan, vaht cumps to mind?'"

He rolled toward me and said, "I guess we do have to just find somebody to trust with all this crap. You're right. That's a good first step. Maybe I'm feeling the way I'm feeling because we're so isolated with our dangerous knowledge, so alone with it. And we don't need a spiritual adviser, we need a good, old-fashioned clean cop. If possible, more than one. Then there'll be at least three of us to get to the bottom of this, and that'll make it easier."

"Timmy, I don't think 'we' have to get to the bottom of anything. All 'we' have to do is find an authority we can trust and tell him or her what we know, and then make sure Maynard is safe and recovering well. I guess we could straighten up his house, too—pick the Indonesian wombat knuckles out of the kitchen sink and so forth. But we can leave it to others better equipped than we are to get to the bottom of things."

This elicited a spontaneous snort, as I suspected it might. "Don't kid me," he said gaily. "You wouldn't miss sticking your nose in this reeking swamp of intrigue for anything in the world." I shrugged. "I know it's only a matter of time," Timmy went on happily, "before you're off to Mexico, and maybe even darkest Central Pennsylvania. I might not be able to tag along—I've got to be back to work on Tuesday. But I certainly wouldn't attempt to restrain you. I know you're in this awful thing to the finish, and I just want you to know, Don, that I'll help out in any way I can, personally and financially, and all I ask is that you get used to the fact that I am scared to death and even acknowledge from time to time that I actually have reason to be."

He seemed more relaxed now, and I was a lot less apprehensive about his mental health than I had been a few minutes earlier.

Then someone knocked at the door.

We both started, and Timmy, big-eyed, whispered, "Who knows we're here?"

"Five friends of Maynard's I just phoned," I whispered back. "The two I talked to and the three I left messages with."

The knock came again, three quick, hard raps.

I got up, went over, and looked through the peephole. I said to Timmy, "Take a deep breath and let it out slowly."

I opened the door and there stood Ray Craig glowering in at us like some grade-B film noir house dick. "It wasn't easy tracking you two down. I had to check half the hotels on the Hill." He must have been upwind of us, for his nicotine stench again rolled into the room.

I gestured for Craig to come on in, and as my glance fell on Timmy, I could actually see his pulse beating in his neck.

# 6

Using the pretext of having to hurry back to the hospital and check on Maynard, we were able to extricate ourselves from Craig within twenty minutes. He told us he wanted to hear our narratives of the shooting a second time. He said sometimes details floated back into memory during the retelling of a traumatic event a day later. This was true, but with Craig the line sounded phony. Again, he sat jiggling his loafer and looking both suspicious of and mildly disgusted with everything we had to say. Then, with barely a word uttered, Craig got up and left. This time, he had asked about Mexico only twice instead of six times.

"What is it with that creep?" Timmy muttered after Craig shut the door behind him.

"I don't know," I said, "but I think it's time we talked to somebody we can trust who'll at least be in a position to offer an informed opinion on Craig—and maybe everything else that's happened. Don't you know somebody in Frankie Balducci's office?" Frankie Balducci was the openly gay congressman from Boston who'd been a relentless voice of sanity on gay matters in an institution where understanding of, and attitudes toward, homosexuality had not yet, as the twenty-first century approached, advanced far into the eighteenth.

Timmy said, "Bob Bittner. He was in my class at Georgetown."

"Can you call him? Don't tell him why, but just ask him if he can find a D.C. police officer who's cleaner than Mother Teresa."

"That treacherous, headline-grabbing, reactionary old crone?"

"All right, then. Cleaner than . . . than any other cop in D.C. Gay might help, too, closeted or not."

Timmy reached his old friend, who agreed to try to track down an indisputably clean cop, no questions asked, and he said he'd get back to Timmy in fifteen minutes. I showered and Timmy went downstairs for a newspaper, and then Bittner called back. The officer we should talk to, he said, was Detective Lieutenant Chondelle Dolan.

After he hung up, Timmy said, "Bob says she's gay, she's smart, and she's squeaky-clean. Dolan is disinclined to rock any department boats, and she goes along and gets along with the mayor and his crowd of leeches and scam artists. But Bob says a woman he knows, Rain Terry, was once involved with Dolan for several months, and Terry swears Dolan is both one of the most uncorruptible people she's ever met and one of the most discreet."

"That's our cop."

"Bob wasn't sure she'd talk to us. Dolan is one for going through channels, he said."

"But if she's that clean, I'll bet our story will pique her interest, at least."

While I dialed Dolan's number, Timmy walked over and yanked open the door to the corridor. Assured that no one was lurking there, he shut the door and came back and sat on the bed while I waited for an answer at Dolan's home.

I was about to hang up when a low, groggy voice came on the line. "Yeah, hello."

"Lieutenant Dolan?"

"Yeah?"

"I'm Donald Strachey, a private investigator, and a friend of a friend of a friend of Rain Terry, who suggested I call you."

"Oh, Rain did, huh?" She sounded as if I had wakened her from a long, drugged sleep.

"I'm looking for the cleanest, most discreet police officer in Washington to talk to about, among other mystifying events, the shooting last night of a gay man by the name of Maynard Sudbury on E Street, Southeast. There may be more to the attack than the police have been told, and I need to bounce some of what I know off somebody in the department I know I can trust. Rain told Bob Bittner, of Frankie Balducci's office, that you are that person. Can we meet somewhere and I can run what I know by you?"

A silence. "Give me your number. I'll call you back."

I recited our hotel and room numbers and hung up. I said, "She's checking on Bittner with Terry and on us with Bittner."

I glanced through the *Post*—Bob Dole was threatening to take off the kid gloves in his second debate with Clinton—and Timmy checked the corridor again and then looked out the window for suspicious characters two stories below on Second Street, SE.

Within minutes Chondelle Dolan had called back and agreed to meet Timmy and me at a Pennsylvania Avenue bagel shop in half an hour. Meanwhile, I checked GW again to verify that Maynard was still stable. He was. With Timmy's concurrence, I went ahead and phoned a number in Tilton, Illinois, and reached, as I hoped I would, old Peace Corps ties aside, Maynard's brother. Neither Timmy nor I wanted to be the one to notify Maynard's parents, if we could avoid it. Edwin Sudbury said he would do that, and he said he and his wife would leave for Washington as soon as they could make travel arrangements.

"Was it a mugging?" Sudbury asked anxiously.

I said the motive for the attack had not yet been determined, but that given Washington's robbery rate, a mugging was what a lot of people seemed to suspect it might have been. Seated nearby, Timmy rolled his eyes.

"You got ID?" she said.

"Sure." I showed her my New York State PI license, and Timmy presented his card identifying him as the chief legislative aide to New York State assemblyman Myron Lipshutz.

"Bob Bittner says you guys have your idiosyncrasies but that you're responsible enough citizens, and I should take you seriously even if what you have to say might sound a little gonzo at first."

"That sums us up," I said.

Dolan looked at me with no hint of enthusiasm but with large dark eyes that were interested and alert. In her midthirties, she had a big, handsome Ibo face with the kind of sharply ridged, ample lips that I'd always found deeply erotic on black men and pleasing in a less hormonal way on black women. Dolan's shoulder-length hair, done in a near-flip, was black and gleaming, and her eye shadow was the same shade of cobalt blue as her two-piece silk suit and blouse. Had it not been for her bulky muscularity, she'd have looked less like a cop than a prosecuting attorney, or a regional administrator of the Department of Labor. She was both cool and formidable—I guessed that even in Marion Barry's age of racial payback in Washington, her rise through the police ranks had not been easy—and it looked as if we had lucked out in hooking up with Chondelle Dolan.

Timmy fidgeted with his bagel and said, "Do you mind if we look at your ID, too, Ms. Dolan?"

"No problem," she said, and flipped open a black leather wallet so that we could examine her name and badge.

"Thanks," Timmy said. "We're nervous—I am, anyway—and when you hear about all this grotesque stuff, I think you'll understand why."

"Uh-huh. Well, you go ahead and tell me your story. I've got plenty of time. I've got a lunch date at one, but till then I'm interested to hear what you got to say about this shooting you mentioned."

I began to speak, but Timmy's eyes darted quickly around the bagel shop at the other customers, and he cut me off with, "You used to date Rain Terry? I just met her a few times and she seemed awfully nice."

"Yeah, Rain's a peach." Dolan picked up on Timmy's antsiness and leaned closer and lowered her voice. "Rain's got two kids now with her partner—two little boys. Did you know that?"

"No, I didn't," Timmy said.

"That's not for me," Dolan said in a matter-of-fact way. "I got nine brothers and sisters, seven of them younger than me. Somebody else wants to overpopulate the world, fine. Me? Uh-uh."

"I'm the father of a child in Edensburg, New York, north of Albany," Timmy said, and with an accustomed gesture whipped out his wallet. "Two lesbian friends asked me to be the father of their child—via artificial insemination, of course—and it turns out I love it. This is Erica Osborne-Kotlowitz."

Dolan glanced briefly at the photo of a tiny person in a white dress and said, "Looks human to me, Timothy. Good for you, honey."

"She'll be seventeen months old this Thursday," he said.

"Uh-huh."

I said, "Chondelle—may I call you Chondelle?"

"Yes, you may."

"Chondelle, to get to the point, a close friend of Timmy's was shot and seriously wounded in front of his house on E Street, Southeast, last night."

"Maynard Sudbury is his name," Timmy put in, leaning close to Dolan. "We were in the Peace Corps together in India in the midsixties. A poultry development project. Few of us had any real experience with farming of any kind. We were what the Peace Corps calls BAGs—B.A. generalists. The Peace Corps philosophy at that time was—"

"Timmy, Chondelle has a date in a couple of hours, so maybe we need to just explain to her what happened yesterday and last night and postpone the theories of rural development until a later date."

"Yeah," she said, "I'd love to hear about you and your friends raising chickens. But let's save that."

I looked around, and nobody was seated at the tables adjacent to ours, and none of the Sunday-morning coffee drinkers and *Post* readers in the shop showed any sign of being aware of us at all. I said, "Timmy is afraid that the shooting and a number of other disturbing events yesterday are interconnected—part of an extensive Robert Ludlum–style conspiracy. I don't agree, but his suspicions are not entirely off-the-wall. It was a pretty wild twelve hours yesterday." Then I laid it all out: the first unexpurgated version of Saturday's events spoken out loud by Timmy or me to anyone.

While Timmy shifted uneasily in his seat, I described to Dolan Maynard's shock at discovering an AIDS quilt panel for Jim Suter; the mysterious appearance at the panel by a woman Maynard recognized as former congresswoman Betty Krumfutz; the letter from Suter warning Maynard that Suter's life was in danger and the admonition not to reveal Suter's whereabouts to anyone, especially not to the D.C. cops or to any people on "the Hill"; the reported vandalism of the Suter panel on the quilt; the brutal shooting; the ransacking of Maynard's house while Timmy and I were at the hospital; the unnerving multiple appearances by D.C. police detective Ray Craig.

Dolan listened to this recitation carefully and with a look of concern and growing distaste. When I mentioned Suter's warning not to reveal any of this story to the D.C. cops, Dolan raised a carefully drawn eyebrow but did not react otherwise.

When I had finished, she said, "I'm sorry about your friend. I hope he makes it. Firearms do terrible damage to human bodies, but at GW they deal with these injuries all the time. So he's in good hands."

"And Maynard's resilient," Timmy said. "He's survived things almost as bad as getting shot—parasites, plagues, guerrilla wars, mobs, you name it. So there's reason to hope he can withstand this attack, too."

"Maynard sounds like a real tough bird."

"So, what do you think?" Timmy said. "Am I crazy, or is there really something big going on here? Something . . . something interrelated with . . . with a lot of people involved in it?" He took a quick look over his shoulder, as if he might catch another patron of the coffee shop in the act of pointing a directional microphone our way, or aiming a bamboo pipe with a poisoned blow dart.

Dolan said, "No, it's not crazy to consider the possibility that there's a connection between everything that went on yesterday. That's not crazy at all. It does sound to me like it's more than a run of bad luck."

"But," I said, "Timmy may be letting his imagination roam a bit too freely, don't you think? Such as imagining, to cite just one example, that some of the GW hospital staff may be out to do Maynard in, and the same for large segments of the D.C. Metropolitan Police Department. I think he needs to be reassured on these points, among a number of others."

Dolan sighed heavily and said, "Look, I gotta make a phone call. I told my date I'd check in with her around now. Come on with me while I make a quick call, okay? There's a phone down at the corner, by Second."

Before we could question Dolan, she stood up and we quickly got up, too, and followed her out onto Pennsylvania Avenue. None of us had finished our coffee, but Dolan paid no attention to that.

As we walked up Pennsylvania toward the Library of Congress, Dolan looked straight ahead and said, "I just wanted to get us out of there. Don't turn around, don't look back, but another plainclothes officer was in the coffee shop. He came in right after I did and sat three tables behind you all. He was too far away to hear much of anything you said, but after you told me what you told me, Donald, I thought, why is this man sitting here? The officer's name is Ewell Flower, and he works under Ray Craig."

Timmy said, "Oh, God," and he appeared to be putting a lot of effort into not looking over his shoulder, as was I.

"Why not let's walk on over to the Capitol," Dolan said. She led us across Pennsylvania, past the library, across the Capitol grounds with their beautifully kept greenery and their antiterrorist reinforced-concrete barricades—would missiles with tactical nuclear warheads explode out of the bushes in the event of attack?—and around the south wing of the great building. The Capitol looked soft and creamy in the autumn morning sunlight, as if it could somehow render benign even the hard-hearted harangues of Jesse or Newt that regularly bounced off the walls inside.

From the high terrace of the west facade, we looked out over the city and the Mall and the AIDS quilt stretching away toward the Washington Monument, and beyond that, Abe Lincoln. Tens of thousands of people milled quietly among the panels. Timmy had remarked the day before that he had never seen so many people in one place remain so subdued. The quiet was partly a sign of respect, we concluded, and of so many of the quilt visitors being lost in memory, but it was also that no words felt adequate to express the quilt's huge and complex meaning.

Timmy said, "It's funny. Five minutes ago I was really frightened, but here I actually feel safe. In fact, this is the first time in twelve hours that I've actually felt safe. Not that I necessarily *am* safe," he added, and took a quick look back toward Pennsylvania Avenue. I looked around, too, but saw no one who stood out among the quilt visitors and other tourists and passersby. Dolan had not described Ewell Flower to us, so I didn't know whom to look for.

Timmy went on, "It's interesting how most gay people aren't usually aware of feeling *un*safe. But at these big, mainly gay events, you're always aware of feeling safe in a way you never do any other time. Do you know what I mean?"

I said I knew, but Dolan just said, "I'll take your word for it."

I asked, "Is this Ewell Flower following us? Have you spotted him since we left the coffee shop?"

"No, and he probably knows I made him. He's a short, skinny African-American man, gray-haired, wearing shades, in a black windbreaker. If they've got a tail on you, he probably switched off with somebody. I don't recognize anybody else from the division just now. I guess they could be using people from outside the division. So, yeah, we could still be under surveillance."

Dolan said all this nonchalantly, but I could all but hear Timmy's sphincter squeaking as it tightened. My own bloodstream was on the move, too.

"What reasons can you think of," I asked, "why Timmy and I might be under surveillance by the Metro Police Department?"

"Craig might suspect strongly that you had something to do with the shooting. Is there any reason he should?"

"Of course not," Timmy said. "That's just wacky."

"No, not wacky, just not real smart. Ray is one of those guys out of another age who think that if you are homosexual, you are, ipso facto, mentally impaired and possibly dangerous. Ray and I have talked about his old-fashioned opinions, which for some reason he seems to want to hang on to."

"Have you been to law school?" I asked Dolan.

"I went to Howard prelaw for a year. I learned a lot of history and a lot of law, and I learned to speak standard American English. But I knew all I ever really wanted was to be a cop, so I switched to an M.A. program in criminal justice. I had an uncle who was an officer in the department until a sociopathic child shot him in the heart in 1989. James Dolan was the kind of man who made police work look like a noble calling. For him, it was a noble calling, I still believe, although for me it's been quite a bit more complicated than that."

"Because you're an African-American lesbian?" I said.

"No, because I'm a woman."

"Oh."

"And now my life is about to become even more complicated in the division on account of you two. I'm not complaining," Dolan said, and hoisted herself, one ham at a time, onto the stone balustrade beneath what must have been the House Speaker's office. "I'm glad you called me. What you told me is interesting. Maybe I can help out a little bit—I don't know yet. But word'll get back to Ray Craig, if it hasn't already, that you guys are talking to me. So we better get our stories straight, right?"

Timmy said, "Absolutely."

"Let's say you heard about me from Bob Bittner, over at Frankie's office—which is true—and you wanted to check in with a gay cop and tell your story to somebody who'd lend a more sympathetic ear than Ray did. That's true, too, and even more important than being true, it's plausible. Ray'll probably just say, 'Oh, they have to go and be PC.' What we don't need to repeat to anybody at this point is all that interesting stuff you told me about this Jim Suter, and the quilt panel, and Betty Krumfutz. Let's keep all that amongst ourselves for now. If there is somebody in the department who is criminally involved, we don't want it to get back, okay?"

We both said no, we didn't want that.

"See, the thing of it is," Dolan went on coolly, "I made a couple of calls before I met you at the bagel shop, and early this morning Craig came up with two witnesses to your friend getting shot. A man and a woman were sitting in a parked car—sharing a joint, it sounds like—about forty yards down E Street. And they saw the whole thing: Sudbury come out his door and walk to his car, a white Honda with Maryland plates roll down the street, stop beside him, and then gunfire. Then the car—which probably was a white Honda stolen earlier in the evening in Kensington—proceeded at a high rate of speed down E Street and turned left at First. The witnesses got a quick look at the driver—who was probably the shooter—and at his front-seat passenger. Both of them, the witnesses said, looked Latino, they thought. Central American, Indian-looking, not Spanish. What the witnesses actually said was, the perpetrators looked Mexican."

Timmy shook his head in amazement. "This is all for real."

I asked Dolan, "If I can locate and talk to Jim Suter and get his story, can you help me find a way to protect him?"

Grimly she said, "Look, this whole episode has drug-operation turf war written all over it. If that's what Jim Suter is involved in, maybe nobody can protect him and you will want to do one thing and one thing only, and that is, stand way clear. You mean this didn't occur to you, Donald? Mexico is now a key transit point for South American narcotics entering the United States. Mexican officials, police agencies, often the narcs themselves, want a piece of this billion-dollar pie. It's a poor country where a lot of people just go ahead and grab what they can. You didn't consider that that might be the source of Jim Suter's troubles?"

"It occurred to me," I said. "But what's a former Republican congresswoman from Central Pennsylvania got to do with it? That part of it makes no sense."

"I guess that's a question you'll have to ask Jim Suter."

"Will you help me investigate?" I said. "I'd like to do what I can to bring in the people who shot Maynard, and to do it without hurting Jim Suter, if that's possible. That's the way Maynard would want me to do it, I think—not that he has any real idea of what Suter's involvement is. The one thing that's certain in all this is that Maynard had no known connection to whatever is going on here, and he does not deserve to be lying shot up in a hospital bed struggling to stay alive."

"Yeah, that's usually the way it goes," Dolan said. "No, I won't help you investigate the case. I haven't been assigned to it, and I won't be, and I've got another six or eight dozen cases open at the moment. What I will do is: I'll keep you up to speed on the department's progress on the case as well as I can without actually doing anything that might jeopardize my job. I'll also try to find out who else in the department is keeping close track of the case, and why. That should help out."

Timmy said, "What if you find out a *lot* of people in the department, especially higher-ups, are keeping close tabs on the case?"

Dolan shrugged. "What if I do?"

"But wouldn't that be significant?" Timmy was pale and looked a little woozy.

"I guess it would be," Dolan said, and caught my eye. She seemed to be thinking what I was thinking, that maybe it was time for Timmy to head back to Albany.

# 7

I know why you're doing this," Timmy said. We were back in the hotel room, where a call to GW had just confirmed that Maynard was unconscious but still in stable condition. "You're acknowledging that there's at least a possibility that some well-connected gang of some type thinks it needs to kill Maynard for whatever weird reason. And you're showing by your actions that the only way to guarantee Maynard's safety—or at least ease my mind about it—is either to disprove a conspiracy, or to expose it and end it. Is that right?"

"Not exactly."

"What do you mean?"

"I mean what you say is partly true, but—Timothy, while the size of my ego may fall within the upper midrange of normal, I do not suffer from delusions of grandeur. I can poke around and try to come up with an educated guess as to the nature of this—thing. But if it's extensive at all, there's precious little I'll be able to do about it. Especially if it's a Mexican drug-gang operation. To those people, I'd be gnatlike, an insect they'd swat. I'm selectively ambitious, yes, but I'm not suicidal."

"Do you think it is a drug operation that Suter's mixed up in?"

"I know too little to have formed a strong opinion, but right now I'd say probably not."

"I don't think so either."

"It's the involvement of the quilt," I said. "And Betty Krumfutz." Timmy nodded enthusiastically. "What could they possibly have to do with drug gangs?"

"A lot of religious-right types are hypocrites," Timmy said.

"But their hypocrisies are usually more mundane—sexual or unsensationally financial. Nobody ever suspected Pat Robertson of running a drug cartel."

"He does have ties with Mobutu in Zaire. Robertson controls mineral concessions there, and he's an apologist in Washington for the tyrant. But, as I understand them, Betty Krumfutz's misdeeds were of a more parochial variety. Or, to be more accurate, her husband's transgressions were. He was actually the only one charged and convicted of the fraudulent use of campaign funds."

"That's right. I don't remember reading about anything international in the Krumfutz case. And they wouldn't have been involved in any CIA–Nicaraguan contras drug connection. Whatever that amounted to, or didn't amount to, it took place in the early to mid eighties—way too long ago."

"On the other hand," I said, "I think we have to take seriously Chondelle's hunch that the actual attack on Maynard was done by drug people. She'd have a reliable feel for that. Maybe Betty Krumfutz wasn't involved in anything really awful. Maybe just her husband was—or is."

"As I recall, Maynard told us Nelson Krumfutz isn't in prison yet, pending the outcome of his appeals. Maybe Betty stumbled onto something—about drug dealing by her husband possibly—and she—what?—heard that some incriminating evidence had been sewn onto Jim Suter's panel in the AIDS quilt. That sounds far-fetched, I guess."

"It does. Although we are talking here about a husband and wife who actually went out and did what people have to do in the United States in order to get elected to Congress—lust after cash like methadone addicts in search of a fix and act civil to some of the biggest assholes in the country. So, where the Krumfutzes are concerned, feel free to give your imagination wide latitude."

"Ah so," Timmy said. "Am I now to believe that you may be ready to entertain the idea of an actual plot? Earlier today my imagination was feverish and possibly in need of medication. Now I'm supposed to give it free rein?"

"Don't go that far. Look, I'm ready to accept that there are connections among several disturbing events here. And speculation on what those connections are can serve as a pastime, for now, in the absence of facts. I'm just not ready—and I don't plan on getting ready—to implicate entire hospitals or entire transportation fleets or entire agencies of government in a monstrous conspiracy."

"I get that. You've made your views plain."

"It's not that I don't believe in conspiracies. I know, recent American history is full of them, from plots to use the Mafia to kill Castro, to the FBI plot to drive Martin Luther King to suicide, to Cointelpro, to Iran-contra. But nearly all human folly and evil, Timothy, is individual—bad or just fallible people caught in the act of being their wicked or weak selves. This has been my experience in life—from crooked pols in Albany, to greedy developers, to people who, when they are backed into an actual or emotional corner, lash out and kill."

"Yes, Don, that's been your experience. But aren't you being just a tad solipsistic?" he said, yet again waving his gilded degree from a Jesuit institution in my face. "Maybe your experience with evil has been relatively narrow, and now it's being broadened. Usually you're as rigorous as anybody I know in insisting on empirical evidence to support your analyses. But this time, you're not. All the evidence here says something complex and very dangerous is happening. I know you think I'm going all nellie and wussing out, but that's not it. It's not me, it's the facts. I *am* afraid, and fear is the only rational reaction to what has happened to Maynard and to you and me over the past twenty-four hours. If you've got facts to the contrary, I'd like to hear about them."

"I didn't say I wasn't afraid."

"No, but you keep acting as if I'm the Grady Sutton character to your Joel McCrea. I saw the way you and Chondelle were looking at me a while ago—as if I were a small child who would probably have to be sent to the countryside until the war is over.

Yes, I am afraid, and I guess I show it, but—I've made a decision about something."

"About what?"

"I'm staying in Washington until Maynard is safe. I'll call Myron today. It'll screw things up in the office, but he'll understand, and Fred Ginsburg can cover for me. I've got three weeks of vacation time coming, and I'm taking it. I'll stay with Maynard—if he lives—and if I have to, I'll hire a private security service to keep us both secure. Also, if you're going to go ahead and investigate Jim Suter and the mysterious quilt panel—which it looks as if you're going to do, because you're a good guy and because you're hopelessly nosy and curious—then I'm going to pay your expenses."

"I guess you have made a decision. More than one decision. For both of us."

"No, I've just decided what I'm going to do. You have to make your own decisions."

"You Peace Corps guys stick together. I've noticed that."

"That tends to be true."

"When we go back to the hospital, we'll probably find Sargent and Eunice Shriver kneeling in prayer at Maynard's bedside."

"I wouldn't be surprised."

Timmy had my number, as always. "So okay then. I'll never be a full-fledged member of the Peace Corps club, but I'll do my bit for the cause, and for Maynard—and of course for you. I'll follow the question wherever it leads. My belief is, it won't lead far. But we'll see."

"Thanks, Don."

Then came a sudden sharp rapping at the hotel-room door. Timmy started, then quietly moaned, "Oh no, oh no."

I didn't want to believe what I thought Timmy was thinking. But as I approached the door, even before opening it, I thought I caught a whiff of Ray Craig's nicotine aura.

We let him in. He sniffed the air. He glared. Without being

invited to do so, Craig took a seat. I thought, he's going to light a cigarette. He didn't, but he fiddled with the pack in his jacket pocket. I wondered if a map was in the packet in the pocket of the jacket—a routine from an old Red Skelton movie—but I decided that mentioning it was unlikely to bring a chuckle to Craig's lips.

He said, "You two had coffee with Detective Chondelle Dolan this morning and went walking around with her. Why?"

"How do you know that?" I said.

His ordinarily dead eyes flashed at my insolence. A Ray Craig of fifty years earlier would have pulled out a sap and worked me over while his goonish partner held me in a headlock. But the times had changed enough for me—if not for every U.S. inner-city resident—and Craig apparently felt not only constrained by the law, he was even unable to avoid answering my question.

"I've had you two under surveillance."

"Why?" I asked.

"For your own protection."

"I doubt that we need protection. What makes you think we might?"

He eyed me coldly, glanced at Timmy, then looked back at me and said, "Washington can be a dangerous place."

"Your decision to have us followed was based on local crime statistics?"

Craig snapped, "I use my professional judgment. If you think I'm some fucking incompetent with shit for brains and my head up my ass, I'd like to hear about it."

This produced a long, strained silence. I knew Timmy would be considering, as I was, Craig's vivid but visually confusing metaphor.

Craig himself finally broke the tension. "Let's talk about Chondelle Dolan."

"Sure. Let's."

"You people stick together, don't you?"

"Chondelle was never in the Peace Corps. For that matter, neither was I."

"You know damn well what I mean. She's a lesbo. She's a big nigger lesbo."

Timmy said evenly, "I'm requesting that you do not talk like that."

"Come again?" Craig eyes were blazing.

"Never mind."

"What do you want with us this time?" I said. "We were just on our way out."

"I've got news concerning my investigation. You'll be interested in this. I've got two eyewitnesses to the E Street shooting. My witnesses say the perpetrators were Mexicans."

Timmy and I feigned surprise. "Oh?"

"Did Sudbury use drugs?" Craig said.

Timmy said, "No."

"Do you?"

"No," Timmy repeated.

I said, "We get high on life. How about you? What do you get high on?"

Craig was seated on the desk chair and I was on the edge of the bed. He flushed and spasmed once, but he didn't lunge at me. Instead, he clapped his notebook shut violently, stood up, and tramped out of the room, slamming the door behind him.

# 8

Log Heaven, Pennsylvania, was up in the thinly populated central part of the state off Interstate 80. The autumn foliage was at its brilliant peak under a high blue sky crisscrossed with big, floating jet vapor trails that looked like ancient glyphs above the earth. I wondered what they meant. Probably Scranton-Pittsburgh, Baltimore-Toronto. The broad highway swept between and sometimes up and down the state's old, worn, friendly mountains, and I wished Timmy were along to enjoy the scenic ride.

He was back in Washington, where we had met some of Maynard's friends when they converged on GW University Hospital. Some of them were going to maintain a watch at the hospital—Maynard's condition was unchanged when I left early Sunday afternoon—and others planned on cleaning up Maynard's house in hopeful anticipation of Maynard's recovery and eventual return.

Neither Timmy nor I told Maynard's friends about Jim Suter's mysterious quilt panel or the letter from Mexico full of warnings. So everyone who knew Maynard remained baffled as to why he might have been shot down in the street and his home ransacked. Some of them speculated on a book or an article he might have been working on that exposed foreign criminality of some sort, but no one could recall Maynard's mentioning any such project. On the contrary, everyone said, Maynard had been doing relatively undemanding straight travel writing since he'd picked up his stomach ailment.

A couple of times I referred to Maynard's recent trip to Mexico. I thought it might jog someone's memory of any remark Maynard might have made about Jim Suter. But Maynard either never told anyone of the odd meeting in Mérida, or none of his acquaintances considered it worth mentioning now.

Chondelle Dolan was able to use her GOP Capitol Hill contacts—she'd once been involved, she had told me that morning, with the first black female member of the Log Cabin Club—to track down former congresswoman Krumfutz. On the staff now of the conservative Glenn Beale Foundation, Mrs. Krumfutz kept an apartment in Washington as well as her Log Heaven home, which she often visited on weekends. She had driven up to Pennsylvania Saturday evening with a friend, Chondelle said, several hours after Maynard had pointed her out to Timmy and me at the Jim Suter quilt panel.

I'd made a plane reservation for a flight to the Yucatán on Tuesday morning. I figured twenty-four hours in Log Heaven would give me enough time to confront Mrs. Krumfutz and extract from her what was extractable concerning her examination on Saturday of the Suter quilt panel and her subsequent panicked, hasty departure from the quilt display and then from Washington. I knew I ran some risk of tipping off the people who had shot Maynard—whoever and whatever they were—and of further endangering Suter. But I convinced myself that the risk was slight and worth taking.

Timmy's Capitol Hill friend Bob Bittner had briefed me on the Krumfutz illegal-campaign-fund scandal—at Timmy's request, Bittner did not ask why I was inquiring about this—and I learned that not only had Mrs. Krumfutz been cleared of any involvement in the scam, but that she had been eager to disassociate herself from her husband, who had spent many tens of thousands of dollars of congressional campaign donations on the home and wardrobe of one Tammy Pam Jameson, of Engineville, near Log Heaven. Mrs. Krumfutz had eagerly testified against her husband at his trial, and I concluded that if she had more recently uncovered additional criminality—by way of the AIDS quilt or otherwise—she would be more inclined to talk about it to me or to the police than to anyone involved in the crime, especially her low slug of a husband. And I did not plan on tracking down Nelson Krumfutz—now residing in Engineville with Tammy Pam, I was told—just yet.

I pulled into Log Heaven in the black shadows of the surrounding mountains under a fall sunset that was a puddle of fire. The sky looked like a Jehovah's Witness's *Watchtower* magazine cover, and I remembered that the millennium was just a few years away. Maybe Armageddon would start off in Log Heaven. It seemed as likely a place as any, despite warnings from the TV preachers that when Good rose up and vanquished Evil, San Francisco would get it first. Then the West Village, the East Village, and Chelsea. Would a wrathful God spare SoHo? Park Slope? TriBeCa? This was unclear.

I cruised down Log Heaven's Main Street, with its three-block-long business district that looked half-dead and half-hanging-on-by-a-fraying-economic-thread. Most of the storefronts were vacant, and the few that weren't were occupied by social-service agencies and businesses with names like Natalie's Nail Heaven, Fenstermacher's Tanning Parlor ("Tan Yer Fanny by the Susquehanny"), and the Mattress Madness Outlet Store. Three big furniture factories I'd passed on the edge of town were dark and boarded up, and the only sizable employer I spotted was a mobile-home assembly plant. I doubled back up River Street. The Susquehanna, one of the loveliest streams in America, was no longer visible from the town that the river had apparently once made prosperous. Somebody—the Army Corps of Engineers, I suspected—had put up a thirty-foot-high, earth-and-stone dike-levee system, a flood-control solution common across floodplain America now, and in its unimaginativeness and inelegance, worthy of the mind of Benito Mussolini. It looked as if in Log Heaven, the walled-off Susquehanna survived largely for the esthetic pleasure of an occasional small-plane pilot and in the minds of the old people.

Back on the outskirts of town, I pulled my rental car into the Bit o' Heaven Motel and checked in. The clerk, a stout, middle-aged woman with a fresh perm and pale teddy bears on her pink blouse, smelled of Ivory soap and Kraft macaroni-and-cheese dinner. When I asked about getting a bite to eat, she suggested that I try Pizza Hut or Karen's Kozy Korner, both up the road. She said they were both good.

I checked the Log Heaven–Engineville phone book and found that Betty Krumfutz was not listed. I told the clerk I was a reporter with the *Philadelphia Inquirer*—it seemed like an efficient enough little fib—and I asked for directions to the Krumfutz residence.

"I feel sorry for that woman," the clerk said. "Betty got a raw deal."

"Yes, her husband was the wrongdoer," I agreed.

"She's a celebrity, but it's taken a toll. Is the *Inquire* going after her now?" She pronounced *Inquirer* "IN-quire," which I'd never heard before, and she seemed ready to be annoyed.

"No, it'll be a favorable piece. Betty's had a tough row to hoe. And far be it from the *Inquirer* to add to her woes."

The clerk told me that her husband's mother "still reads the *Inquire*"—an eccentricity of the elderly, it was made to sound like—and she'd ask her to save my article. Then she told me how to find the Krumfutz house on Susquehanna Drive in Log Heaven. She said she thought Betty would be home; the clerk had a friend who was in Betty's target-practice group, which met on Sunday afternoons. So Betty always made it a point to be in Log Heaven on Sundays, "for church and target practice."

"What do they shoot?" I asked.

The clerk looked puzzled. "Bottles and cans and things like that, I guess."

"With guns?"

"Why, yes. It's the gun-club members."

"Who all is in the gun club? Hunters? Sportsmen?"

She nodded, beginning to look a little suspicious of this interrogation.

I took a wild stab and said, "An American citizen's constitutional right to bear arms is the envy of the world. I was speaking to a Canadian recently who was thinking of emigrating to the United States so that he could keep his own firearm for self-protection. He drives down to Watertown, New York, once a week for target practice there. Are there any foreigners like that in the Log Heaven gun club? Or, I guess Log Heaven is too far from the border for that."

"Funny you should ask that," the motel clerk said. "Both Luis and Hector are in the gun club, I know. They work in the kitchen at the Kozy Korner. Karen's in the gun club and she got her two Mexicans to join, she told me. But she said they already knew how to shoot, and they actually taught her a thing or two. But I doubt if they came to America for target practice. They came to get work. Which I say, more power to them. You try to get our kids to wash dishes these days, and you might as well ask them to fly to the moon. It's even hard to get kids these days who'll rake and bag leaves. They might get their hands dirty. But Luis and Hector, why they'll even do yard work. As a matter of fact, they've been doing work lately around the Krumfutz place. Karen said Betty had hired Hector and Luis for some type of work she had, and Betty told Karen that she was quite satisfied with the good job they did."

# 9

Mexicans with guns? I locked the door behind me in my room at the Bit o' Heaven and sat on the edge of the bed. I held my right hand out and checked it for steadiness. The tremor was minor but discernible. My Smith & Wesson was back in Albany—why would I have carried a firearm to a display of the AIDS quilt?—but suddenly up in Log Heaven what I was thinking hard about was protecting myself. Was I panicking, like Timmy? Was I reacting stupidly to an ethnic stereotype?

I made a credit-card call to Timmy's and my room at the Capitol Hill Hotel but got no answer. I guessed Timmy was off at GW with Maynard and his friends and, maybe by now, Maynard's brother and sister-in-law. I got hold of the hotel desk and left a message for Timmy, informing him that I would not be staying over in Log Heaven that night after all, but would be returning to Washington late. I did not explain that I was afraid of being unarmed in a town where two Mexican sharpshooters with connections to Betty Krumfutz were on the loose; I kept it vague. Then I called GW and learned that Maynard was still "stable," a promising sign.

I showered, rumpled the sheets to make the bed look as if it had been slept in, repacked my bag, left the key on the desk, and went out into the cold, black Pennsylvania night. I threw my bag in the car and drove away from the Bit o' Heaven Motel. The next day, Monday, was going to be Columbus Day, but I figured that even if Betty Krumfutz remained in Log Heaven for the holiday, she would probably not run into Karen, of Karen's Kozy Korner, until the following Sunday at target-shooting practice and possibly learn that a *Philadelphia Inquirer* reporter had been in Log Heaven intent on interviewing her—a reporter who had then mysteriously failed to show up at Mrs. Krumfutz's door.

I drove up the highway past K Mart, past E-Z Mart, past Pizza Hut, Valu-Video, and Hall's Beer Distributor to the Kozy Korner. It wasn't on a corner and with its cold-white-light and Formica interior it wasn't cozy. Two specials were scrawled on a blackboard propped next to the cash register. The fried haddock with FF & apple sauce was $3.85. The ham croquettes with mac and cheese was $3.15.

I asked the round, clear-skinned young woman who took my order—I couldn't resist the croquettes—if she was Karen. She smiled, showing me her braces, and said uh-uh, she was Stacy; Karen didn't come in on Sunday.

While I waited, I read the ads on my place mat for a tire store, a sealer of driveways, and, among others, Ron Diefenderfer, CPA, and Helen's Pitch-n-putt. The other tables and booths at the Kozy Korner were occupied mainly by middle-aged and elderly married couples who had apparently run out of anything to say to each other some years back. They seemed to take their gratification from their haddock, which I figured they knew they had earned. At a table near the back, three voluble older women sat, loudly comparing doctors with Indian names. They liked Dr. Patel best because, one woman said, he didn't give you the bum's rush.

I could see over the counter and through a big window into the kitchen. I saw no Mexicans there, just a woman in a blue smock; her origins looked local. She seemed to be the cook, and a skinny teenaged boy in a baseball cap that was on frontward—was this a clue?—washed dishes.

I enjoyed the comfort food, which I followed with plain coffee—no sign was up announcing "brussels sprouts" or "Robitussin" as the ground-roast flavor of the day—and I had a small saucer of rice pudding. The bill came to just over five dollars, including tip. Driving back into Log Heaven, I exercised my tongue as I attempted to pry loose the mac and cheese still stuck to the roof of my mouth. I got most of it.

Just after nine o'clock, I parked the car along Susquehanna Drive across from the address for Betty Krumfutz that the motel clerk had given me. I was up on a bluff on the western outskirts of Log Heaven. To my right was a sharp drop-off, with the river in the darkness below. Across the street to my left was a wide, split-level flagstone ranch house on a partially wooded hillside. A broad driveway, newly tarmacked, ran up to a two-car garage. A gray Chrysler LeBaron with Pennsylvania plates was parked on one side of the driveway, a Chevy pickup truck with plates I didn't recognize was on the other.

Lights were on behind the drawn drapes in the big picture window. Another room was lit—the kitchen?—between the living room and the garage. There were no floodlights or other illumination outside the house. Clouds had moved in, and I decided that I could get away with a quick bout of voyeurism under cover of the October darkness. I knew that if I was caught by the Log Heaven police, I would have no plausible explanation I could safely provide them for spying on former congresswoman Krumfutz. And if Mrs. Krumfutz and her two Mexican shootists got hold of me, I might long to be in the custody of local law officers. But a quick look around seemed minimally risky, so I got out of the car and shut the door quietly.

Susquehanna Drive was also the main road to Engineville, twenty-six miles upriver, where Nelson Krumfutz and his girlfriend, Tammy Pam Jameson, now consorted. Traffic to Engineville on Sunday night was sparse, so I had no trouble ambling across the road apparently sight unseen. The nearest streetlight was a quarter of a mile east, and the houses on either side of the Krumfutz place were lit inside but with the shades drawn. I strode directly up the Krumfutz front lawn, passed under a good-sized maple—black trash bags apparently stuffed with fallen leaves had been piled up alongside the driveway—and on to the back of the property. I lingered there for a couple of minutes getting used to the darkness and listening for any pets Mrs. Krumfutz or her neighbors might have had on the loose. I'd once had, in a similar set of circumstances, an encounter with a warthog in a poodle suit that I did not want to repeat.

I went around to the darkened rear ell section of the house. I passed an air conditioner jutting out from a window—I could just make it out in the near-darkness—and I was careful not to whack into it. What if, when he hit the air conditioner, O.J. had been knocked unconscious? What if Kato had gone out with a flashlight and discovered O.J., knocked out, with a bag full of bloody clothes? Whom would Kato have phoned? Nine one one? William Morris? O.J.'s dry cleaner? How might it all have turned out differently? I wondered.

Staying close to the wall of the house, I moved across a stone terrace to the sliding glass doors that I estimated were opposite the picture window out front. Heavy white drapes blocked my view in—and Mrs. Krumfutz's view out—so I continued on beyond the doors to a smaller, darkened window that looked in on what appeared to be a breakfast nook. The venetian blinds were only half-shut, so by standing close to the window on the far side I found an angle that afforded a line of sight into the living room behind the drapes.

"Don't move!"

I turned, and a bright light hit my face.

"I want to see your hands!"

"You bet."

"Both of them!"

"Two is my limit."

A floodlight mounted on the side of the house came on, illuminating the entire terrace, and I saw that the man with the flashlight in one hand and a drawn revolver in the other was wearing a police uniform.

"Assume the position!" the cop barked.

That phraseology had always sounded like something out of my high school debating-club days, but I knew what this man meant.

"Spread 'em! Get 'em up!"

I pressed my palms against the wall of the house as the cop patted me down. He had pocketed his flashlight, but he still held the police special. A door opened off to my right, and I heard a nasal female voice say, "What's going on? Horse, what in the world are you doing?"

"Speck Spindler saw somebody in your yard, Mrs. Krumfutz, and called it in. It's this guy here!"

"Oh, for heaven sakes!"

As the cop yanked my wallet out of my jacket pocket, I turned far enough to catch sight of a bulky woman in a pale green sweat suit. With her small mouth open in a look of shocked surprise, she was identical to the woman I'd seen the day before at Jim Suter's quilt panel, minus the shades and the golf-cart-motif head scarf. Mrs. Krumfutz did have a bandanna tied around her head, but instead of golf carts it had pictures of cherry pies all over it. I knew they were cherry because each pie had a C carved in the crust.

"Are you all right, Mrs. Krumfutz?" the cop said as he flipped through my wallet with one hand.

"Yes, Horse, I'm just fine. Don't worry about me. Who is he?"

"Is there someone else here with you?"

"No, but this fella didn't get inside. Who is he?"

It was not true that Mrs. Krumfutz had been alone in her house. In the instant before the cop—Officer "Horse" seemed to be his name—came upon me and shouted, I had caught a fleeting image of two figures in the Krumfutz living room. They had seemed to be kneeling on the floor side by side, but it all happened so quickly that I couldn't be sure of what I had seen.

"His name is Donald Strachey." To me the cop boomed, "Are you Donald Strachey?"

"Yes."

"What do you think you're doing on this property?"

"Conducting an investigation."

"An investigation? What do you mean, an investigation?"

"I'm a private investigator licensed in the state of New York.

My card is in the wallet." At this, Mrs. Krumfutz, I thought, flinched.

"If the laws of New York are anything like the laws of the Commonwealth of Pennsylvania, I don't think you're licensed to trespass," the cop said. "Now turn around slowly and look at me."

I turned and faced a big, ruddy-faced youth with clear blue eyes and a name tag that read "Patrolman Lewis Henderson Jr."

"What you and I are going to do now, Donald, is we're going to walk out to my patrol car—you walking ahead of me—and you're going to get into the backseat, and you're going to sit down there while I shut the door. Do you understand that, Donald?"

"Yep."

"Just a minute," Mrs. Krumfutz said, and walked closer to the cop and me without ever quite joining either of us. "Let's just have a look at that license of yours, Mr. Donald-the-Private-Investigator."

As the cop held open my wallet, Mrs. Krumfutz came closer to him and squinted at it briefly. She said to me, "Donald Strachey. Why, I think I know just who you are."

"Oh?"

"Who is he?" the cop said.

"Horse," she said, forcing a tight grin, "I think this might be all right."

"Oh, yeah?"

"Could I speak to Donald privately for just a second? This may be just a teeny-tiny bit personal. If you know what I mean," she added, and let loose with an outburst that was half cough and half cackle.

Officer Henderson didn't seem to like the way all this was heading. Clearly, the correct procedure here was to lock me in the cruiser while he ran my name through the computer. But, owing to her celebrity status—not just as a pro-life, pro-gun former congresswoman but as a pro-life, pro-gun former congresswoman who had been involved in a scandal that had gripped the Susquehanna valley at six and eleven for many weeks—Mrs.

Krumfutz was a woman whose wishes could reasonably be viewed as something akin to authoritative and would thus supplant any normal routine.

Henderson said, "He's not armed. If you'd like to step inside, I'll stand by. Holler if you need help."

"Thanks, Horse." Mrs. Krumfutz gestured for me to follow her.

We went into the house and she shut the door behind us. Instead of remaining near the door, she led me across the kitchen, through another door, and into the garage. A dim overhead light went on automatically.

I said, "You don't want us to be within earshot of Officer Henderson. Is that right?"

"Yes," she hissed, and her black eyes bore into me. "All right, Mr. Peeping Tom, you can spit it out right now. Are you working for Nelson?"

"I am unable to identify my client, Mrs. Krumfutz. I'm sorry."

"Maybe you'll be able to identify your client," she said evenly, "if I go get my Walther PK-38 and threaten to blow your face off. Would that make a difference?"

She talked like an NRA fund-raising letter, and I'd run into gun people before and knew they could be dangerous. Also, I wasn't sure there weren't two Mexican hit men somewhere in the house. I looked at Mrs. Krumfutz and wondered if I should make a break for it out the front while she was still unarmed and before Luis and Hector appeared. The problem was, the cop knew my name and had my car ID—in fact, he was still holding my wallet.

Mrs. Krumfutz said, "Cat got your tongue, dog's breath?"

Recklessly I said, "I saw you."

She went white. Then suddenly her color returned with a rush, and she snapped, "I don't give a hoot! It doesn't make a bit of difference. I've got plenty on Nelson. I know it and he knows it!"

"What have you got?"

"I've still got my scrapbook, and Nelson knows I've got it. If that man messes with me, believe you me, I'll put him in the hoosegow for the rest of his life. Just don't tempt me, Donald. You tell him that. Just don't tempt Betty, tell him. And if anything happens to me—if they find my body dumped on the Log Heaven levee some fine morning—that's it. It all goes to the prosecutors, the whole kit and caboodle. Friends of mine have their definite instructions."

"You seem to have made thorough arrangements, Mrs. Krumfutz. I'm impressed. You're quite a force to be reckoned with. Tell me more."

"I'll tell you not one more blessed thing. Now get out of my house and out of Log Heaven, and take your filth with you!"

"My filth?"

"You tracked mud through my kitchen! I'd make you stay and mop it up, but I'm sick to death of you and everything you and my husband represent, and I want you out of here *now*. I'll fix it with Horse Henderson. I just want you out of my house!"

"I'll be happy to go, but I want you to understand one thing, Mrs. Krumfutz, and understand it clearly. If you unleash your Mexican paid killers, and if anything happens to Jim Suter—anything at all, now or in the distant future—I will expose you. You'll pay. You'll go down the rest of the way. *All* the rest of the way. Do you understand me?"

She stood there looking baffled. "Hit men? My Lord, is that what Nelson thinks? Don't be silly. And Jim Suter? You mean Jim Suter the writer?"

"Who else?"

"Donald, I don't know what in the Sam Hill you're even talking about. One of us must be crazy as a loon. What's Jim Suter got to do with it?"

# 10

Mrs. Krumfutz just snickered at the idea of Mexican paid killers, and she found it preposterous that Jim Suter had any connection at all to her husband's criminal activity, the exact nature of which I could not get her to specify. I thought her repeated references to "my scrapbook" referred to additional records she had kept on the campaign-finance scam, but I wasn't sure of it, and as she began to sense how little I actually knew about her husband's activities, she grew even cagier and less forthcoming on that subject. Nor did Jim Suter seem to have anything to do with whatever it was that had gone on in Mrs. Krumfutz's house that night and which I pretended to have witnessed but hadn't actually. I had only just seen two people kneeling side by side, or so it seemed.

Moreover, Mrs. Krumfutz denied visiting the AIDS quilt the day before and having fled in fear from Jim Suter's panel. Nor could she imagine why anyone would sew a section of her campaign biography on an AIDS quilt panel.

"Is Jim dead from AIDS?" she gasped. "But you just talked as if he's alive."

"He is alive, but he's in danger."

"What do you mean? How do you know?"

How much could I tell her? It had all gotten too confusing. Was she putting on an act? This was possible. Here was a woman who had been elected to Congress with the backing of the pious religious right, yet in private she connived like and spoke in the language of an Albany Democratic-machine ward healer, circa 1935.

Taking no chances, I said, "Jim may be in trouble, but I don't know where he is or exactly what the problem is. On behalf of a mutual friend, I'm watching out for him and his interests."

Now she looked perplexed all over again. "Nelson is taking an interest in Jim Suter? That's hard to believe. Nelson always called Jim 'that fairy writer.' Jim's a homosexual, you know."

"I know."

"As far as I was concerned, Jim being a homo was up to him. I hired him to write literature for my congressional campaign."

"Uh-huh."

"Homosexuals always end up in trouble."

"Where were you yesterday afternoon," I asked, "if you weren't at the AIDS quilt?"

"That is none of your concern. None whatsoever."

"Three people saw you at the quilt."

"No, they didn't. They might think they did, but they didn't. Or, those three people are bald-faced liars."

I had been one of the three—Timmy and Maynard were the others—who had seen a woman Maynard had identified as Mrs. Krumfutz examining Jim Suter's quilt panel on Saturday and then rushing away, frantic and distraught. And yet, when I'd turned up spying on her through a rear window of her house fifteen minutes earlier, Mrs. Krumfutz gave no indication that she had ever seen *me* before. Or was that an act? And if it wasn't—what? Were there two Betty Krumfutzes?

"Have you got any sisters, Mrs. Krumfutz?"

"Yes, why?"

"Do you have a twin?"

"You mean an evil twin, Donald? No. My sister, Fran, is older and a good bit heavier than I am. She lives in Engineville and she's never been farther south than Harrisburg. So nobody saw her at the AIDS quilt, that's for darn sure. Anyway, she'd be afraid of catching it."

"I understand that you ran an antigay TV ad against your

opponent in your first Republican primary. He'd accepted a donation from a college gay group, and you hit him hard for it, saying this showed he would support same-sex kissing instruction in the public schools. Wasn't that unfair?"

"Sure, it was unfair. So what? Advertising is unfair. Politics is unfair. Life is unfair. I'm not here to promote fairness. I never said I was."

"Oh, I see. What are you here to promote, Mrs. Krumfutz?"

I'd walked right into it. She gazed at me serenely out from under her cherry-pie-motif head scarf—she seemed to have some device stuck in her pinned-back hair, but I couldn't make out what it was—and said, "I believe I have been put on this earth to promote the right to bear arms and the rights of the unborn. I know in my heart that in both cases—no matter how ruthless and cold-blooded my means may seem to some people—I am doing the Lord's work. Any other questions?"

I couldn't think of any.

Mrs. Krumfutz was able to convince Horse Henderson that my spying was just one unsavory feature of a nasty divorce proceeding, and she told him that she preferred not to press charges against me. She said she had nothing to hide and that her prosecuting me locally might suggest to some people that she did have some dirty laundry to cover up, even though it wasn't true. "You know how people are," she said, and Officer Henderson said he did. He returned my wallet and let me go, although plainly he wasn't happy about it.

I drove back into downtown Log Heaven and stopped at the only eatery open on Main Street, an old greasy-elbow diner called Teddy's. It had a grill in the steamed-up window laid out with rows of wieners, the ones on the left burnt umber, the ones on the right mauve. I went in and had two burnt umber ones with chili sauce, plus a cup of high-octane coffee. There would be plenty of opportunities back in Albany for arugula and bent-twig tea. To deal with the Krumfutzes, I needed fat and caffeine.

When I came out of Teddy's, a squat man who'd been leaning against the building when I went in spoke to me. He said, "Duh-*buh*." His hand came out of his windbreaker pocket and he tipped his porkpie hat.

This one, I was sure, wasn't part of any plot, big or small. He was just a contemporary fixture of Main Street America. I said, "Nice night."

As I got into my rental car and drove away, the man watched me go.

I gassed up at a convenience store, punched sixty or eighty digits into a pay phone, and reached Timmy. It was after ten and he was back in our room at the Capitol Hill Hotel.

"Maynard is showing signs of regaining consciousness. We're all trying to be optimistic." Timmy added some clinical details, then said, "I've also been doing some discreet detective work that's paid off."

"Hey, good for you."

"I've gotten to know a lot of Maynard's friends and his brother Edwin, and Edwin's wife, Laurie. They're a good bunch, and being with them today has made this thing a whole lot easier."

"Great. What was the discreet detective work that paid off?"

"It turns out that one of Maynard's friends knows Jim Suter, too."

"You brought Suter's name up? Isn't that risky?"

"Why? Do you suspect there's a big, wide-ranging, monstrous conspiracy under way involving dozens of corrupt and dangerous people? Hmm."

"You know what I mean." I hadn't even told him yet that since my confusing encounter with Betty Krumfutz I no longer had any idea what to think. "I just thought we had agreed to play it safe and not bring Suter into it until I had caught up with him in Mexico and heard his end of the story."

"The thing is, I didn't have to bring Suter's name up. People had seen the quilt vandalism story on television, and when they were discussing it, one guy mentioned he knew Jim Suter and he was shocked. He didn't think Suter had AIDS and he didn't think he was dead. This guy, Bud Hively, a writer at the *Blade,* the D.C. gay newspaper, said he had seen Suter six or eight weeks earlier, and that Suter had told him he was leaving soon for Mexico. Suter didn't mention any danger he was in—or at least Hively never brought it up. Suter just told Hively he had a boyfriend in the Yucatán and he was planning on spending the winter down there."

"Did you extract any other details, I hope? Such as who's the boyfriend, or what he does or where he lives?"

"I didn't learn as much as I'd have liked. I mean, how nosy could I afford to appear?"

"Not very."

"I did find out that the boyfriend's first name is Jorge and that he and Suter would actually be living in two locations. The boyfriend has a place in Mérida as well as a beach house on the Caribbean coast south of Cancún. And he's financially well-off, Hively said."

"This is a start. All I have to do to locate Suter is find well-off Jorge of Mérida and Cancún."

"There are two other possibly helpful shreds of data. One is, Maynard's friend Dana Mosel, a *Post* reporter who was at the hospital with us, is doing a follow-up story on the quilt vandalism. She was as intrigued as everybody else by the idea that an AIDS quilt panel had shown up memorializing a living person. She asked Bud Hively for a list of Suter's family, friends, and acquaintances, and as Hively was reciting those he knew, I memorized them and later I wrote them down. I think I bollixed up only a couple of the names."

"That is good work, Timothy. You'll be rewarded for this."

"Thanks. I'm keeping my head, Don. I really am. Even if I'm really still quite frightened. I'm chained and dead-bolted in our room and I can't wait for you to get back here. So you're actually coming back to D.C. tonight? I got your message. How come you're not staying up in Pennsylvania?"

I gave him a ninety-second version of my abbreviated visit to Log Heaven: how I had learned of the sometime-gun-toting

Mexicans who'd done a "job" for Betty Krumfutz; how I had been caught prowling behind her house and ended up confronting her; how she assumed I was working for her husband and I let this misapprehension stand in order to facilitate my escape from the Log Heaven Police Department; and how it now appeared that Mrs. Krumfutz had no connection to Jim Suter's danger and that the job the Mexicans had performed so ably for the former congresswoman seemed to have been no more than yard work.

But, I told Timmy, Mrs. Krumfutz had lied to both me and the Log Heaven cop when she said she was alone in the house. And she did have, I had learned, a guilty secret that her husband could blackmail her with once he discovered what it was, which she now believed he had—although she had the goods on him, too, and their battles with each other now appeared to be stalemated.

Timmy said, "So you don't think she's involved in Jim's danger or the attack on Maynard?"

"I'm inclined to doubt it. Anyway, I think I am. For now."

"Then who was that frightened woman at the quilt that Maynard thought was Betty Krumfutz?"

"Beats me."

"So you've more or less decided she's not involved at all in what's going on here?"

"I think I've decided that. But I'm not sure."

"Hmm."

"Mrs. Krumfutz is certifiably amoral and devious on behalf of her causes. She brags about that. And her husband I'm even less sure about. Also, according to the missus, Nelson Krumfutz has been up to his neck in something that could land him in prison for the rest of his life. She says she's got proof, so my guess is it's more campaign-fund chicanery. And this might or might not be the criminality that Jim Suter says certain dangerous persons think he knows about. Anyway, I'm not getting anywhere near Nelson just yet. First it's important that I talk to Suter."

Timmy breathed deeply. "Well, I hate to say this."

"What?"

Two more noisy inhalations.

"What? What?"

"The other thing I found out from Bud Hively about Suter and his Mexican boyfriend is this: Jim met his terrific new boyfriend, he told Hively, through a friend who Jim wouldn't normally have thought of as a person who'd be serving as a gay dating service. And that friend is—you don't want to hear it—Betty Krumfutz."

"Oh?"

"Oh, yes."

"Hell."

"Yeah."

"Well, it'll all come clear. But not tonight. I'm leaving Log Heaven now. I should arrive down there between two and three. I'll ring you from the hotel lobby so you can let me in. Okay?"

"Sure. Drive carefully."

"I will. Traffic will be light."

As I rang off, I remembered something. I pulled from my pocket the letter Jim Suter had sent to Maynard from Mexico. I looked at the way he had signed it: "Your friend Jim, still unlucky in love." Did that mean, as it seemed to, that the wonderful boyfriend had not worked out?

Before I left Log Heaven for the drive to D.C., I made a final swing past Mrs. Krumfutz's house on Susquehanna Drive. All the lights were out now—it was just past ten-thirty—but the pickup truck was still in the driveway next to the Chrysler. I made a U-turn and pulled up the driveway so that my headlights caught the truck's rear plate. I noted the number and the state, Texas, then backed out and drove quickly—but not so quickly as to attract attention—out to the interstate.

# 11

I awoke midmorning on Monday to a warm and hazy blue day, with the Washington outside my hotel window all but shut down for the federal holiday. This twenty-four-hour memorial to Christopher Columbus was primarily an Italian-American holiday, even though Columbus had been on the royal Spanish payroll in 1492 and had actually opened up the New World for Spanish, not Italian, conquest. What if Columbus had sailed west, say, on behalf of the Venetian Republic? How would the Americas be different today? Politics and government in many nations might more readily be carried out with the consent of the governed. For hundreds of years people would have traveled up and down the North and South American continents not on horseback but in gondolas, and later vaporetti. Instead of eating rice and beans, people south of the Rio Grande would sup on *brodetto* and *seppie alla veneziana*.

I laid out this historical conjecture for Timmy over good coffee and even better croissants at a Second Street café. He explained to me that in 1492 Venice had its own lucrative easterly routes to Asia and would have had no need to go sloshing off into the unknown western seas. I told him he was missing my point. He wouldn't drop it though and insisted on asking what my point was.

Luckily, Chondelle Dolan showed up just then. She had joined us at my request, to give us an update on the police investigation of Maynard's shooting. We preferred her company to Ray Craig's. We sat around one of the little tables on the sidewalk in front of the café, and we quickly spotted Craig repeatedly circling the block in an unmarked car; he cruised by and peered over at us every three or four minutes. This made Timmy nervous, but Chondelle said, "It's just Ray being Ray. When he's out in public, the department should make him wear a sign letting people know that he's relatively harmless."

Timmy said, "Relatively?"

"Yeah."

"Relative to what?"

"To a couple of other people in the department whose names I won't mention. The names wouldn't mean anything to you anyway, Timothy."

Timmy shook his head, then changed the subject. He had gotten up early to go check on Maynard, and he said Maynard had opened his eyes several times, although he had not yet spoken.

"It looks like he's going to be okay," Chondelle said. "That's the good report the division is getting, too."

"I noticed," Timmy said, "that a D.C. police officer has been posted outside Maynard's room. Who arranged that? He wasn't there yesterday."

"That was recommended by Lieutenant Craig."

"Why?" Timmy said, looking up with a cappuccino mustache.

"Ray's pursuing the drug-gang angle, and he told the captain he didn't want to risk losing a witness."

I said, "Craig thinks Maynard might be a member of a drug gang? He tried that one out on us, too, but he seemed to have no basis for the theory other than that Maynard was shot by a man who looked Mexican."

"Ray paints with a broad brush," Chondelle said. "A cousin of mine in the narcotics division told me Ray had requested any information they had on Maynard Sudbury, but the inquiry drew a blank. It's possible the request was just Ray covering his behind to justify the order for the hospital guard, which he wanted for some other reason."

"Which might be what?" I asked.

"Dunno. But I'd like to find out. One good thing, as far as you two are concerned, is this: Jim Suter's name hasn't come up anywhere in the Sudbury shooting investigation. Or anywhere else in the system. So if your aim is to keep his name out of this until you get to him, you're doing okay."

"I'm going down to the Yucatán tomorrow," I said. "But it's a big place and I haven't got much of a lead for tracking Suter down. The problem is, if I try to get information by approaching people in Washington who know him, they might have connections to the people he says are trying to kill him. I'd tip them off to his location—or, if they already know where he is, to the fact that he's letting people know that he's in some kind of bad trouble. And they might just finish him off."

I went on to describe to Chondelle my trip to Pennsylvania and my bewildering encounter with Mrs. Krumfutz. I told her how, despite Mrs. Krumfutz's essentially plausible denial of any knowledge of Jim Suter's current troubles, it was she, Timmy had learned, who had introduced Suter to the Mexican boyfriend Suter went to Mexico to be with—now, apparently, to hide out with.

Chondelle said, "It sounds like it won't hurt if you just go ahead and ask Mrs. Krumfutz who the boyfriend is and where they are. If she's not involved in whatever it is Suter is afraid of, there's no risk at all for him or you. If she is involved, you've already alerted her that you're interested in Suter and there's not much more damage you can do than you've already done. Of course, if she thinks you've got something on her, then you can bargain with her. Unless she just lets on that she's going along with your wishes and then has Jim Suter shot dead and, just to be on the safe side, she arranges to have you blown away, too."

Timmy flinched. I reached for my coffee cup.

Chondelle went on, "But it sounds more like her husband is the baddie here, if anybody in the family is. So both of you are probably okay for now. Anyway, look—how about if Sudbury's friend Hively, the writer for the *Blade,* calls up Mrs. Krumfutz? Hively can say he's doing a story on the mysterious Jim Suter quilt panel, and he heard Suter was in Mexico with his boyfriend Jorge, and does she know how to get in touch with Jorge? Why wouldn't that work?"

Timmy looked doubtful. "I don't think Hively would call Mrs. Krumfutz without some explanation from us as to what this is all about. He's a nosy reporter, after all. And if we tell him the truth, then he's involved in this—whatever it is—too. I don't want to do that to anybody else."

Chondelle sipped from the second of the two double espressos she'd ordered, then said, "So what if Hively didn't call her, but somebody *saying* he was Bud Hively of the *Washington Blade* did? That would work just as well, if you ask me." She set her cup down, winked at me, and gazed at Timmy, waiting.

Timmy said, "Uh-uh. Not me."

"Why not?" Chondelle asked.

"For one thing, I've always been a terrible liar."

"It wouldn't take but a minute. You could prevaricate for one little minute, I'll bet."

I said, "Timothy, it would just be a small social lie."

He reddened. "No, it wouldn't. It would be much more than that."

I said, "You see, Chondelle, he went to Georgetown. He was educated by Jesuits."

"Yeah," she said, "Clinton went there, too, I hear."

"Look, I'm not all that pompously self-righteous," Timmy said. "Jeez, give me a break. It's not that I've never told a lie. It's that I'm really bad at it. I'll blush and probably stutter."

"Mrs. Krumfutz will never see you blush over the phone," I said. "And to her, you'll sound as if you're just another homosexual with a speech impediment."

Timmy fumed for another minute, but finally agreed to impersonate newspaper reporter Bud Hively and phone Mrs. Krumfutz. He said he guessed the morality of his doing so was sound overall, though muddy, and his biggest concern was his ineptitude as a liar as a result of a paucity of experience. We kidded him some more about the lofty moral plane he lived on. It was one of the characteristics that had drawn me to Timmy nearly twenty years earlier, and which had made me want to remain with him through hard times and easy, except, of course, whenever his rigidity made me want to flee the sound of his voice.

Five minutes later, after Chondelle had obtained Betty Krumfutz's Log Heaven phone number through a police department source, we sent Timmy to a pay phone around the corner on Pennsylvania Avenue to lie through his teeth.

While Timmy was gone, Ray Craig made another pass and squinted over at us. He must have spotted Timmy at the pay phone and wondered what we were up to now. But Craig didn't stop. He just continued on down the block and hung a left at the corner.

Timmy was back in three minutes. He was wearing a half smile as he seated himself. He slurped up some cappuccino from his cup.

I said, "So?"

He grinned a little dementedly. Now he knew he'd go to hell, but apparently he didn't give a fig. "Jorge is Jorge Ramos. Ramos and Suter met in her office, yes, but Mrs. Krumfutz doesn't know Ramos very well. He's a friend of Alan McChesney, who used to be her chief of staff in the House. McChesney now runs the office of Congressman Burton Olds. McChesney often vacations in Ramos's house on the Caribbean coast, below Cancún, and Mrs. Krumfutz said that if Jim Suter is with Ramos, that's probably where they are. She gave me the name of the village near Playa del Carmen." Timmy lifted his cup again and drank from it.

Chondelle said, "Nice work, Timothy. No offense intended, but it looks like you're a better fibber than you thought you were. It's nothing to be proud of, but it can come in handy, can't it?"

I said, "So you *are* adept as a liar. This changes everything. I may never believe another word you say."

"Neither of you two guys ever told a lie to the other one?" Chondelle asked.

Timmy said, "No."

I said, "Not for many years, so far as I am able to recall."

"It was amazingly easy getting the information out of Mrs. Krumfutz," Timmy said. "She asked me if our conversation would be off the record, and I said yes. She said she did not wish to be quoted in the *Blade* on anything having to do with the AIDS quilt, and she did not wish to have her name mentioned at all in connection with it. I said that was fine, that I just wanted to track down Jim Suter for a story I was writing about a quilt panel that had mysteriously appeared with Jim Suter's name on it, even though he is believed to be alive and well.

"She said wasn't that odd, as if she'd never heard of the Suter panel. Obviously, I didn't mention your encounter with her, Don, and I didn't say anything about pages from Suter's campaign biography having been ripped off the panel—Bud Hively wouldn't have known about the campaign-bio pages. But I did ask her if she had visited the quilt display. She said no, she'd never seen it, but she said she'd heard it was big and colorful. Then I thanked her and said I supposed she was enjoying the fall foliage up in Pennsylvania—nature's quilt. She said, oh, yes, she certainly was."

I said, "You actually called the Pennsylvania fall scenery 'nature's quilt'?"

Timmy smiled slyly.

Chondelle said, "Timothy, it sounds to me like you're a natural at this. If I ever need somebody to tell a big fat lie for a good cause, I'm gonna call you."

Still looking almost smug, he said, "Don't bother. In the future, I'll only lie for Donald. This is something that's just between me and my honey pie here."

I said, "What in God's name have I done? I may need to take you back to the priests, Timothy, and sign you up for an ethical tune-up."

He chuckled, but then Ray Craig rolled slowly by, and Timmy's mood abruptly darkened again. He said, "What does that man *want* with us?"

# 12

Bud Hively, the real one, was among Maynard's friends gathered at the ICU lounge outside the George Washington University Hospital unit where, by one o'clock Monday afternoon, Maynard was awake and answering yes-and-no questions by blinking. He had a black tube down his throat that looked like a creature from *Alien* emerging from his gullet, and so he was unable to speak. Only immediate family members were allowed into Maynard's room, two at a time, but Edwin Sudbury told the nurse in charge that we were all Maynard's siblings. "We're farmers," he said. "Big family." The nurse looked as if she had heard this many times before and did not find it clever, but she let us go in.

A District of Columbia police officer was seated on a desk chair that had been wheeled over to the entrance to Maynard's room. He gave each of us who entered the room a quick once-over, but he made no body search and failed to conduct even perfunctory interrogations of Maynard's visitors. Were Maynard to be finished off by a visitor, the cop would be good for a vague description, I guessed, but not much more.

Timmy and I went into the room together for a brief stay. Timmy spoke reassuring and affectionate words to Maynard, who stared up at us weakly, quizzically. He obviously had questions but no way of asking them. When Timmy asked him if he'd like an explanation as to why he was lying badly wounded in a hospital bed, Maynard blinked furiously, yes, yes. Timmy gave him a quick rundown of the shooting and the confusing aftermath. Maynard shook his head in amazement at Timmy's story.

Then, apparently exhausted by his attempt to make sense of what had happened to him, he drifted off again. We gazed at Maynard a moment longer, outraged and sickened all over again at what had happened to our friend.

Back in the ICU lounge, Timmy and I managed to maneuver Bud Hively, the *Blade* writer, and Dana Mosel, the *Post* reporter, into a corner and then brought the conversation around to Jim Suter and the mysterious quilt panel. Hively was interested in Suter's fate because he knew him, and Mosel had managed to wangle an assignment from the *Post* metro editor to follow up on the odd panel and the just-as-peculiar act of vandalism.

"I talked to a woman at the Names Project in San Francisco," Mosel said, "and she gave me the name and address of the man in D.C. who submitted the panel last May. But there's no record of a David Phipps in or around the District. The phone number, which I called, is a fake, and the address is at a Capitol Hill Mailboxes, Etcetera. It would take a court order to find out who actually rented the box. Those private outfits contract with the Postal Service and they're subject to the same federal privacy laws that a post office has to observe."

Mosel, a slender, pretty, auburn-haired woman in a linen suit and a pair of well-worn tennis shoes, had her notebook out and flipped through it in search of additional details she thought might interest us. She had told Timmy earlier that she'd been in the Peace Corps in Malawi in the midsixties, and she'd gotten to know Maynard through the former-Peace-Corps-volunteer writers' network. This was a web of several hundred people whose reach into U.S. journalism and letters seemed to resemble, as Mosel had described it, Pat Robertson's idea of the grip of the Illuminati on eighteenth-century Europe.

"Amy Chavez, the Names Project staffer," Mosel went on, "was as mystified as everybody else by the Suter panel, and she said a lot of their people are unnerved by this thing. But they've never asked for death certificates or other documentation in the past, and she doubts they'll start doing it now. This type of weirdness just hasn't been a problem."

Bud Hively said, "There's a respect for the quilt—a reverence almost—that's felt even by most of the people who think it absorbs angry emotions that should be fueling political action instead. There's one panel made by a dead man's friends who wrote on the panel, 'He hated this quilt and so do we.' But they're still part of it, even if they think it's wrong, and I don't think they would play games with the quilt or desecrate it."

"No," Timmy said, "that would feel like an insult not to the quilt project but to all the people whose names are there."

Hively, a muscular, pug-nosed man with a shaved head and a mustache the color and shape of the pyramid at Chichén Itzá, said he thought whoever had sent in the panel memorializing a man who'd been alive when the panel was submitted must have been consumed with bitterness. Hively said, "He must have hated Jim deeply to do a thing like that. And I guess he must have hated the quilt, too, to have used it so selfishly."

I said, "Do you know people who disliked Suter? Is he a man who makes enemies?"

Hively smiled knowingly and a little sheepishly. "Jim Suter broke a lot of hearts in gay Washington over the years."

"Yours included?" Mosel said. She still had her notebook out and added, "This is all on background, of course."

"Yeah," Hively said, and laughed uneasily. "I had a fling with Jim ten or twelve years ago. He was—to put it mildly—one of the most attractive men in Washington, Maryland, and Virginia back then. Really one of the most dazzling-looking men I'd ever seen. He still is, in fact—or was the last time I saw him. Jim was also smart, sexy, energetic, and he knew everybody and everything that went on in this town. And he wasn't shy about letting you know how popular he was either. I spent a night with him one time, and I wandered into Jim's kitchen around ten on a Sunday morning. He was there fixing breakfast while he was dishing the dirt on the speakerphone with—guess who? Nancy Reagan."

Timmy said, "God."

I said, "I don't suppose Suter is as wired into the Clinton White House as he was back in the Reagan era, or is he?"

"No, the Clinton gay mob—a large, moody, disappointed bunch of nice people, by and large—don't care much for Jim. His most intimate nonromantic ties have all been with Republicans," Hively said. "They knew he was gay, of course, but that didn't matter much to the Reagan crowd. These were Hollywood people. The Bush White House was stuffier, but even there Jim had his admirers."

"And his enemies?" I said.

Hively looked at me a little sadly now. "The people I know who didn't like Jim—and some of them loathed him deeply—were not political or professional or social enemies. They were all men who had fallen in love with him—which is the easiest, most natural thing in the world—and whom he had led on, and taken into his arms for a time, and then abruptly dumped. Jim seemed to take a kind of sadistic pleasure in doing that. Over the past twenty years, a lot—I mean a platoon, a battalion, a small army—of men have gone gaga over Jim Suter, and there were very few—only the dregs of the dregs really—that he ever turned away.

"But then, after a week or two, that was it. He wasn't a one-night-stand-then-never-again man, he was a two-week-stand-then-never-again man, a very, very cruel thing to be. It was always a week or two of bliss, then suddenly—nothing. You are among the disappeared. He doesn't return your calls, he ignores you in public. And I am speaking to you not just from hearsay—although that's plentiful—but from grim experience. I'm over it now, I think. But for years I despised Jim Suter because he did to me what he always does to men. He wrecked my head and then he broke my heart."

Mosel said, "Doesn't word get around that guys should avoid this shithead?"

"Sure," Hively said, "but in a transient town like D.C. there are always new heads arriving to be turned. And Jim has always been such a hunk that even men who know what they're in for often can't resist him. And even some who've heard of his rotten habit have to see for themselves what the big attraction is, and the repulsion, too."

Timmy said, "Maynard doesn't seem all that bitter about his affair with Suter. He said it didn't work out because he didn't like Suter's politics and he thought Suter was emotionally erratic. But it sounded as if it was a mutual parting of the ways and that was all."

"Maynard was a special case for Jim," Hively said. "Maynard is so self-confident and self-contained that as soon as Suter turned distant, Maynard just let it go. He once told me that *he* began to lose interest in *Jim* as soon as Jim started ignoring his calls. Maynard said that in Southern Illinois people just don't treat each other that way. It's rude, he told me. But then Jim turned around and started pursuing Maynard again. *He* always had to be the one doing the rejecting. So Maynard came back for a while, and then Jim backed off again, and soon afterwards, that was that. They both saw the game that was being played, and soon they'd both had enough of it."

"It sounds," I said, "as if Maynard came away from his affair with Suter uncharacteristically unscathed. So, who among Jim's long list of boyfriends that you know of was permanently embittered, even traumatized?"

Mosel still had her notebook on her lap, and when Hively glanced at it apprehensively, Mosel said, "I'm just listening."

"I hope so," he said. "If anybody asks, none of what I'm about to tell you came from me. I could probably name fifty gay men, if I really thought about it, who have been shit on by Jim Suter over the past twenty years. And most of them, if I asked them about it today, would probably chalk it up to experience and let it go at that. They'd just laugh it off and say, yeah, they had their own heartbreaker of a Jim Suter story, too. But four or five people that I know of were devastated by the way Suter treated them and are very, very angry. And one of them might still be mad enough to play a macabre joke on Jim, such as sending a panel to the AIDS quilt with Jim's name on it."

Mosel had shut her notebook, but now she was flipping its cover up and down absently. Hively's refusal to be used as a source for anything he had told her was plainly driving Mosel nuts. She blurted out, "Oh, come on, Bud. Let me have the names. I promise I'll keep you out of it and I can check them out discreetly."

"You can? I doubt that that's possible."

"All right, so maybe it wouldn't be so discreet. But I won't mention your name. I can just call these guys up and say, 'I heard you dated Jim Suter and it ended unhappily, and do you have any idea how a panel with Suter's name on it made its way into the AIDS quilt?' Maybe I won't find anybody who'll admit it, but I might come across a Suter hater who knows who did do it, and who's mad at that guy, too, and who'll rat on him to the *Post.*"

I said, "That sounds like a promising approach to me."

Hively slowly massaged his hairless head, as if to stimulate the cells responsible for decision making. "We can't be sure, of course, even that it was one of Jim's wounded lovers who sent in the quilt panel. The quilt stunt could be totally unrelated. And if it was an old boyfriend who did it, why would he and somebody else then vandalize the panel at the D.C. display?"

"To call attention to it," Timmy said. "So nobody in Washington would miss the act of revenge."

Hively let loose with a little sigh and said, "I guess you might as well go ahead. I'll give you the names. Just don't tell anybody the names came from me."

"Agreed," Mosel said. "I'm wondering something, Bud. Is there any particular reason, other than mere privacy, why you don't want these guys to know it was you who ID-ed them as former Suter boyfriends?"

Hively laughed. "It's not the ex-lovers I'm worried about. The problem is, I already gave the names to the *Blade* reporter covering the quilt display, and I don't want her to find out I also turned the names over to the *Post.*"

"I guess I'm going to have to work fast," Mosel said dryly. "Anyway, thanks."

Hively grew serious and said, "I'm telling you because I want to do everything I can to help expose the person who used the quilt in such a shabby way. I've got too many friends on there not to care a lot about this. I know that in the big picture the quilt is indestructible, and what it means is indestructible. But this was a miserable, selfish stunt, and it just hurts. I'm sure an awful lot of people have been sickened by it."

"I think so, too," Mosel said, "and so does my editor. That's why it's news."

As Bud Hively described the five men whose detestation of Jim Suter was, Hively believed, abiding and even potentially violent, Mosel took notes on—and I carefully memorized—the sketches of Jim Suter's attenuated love affairs with Martin Dormer, Graham Houston, Jason Leibowicz, Bill Walker, and Peter Vicknicki.

As Hively spoke, I listened for any biographical suggestion that any of these men might be connected, however slightly, to Betty or Nelson Krumfutz, to Maynard, or to Mexico. I didn't hear any. But I picked up plenty of data to serve as a conversational icebreaker with Jim Suter, well-known Washington writer, heart-throb, and—the word that came to mind was an oddly old-fashioned one—cad.

# 13

By four Monday afternoon, I was back in the hotel room working the phone. Timmy had the list of Jim Suter's family and friends that Bud Hively had given Dana Mosel on Sunday, and I had the names of the five embittered Suter ex-lovers that Hively had described to Mosel earlier on Monday. After several unproductive calls—answering machines and services, or no answer at all—I reluctantly called the airline and postponed my reservation to Cancún from Tuesday to Wednesday morning. I immediately felt pangs of regret, even irritation—mixed with a strange but powerful sense of relief—that I would not be leaving for the Yucatán first thing in the morning. But at the time I didn't realize what those pangs meant.

I was able to reach two of Jim Suter's friends, as well as his mother and brother in Maryland. With the friends and relatives I identified myself as a reporter for the *Baltimore Sun*. This was a low subterfuge that would have disgusted my journalist friends but which I justified by Suter's own alleged precarious life-or-death situation. Admitting that I was a private detective might have tipped off one of the people Suter was afraid of that someone besides Maynard might be aware of Suter's terrible danger.

I guessed, though, that the angry ex-lovers would be unwilling to speak with a reporter, so I told the two I reached late Sunday afternoon that I was a private investigator employed by Jim's mother to look into the disturbing AIDS quilt panel. Timmy termed this particular lie "squalid," but he couldn't come up with an approach that was morally superior.

Anyway, it worked. By 5 P.M. Monday, I had interviews lined

up with Suter's mother and brother at six-thirty, with Peter Vicknicki and Martin Dormer, two of Suter's angry former lovers, later in the evening, as well as two of Suter's friends at lunchtime Tuesday.

Timmy phoned his boss, state assemblyman Myron Lipshutz, in Albany and requested several days off "for personal reasons." He told the politician he was unable to explain exactly what was going on, but he said he wanted Lipshutz to know how gratifying it had been working for him over the years and how much respect and affection he felt for the assemblyman.

It was obvious from Timmy's end of the rest of the conversation—"No, don't worry, I'm fine, Myron, really"—that Lipshutz had been unnerved by Timmy's remarks, which could easily have been interpreted as *(a)* a prelude to suicide, *(b)* the veiled announcement of a fast-moving terminal illness, or *(c)* an indication that Timmy had fallen under the influence of Deepak Chopra.

Afterward, I said, "It sounds as if you may have scared Myron to death."

"I guess I did leave him a little bit shaken. I didn't mean to frighten Myron. But after what happened to Maynard, I've got this heightened sense of the fragility of human existence—everybody's, including my own—and I feel impelled to tell people how I feel about them before it's too late."

I had never been seized by the need to exclaim my love to anyone other than my lover—for a WASP Presbyterian from New Jersey, that was chore enough—but I liked that Timmy could be selectively, though not promiscuously, spontaneous with his affections. He didn't need to tell me how he felt about me—he'd done it countless times over the years with all the force and clarity of his strong Irish heart—but he did tell me yet again, and I replied unexpectedly in kind. We made love, and it was excellent.

Soon, though, my mind divided, and part of it began to wrestle with ways of clearing up the Jim Suter–Maynard Sudbury complex mystery at the earliest possible moment, and of extricating Timmy and me—and Maynard—from it. Just as I did not want to live in a state of fear and paranoia, neither did I want to live with—or to live with a man with—a twenty-four-hour-a-day overwhelming sense of doom. As Timmy and I excitedly generated sweat and other fluids, I also couldn't seem to help imagining, a bit guiltily, my upcoming encounter with the beringleted former wrestling star, Jim Suter, although I did that only for a fleeting moment.

My six-thirty meeting with Jim Suter's mother and brother at Mrs. Suter's condo in Silver Spring was not only unhelpful in any specific way—neither George nor Lila Suter knew much about Jim's private life, they told me several times—but I immediately sensed that both of them were continually lying, at least by omission.

Both Suters were handsome, conservatively dressed people who looked as if they would have been comfortable posing for a Buick ad in *Town & Country*. They served cocktails and hors d'oeuvres and chatted volubly about themselves in a way that felt just a little forced. Mrs. Suter was a real estate agent and George a computer-program analyst for a big Maryland HMO. It came out in the conversation that Mrs. Suter had been married four times and George twice. Both were currently unattached.

Mrs. Suter had agreed to meet with a reporter, she said, in order to reassure me. She said she was certain that the quilt panel with her son's name on it was "a prank." The vandalism of the panel was harder to explain, she said, but "nothing James gets mixed up in ever surprises me," she added with a laugh. "James has always gone his own way." She said she had told the *Post* reporter the same thing and was surprised that editors might continue to consider the incident newsworthy.

"I've been told," I said, "that Jim may be out of the country, and that's why he hasn't responded personally to the quilt-panel mystery. Is that the case?"

George Suter glanced at his mother, who hesitated for just an instant before replying, "I think he is, yes. That's the case insofar as any information I have." Her language was flat and without nuance, but she spoke to me in the "gracious" tone I guessed she employed with potential buyers and sellers in her real estate business.

"You aren't sure where Jim is?" I asked.

"No, not precisely," she said. "He did say he thought he might be abroad for some time. But Jim's travel plans hadn't quite firmed up the last time we spoke." Mrs. Suter and her son both peered at me now in a way that said no additional information would likely be forthcoming on this topic.

"When were you last in touch with Jim? Either of you."

"To tell you the truth," George said, "I haven't seen Jim—or talked to him at all—since early summer sometime, I'd say it was. I don't recall his discussing any particular trip he had planned. But Jim has always been something of a gadabout, and he doesn't always inform me or Mother where he's off to or when he'll be back. It's actually a rather annoying habit Jim has." Suter, who appeared to be in his midthirties, had a head full of the famous male-Suter locks, and they were indeed golden and fell across his brow fetchingly.

"So Jim might not be out of the country, just out of the Washington area?"

"That's right," George said. "Jim hasn't answered his telephone or returned messages for some time. So I'd say there's a good possibility that he's out of town."

"That would be my guess, too," Mrs. Suter added.

Jim Suter's mother and brother sat watching me with eyes that looked as if they were going to reveal nothing because the Suters did not intend for them to reveal anything. I guessed they were not only lying—poorly—but that they knew Suter was in trouble and probably that he was in trouble in Mexico. But if that's all they knew, then there was no point in pressing them, for I already knew that much and more. And if they knew more than I did, they certainly weren't about to reveal it to a newspaper reporter from Baltimore. They had agreed to see me, they said, only to dampen interest in the strange quilt panel and the vandalism, and maybe also to find out if I was really a reporter. Although, when I arrived, they did not—luckily—ask to see my press credentials.

I considered confiding in the Suters—telling them I was an investigator and I knew Jim was in some kind of ugly fix down in the Yucatán—but that might simply have spooked them. If Jim had written his family a letter similar to the one he'd sent Maynard—"You must tell no one in Washington where I am," etc.—George and Lila might have been afraid I was not part of the solution to Jim's problems but part of the terrible problem itself, and they might become terrified uselessly. There was also the unsettling possibility that the Suters themselves were part of Jim's problem—I had no idea what his relationship with his family was—and that opening up to them would not only further endanger Jim but put Timmy and me at risk, too.

So, unable to find a safe and reliable way of extracting any useful information from the Suters, I thanked them and got up to leave.

"When will your article appear in the *Sun*?" Lila Suter asked. "Ordinarily, I don't buy the Baltimore paper. But I'll certainly be interested to see what you wrote about George and I and about James."

She eyed me levelly but noncommittally in a way that could have meant she shared the widely held American belief that reporters were lunkheads who rarely got anything right, or it could have meant she doubted I was a reporter at all. Mrs. Suter's cool look also could have signaled—this would have been Timmy's take—that she knew exactly who I was and she didn't care if I knew she was onto me.

"When the piece runs will be up to my editor, and no sane reporter ever tried to read the mind of an editor." I grinned, but neither Suter smiled back. "It's possible that we won't run anything more on the quilt or on the mysterious panel. At least, not until all the unanswered questions have been answered—whenever that might be."

Both Suters nodded. Then they wished me luck in my investigatory quest, and I headed back out in the direction of the Silver Spring metro station.

As I walked away from Mrs. Suter's building—La Fuente, it was called, spelled out next to the entrance in a silvery script—I turned and looked up at the location where I estimated her third-floor balcony must have been. In the dimness behind the glass door at the rear of the balcony, two figures were standing and seemed to be watching me go.

# 14

When I met Timmy at eight at a Thai restaurant near Dupont Circle that had been recommended by one of Maynard's friends, he was despondent. He told me that he had just visited Maynard again. And while Maynard's condition had been upgraded from stable to fair, Timmy hated seeing his friend so weak and damaged, so helpless, so not the person Maynard had always been.

" 'Fair,' they're labeling him," Timmy said. "He didn't seem so 'fair' to me. I asked him if he felt 'fair,' and he shook his head. But I told him he was improving, day by day, and he nodded and—I think—tried to shrug. But if what Maynard is is 'fair,' I'd hate to see him doing poorly."

"You did see him doing poorly Saturday night, on that sidewalk in front of his house. 'Fair' is preferable to that."

"True."

"Any estimate on when Maynard will be able to speak?"

"Maybe tomorrow, the nurse said. And I'm not the only one waiting to talk to Maynard. You-know-who was up in Maynard's room nosing around a while ago."

"Ray Craig?"

"Smelly Ray."

"When you and I met, I must have smoked as much as Ray does. I must have stunk that way, too."

"You did. It was awful."

"How did you stand it?"

"You said you intended to quit. And you did. Anyway, I'd spent a month once visiting an Indian friend who lived next to a chemical-fertilizer factory in Poona. So I'd developed an adaptability toward vile odors when the cause was good."

"Lucky for me."

"Yep. Me too."

Timmy and I were seated at a table for four against a side wall at the Bangkok Flower. We were waiting for our two dinner companions, Martin Dormer and Peter Vicknicki, two of Jim Suter's embittered former lovers who had since met and become friends. We didn't know what they looked like, but the maître d' had been alerted to send them our way.

I asked Timmy if Ray Craig had spoken to him, and he said, "Yes, and he asked where you were."

"What did you say?"

"I told him you were dropping some clothes off at the dry cleaner's."

I laughed. "Why did you say that? I think I know."

Timmy laughed, too. "You probably do. It was the first thing that popped into my head, and I guess I was trying to plant the idea that maybe Ray ought to have some clothes dry-cleaned, too. Although, Don, even Freud said, sometimes a cigar is only a cigar."

"No, I don't think Freud ever actually said that. That was disinformation put out by the behaviorists."

"Right. Next you're going to tell me Freud never said, 'Round up the usual suspects.' Or, 'At least we had Paris.' "

"No, those are both Freud."

"Anyway," Timmy said brightly, "if Craig was in the hospital checking up on Maynard, that means he wasn't following you. That's reassuring."

I could have said, "Yes, but maybe Craig had you under surveillance and one of his junior officers was following me," but Timmy already had enough gnawing on his mind. Anyway, I had watched carefully for a tail out to Silver Spring, and I hadn't spotted any.

I said, "I suspect maybe Ray has done some checking on us, Timothy, and he's been reliably informed that we're not likely to turn out to be agents for the Medellín cartel. Did he say anything to you about how the shooting investigation was going?"

"No. I asked, but he didn't answer me. He just asked where you were. Maybe it's because he's an orthodox Freudian that he always answers a question with a question."

I said Timmy's analysis of Officer Craig sounded as good as any I could come up with and went on to describe to Timmy my unsettling meeting with Jim Suter's chilly and unforthcoming mother and brother.

"Jeez," Timmy said, "it does sound as if they know more than they're letting on. Do you think they're protecting Jim, or even that they're in on it?"

*It* again. "I'm clueless. I was able to extract precisely nothing out of them. In fact, that's what made me suspicious, the care they took in chatting me up lengthily about themselves while revealing no fact at all about Jim."

"So I guess it's more urgent than ever that you track Suter down yourself."

"That's what I think."

The maître d' now appeared briefly alongside our table and left behind two men. The shorter and more compact of the two, a tidy, clear-skinned, strawberry-blond, preppy-looking man with a cream-colored sweater tied around his neck, said, "Don Strachey? I'm Martin Dormer."

There were introductions all around, with Dormer, and with Peter Vicknicki, a tall, thin man with a bushy, dark beard and small black eyes behind wire-rimmed glasses. He had on faded jeans and a well-worn black sweatshirt with SWEATSHIRT spelled out across the front.

I thought about the four former lovers of Jim Suter that I had laid eyes on—these two, Bud Hively, and Maynard—and saw no physical resemblance among any of them. I guessed that the men who turned Suter on were simply those men who were strongly attracted to him, and they had come in a broad spectrum of types.

As soon as we'd all been seated, with no preliminaries,

Vicknicki asked, "Is there something really weird going on? The *Post* story on the quilt said a panel with Jim's name on it had been vandalized. And then somebody told me that a detective—I guess that's you—was asking around about Jim, who seems to have disappeared. At least, nobody we know has any idea where he is."

"And," Dormer added, "we heard that Maynard Sudbury, another one of Jim's exes, was shot in front of his house Saturday night and he's in the hospital in bad shape. Although I don't suppose there's any connection between that and Jim's disappearance and his name turning up on the AIDS panel. Is there?"

"We don't know if there's any connection," I was able to say honestly.

"I just hope there's not some bizarre conspiracy unfolding here," Vicknicki said, and I glanced at Timmy, who looked alert. "Jim Suter probably has more ex-lovers in Washington than all the Kennedys combined—a very large number of people fall into this category—and Sudbury was the second one of them inside of a year to be shot on the street on Capitol Hill. Maynard's expected to live, though, unlike poor Bryant Ulmer."

Timmy fidgeted with his water glass and said, "Who's Bryant Ulmer?"

"You haven't heard about Bryant?" Dormer asked. "Where are you guys from?"

"Albany, New York," Timmy said, and Dormer stared at him as if Timmy had announced that we were down for the weekend from Bleeding Gums, Ontario.

"Bryant was quite well known on the Hill," Dormer said, "and he was Jim's boyfriend for a month or so . . . a couple of years ago, I'd say. Then last winter Bryant was murdered. It was horrible. Bryant was shot in front of his house, too, about eight blocks from Maynard's. The police said it was a mugging and they never got whoever did it. But now with Maynard Sudbury getting shot the same way, some of us are beginning to wonder."

"Tell me again," Vicknicki put in, "what your connection is with Jim. Did you say his mother hired you to find him? From what I heard from Jim about Lila, I'm surprised she'd hire a gay detective. She's extremely homophobic and never wanted to know anything about Jim's personal life. You two are a couple, aren't you? You seem like you are." The deep black eyes behind Vicknicki's specs had hardened as he waited for one of us to answer.

I said, "We're partners, yes, and we're actually friends of Maynard's. The business about Mrs. Suter hiring us was a line to get you here. Sorry about that."

"Oh. I see."

"We were with Maynard Saturday when he discovered the quilt panel for Jim, and he was upset and concerned. He wanted to find out what had happened. Then he got shot, so we're investigating on our own. I am, at any rate. I'm a licensed private investigator in the state of New York." I took out my wallet and held up my license with its photo ID, and Dormer examined it with interest.

Vicknicki still looked skeptical. "You could have been honest with us."

"I can see that now," I said.

The waiter appeared, a slight Asian man in shiny black pants and a white shirt with a speck of cilantro on his sleeve. "Are you ready to order?"

"We haven't looked at the menu," Timmy said. "Sorry."

"Take your time," the waiter replied, and zipped away.

I said, "Martin, how come Bryant Ulmer was so well known on the Hill? Maybe we ought to be aware of who he was. Timothy and I do read the *New York Times* every day and when channel-surfing we pause from time to time at C-Span. But you can help us out by reminding us of exactly what Ulmer's claim to fame was."

"He was Burton Olds's chief of staff," Dormer said, then sat looking at me as if no further explanation were needed. I did recognize the name as that of an influential Republican congressman from Illinois who was chairman of an important House committee, although I couldn't remember which one. His name had also come up as the current employer of Alan McChesney, Betty Krumfutz's former chief of staff who was a friend of Jim Suter's boyfriend Jorge Ramos.

I said, "Olds is head of what? The banking committee?"

"Commerce," Dormer said. "And since Olds is both lazy and preoccupied with skirt-chasing—as men of Burton's generation in the House like to term it—Bryant Ulmer pretty much ran not only the office but the congressional seat. Bryant's murder was a real blow to Olds."

"Who," Vicknicki added, "is one of more than a few elected representatives serving in this city who possess, instead of a brain, an effective staff."

"Luckily for Olds," Dormer said, "Ulmer had a deputy who was able to step into the job when Bryant died. Alan McChesney is every bit as tough and capable as Bryant was. If not quite so nice."

Vicknicki said, "And like Bryant, Alan knows where all the bodies are buried." We stared at him, and Vicknicki added, "Figuratively speaking, I mean. I mean, I think I mean."

Timmy said, "Alan McChesney—isn't he another one of Jim Suter's exes? I've heard that name somewhere recently."

"They were briefly an item," Dormer said, "back when McChesney worked for Betty Krumfutz. Do you know who she is?"

"Yes, we do," I said.

Vicknicki said, "If it's beginning to sound as if Jim Suter fucked half the gay men on the Hill, that's probably about right. Between a half and two-thirds, I'd say." Dormer nodded thoughtfully, as if the figure sounded within ballpark range. "Which is not to say," Vicknicki went on, "that Jim ever slept with anybody more than, say, ten times."

"No." Dormer shook his head emphatically. "Ten tops. With me it was six."

"Me, too," Vicknicki said. "When Jim met you, it was, 'God, where have *you* been?' Then it was a week or so of rapture—with Jim's intense focus on you, and those eyes, and that hair—and then nothing. No thing. He'd never return your calls, and when you ran into him, he'd glance your way and say, 'Hi, nice to see you,' as if you were someone he'd once been introduced to at a reception at the National Bee Balm Association or whatever."

Timmy said, "Suter sounds perfectly infuriating. Neurotic and nasty and infuriating."

"I despise Jim Suter," Dormer suddenly sputtered, his face red with anger. "I am not a man who holds grudges normally. But I can honestly say I hate Jim Suter now and I will always hate Jim Suter. When I met Jim three years ago, I had just come out of a seven-year relationship. I was lonely and desperate and without hope. I felt like the breakup was my fault. Now I know it was both our faults, but at the time I was convinced I was a worthless piece of shit.

"Then I met Jim. And for exactly one week I felt human again. I was in love, and I felt loved. Until, that is, Jim stopped answering his phone with no explanation. And when I camped outside his door until he came home late one Sunday night—with another guy I recognized as the day-shift supervisor at the Capitol South metro station—Jim just took me aside and said he really didn't appreciate being stalked. Stalked! He said he wasn't comfortable with people who were as obsessive as I was, but he wished me luck finding someone who was into that type of thing."

"Into obsession?" Timmy asked, incredulous.

"Yes!"

Vicknicki said, "Martin's story might sound extreme, but mine was similar. Nearly identical, in fact."

"I guess it's safe to conclude," I said, "that Suter has a lot of people in his life whom he's hurt so badly that they might be compelled to get even."

"Revenge-wise," Dormer said, "Peter and I have to be just the tip of the iceberg."

"But you didn't submit the AIDS quilt panel as a kind of macabre joke to embarrass or hurt Suter?"

"Of course not. Don't be ridiculous," Vicknicki said quietly.

He paused and went on, "Martin and I are both HIV-positive. That's where we met, in an HIV support group. And while, yes, there's a lot of sardonic humor about HIV among people who are infected, it's not really a condition that anybody I know of would use against another person, even metaphorically. Oh, Hitler, sure. Or Pol Pot. But not some ordinary piece of shit like Jim Suter. Who, by the way, was not and is not, to the best of my knowledge, infected. Jim was always extremely careful, I think. I was, too, mostly. Mostly but not always."

"Do you know the old Comden and Green song 'Carried Away'?" Dormer asked. " 'Carried away,' " Dormer sang mournfully, " 'carried away—I got carried away.' "

Timmy said, "I'm sorry to hear that you're paying such an absurdly high price for such an understandable kind of slip."

Vicknicki smiled ruefully. "Martin and I both have good insurance coverage. I'm at the Library of Congress and he's in congressional liaison at Labor. So we can afford the regimen with the full cocktail. Both our numbers are fair and improving, we feel good, and we're optimistic."

"We're lucky," Dormer said. "We've both lost a lot of friends over the last ten years."

"Us, too," Timmy said. "And the two of us only escaped by the skin of our teeth." He meant the skin of *my* teeth but was too nice a guy to make the distinction among people who had no need to know of our complex history, and of our sexual philosophies that differed in the late seventies and early eighties and then largely merged in the late eighties.

Timmy said, "It sounds as if there must be almost as many Washington gay men eligible for Jim Suter–survivor support groups as there are for HIV support groups."

"As plagues go," Vicknicki said, "Jim's a minor one. And I don't suppose the Suter plague has spread through Asia and Africa."

"Do you have any idea where Jim might have disappeared to?" I asked. "Everyone we've talked to, including Jim's family, seems stumped over his whereabouts."

"I heard back in the early summer that he had a Mexican boyfriend," Dormer said. "So Jim might have gone south of the border to spread heartbreak down there. Maybe it was part of the deal on NAFTA, which Bryant Ulmer and Alan McChesney both worked on: Mexico gets several hundred thousand jobs without having to commit much in the way of environmental protection, and as compensation it has to accept Jim Suter's exile. And when Mexican gay men start to complain about Suter, the government can tell them to go fuck themselves."

"I doubt that that last part would have to be included in any treaty," Vicknicki said.

I asked Dormer and Vicknicki if they thought Suter, who had close connections with former congresswoman Betty Krumfutz, could have been involved in the campaign-finance scandal that had brought her down. They both said they doubted it, that Jim had been closer to Mrs. Krumfutz's staff than to her, and that none of her aides had been implicated in the scam. That had been the dirty work of her shady husband, Nelson.

I told Dormer and Vicknicki that I'd been given the names of three other men—Bill Walker, Jason Leibowicz, and Graham Houston—who were angry ex-lovers of Jim Suter's, and that I'd been having trouble tracking them down.

"I don't know about the other two," Vicknicki said, "but Graham Houston is dead."

"Was he shot?" Timmy asked.

"No, it was AIDS. He died about six months ago. I saw it in the *Blade*. I thought about him a lot after I read his obituary. I'd slept with Graham once about five years ago, and when I saw that he died, I wondered if maybe he infected me or maybe I infected him."

"I know Jason Leibowicz," Dormer said, "but I think I heard that he's in Uzbekistan or somewhere. He's State Department, and I'm pretty sure he was sent out to the ends of the earth a year or two back. As for Bill Walker, I don't know the name."

"If you're looking for people who loathe Jim," Vicknicki said, "the guy at the top of the list really ought to be Carmen Lo-

Bello. He was burned by Jim in Jim's characteristic fashion eight or ten months ago, and the last time I saw Carmen the wounds were still raw."

"Who's he?" I asked.

"Carmen's a drag queen and cabaret performer who used to be popular in local clubs. He specialized not in Barbra and Judy and Joan Crawford, but in doing D.C. power queens: Hillary, Nancy Reagan, Meg Greenfield, Liddy Dole. Donna Shalala would never have shown up at a performance, but I heard she got hold of a video of Carmen doing her one night and reportedly the Secretary of Health and Human Services was not amused."

Timmy said, "This is some inside-the-Beltway esoterica I've never heard about."

"Carmen was really brilliant. He had one routine where he did Cokie Roberts, then Nina Totenberg, *and* Linda Wertheimer."

"I'm truly impressed," Timmy said. "This is not the Washington I knew when I went to school here in the sixties. This Carmen LoBello would have been considered far ahead of his time at the Georgetown Grill."

"But then when his affair with Jim ended last winter," Vicknicki went on, "something seemed to snap in Carmen. People who know him said sometimes he was enraged—kicking and throwing things and cursing Suter's name. And then other times Carmen was depressed and withdrawn. Anyway, Jim's dumping him apparently left Carmen completely unhinged, and his cabaret act changed almost overnight. He stopped doing Hillary and Cokie and Barbara Boxer, and instead he just did one bizarre character over and over again, a surreal composite of two famous Washington figures that he called G. Gordon Liddy Dole.

"It was basically Liddy Dole, of course—who'd been one of Carmen's audiences' favorites—with the sugarcoated Southern faux-sincerity and the hairsprayed soul and the pretty red power frock. But suddenly Liddy also had a big slab of a mustache and smoked a fat cigar, and she ranted about Vince Foster, and about nuking China.

"Carmen never gave a reason, but he absolutely refused to do anybody but this one weird character over and over again. Audiences soon got tired of it, and even Carmen's die-hard fans gave up on him. Carmen was fired from Starkers, the club where he worked, and the last time I heard, he still had his day job at the Bureau of Mines, but he wasn't performing at all anymore. I know that Carmen still explodes into a tirade whenever Jim Suter's name comes up. So if you're looking for people who hate Suter, Carmen should move swiftly to the top of your list."

I said, "LoBello can be reached at the Bureau of Mines?"

"That's where I'd try first," Vicknicki said. "A friend of Carmen's said his home number's been changed and is now unlisted."

I asked Vicknicki for the names of a couple of LoBello's closest friends, and I wrote them down.

Dormer said, "The TV news also reported that the quilt panel with Jim's name on it had been vandalized—parts of it ripped off. Do you guys think that has anything to do with Jim's disappearance and two of his ex-boyfriends getting shot? It's hard to imagine Carmen being mixed up in anything violent. But he's always been a strange man. Creative but strange."

Vicknicki and Dormer both watched me carefully as I replied, "I don't know yet what to make of any of these violent and destructive events. But it wouldn't surprise me at all if it turned out to be a string of ugly coincidences."

Dormer considered this gravely, Vicknicki continued to gaze at me with a look of penetrating curiosity, and Timmy gave me his droll, skeptical once-over. Lucky for me, the waiter reappeared and, a little more insistent than he'd been the first time, asked if we were ready to order yet. We made some snap decisions, none of which we came to regret.

Between the soup course and the entrées, I excused myself, found a pay phone, and tracked down Chondelle Dolan. I asked her about the murder of Bryant Ulmer and what she knew about Alan McChesney. Ulmer died in an unsolved street robbery on a Capitol Hill side street the previous January, Dolan recalled. But it wasn't a case she had worked on, so she said she would have to look into the file and check on the investigation's current status.

Alan McChesney, Dolan said, was a formidable if not particularly well-liked man on the Hill. As Burton Olds's chief of staff, McChesney was also one of the most influential homosexuals in official Washington, not counting, of course, those six or eight or ten gay or lesbian representatives and senators who were either un-, discreetly, or pathologically closeted. I asked if McChesney's moving into Ulmer's job after his death had had any political, professional, or personal repercussions that Dolan knew of. She said she didn't know but she'd check.

Then Dolan said, "Donald, you don't want to hear this, but you better know it. Ray Craig had you tailed out to Silver Spring earlier. Ray stayed with Timothy at GW, and an officer I know named Filbert Furlong tailed you to the apartment of Mrs. Lila Suter."

"Tell Filbert he does good work. I had no idea. What's he look like?"

"Oh, he's the invisible man."

"I'm calling from the Bangkok Flower, up from Dupont Circle. Is Filbert skulking in here somewhere, wearing a camouflage of peanut sauce and tiny prawns?"

"No, he's off duty now. It's probably some other officer there amongst the rice noodles."

"Do you have any clearer idea of why Craig is so suspicious of Timmy and me?"

"Wish I did. Like I said, it's probably a failure of imagination. But I've got other bad news for you, too, Donald."

"What's that?"

"Ray's been talking to a captain he's tight with by the name of Milton Kingsley. Kingsley is probably well aware that Ray and another Caucasian lieutenant do imitations of the captain that are what you really have to call unflattering. But these two use each other and need each other, so the captain puts up with Ray. But now, a buddy of mine in administration told me today, Captain Kingsley is taking a trip. Papers have been processed for a plane ticket and expenses for—I hate to say it."

"Don't tell me."

"Yep. Cancún, Mexico."

"When?"

"Wednesday."

When I got back to the table, Timmy, Dormer, and Vicknicki were busy conjuring up conspiracy theories—most of them political and far-fetched—that might explain the connections between Bryant Ulmer's shooting, Maynard's, and the Jim Suter quilt panel and vandalism. And Dormer and Vicknicki didn't even know about the mysterious appearance of Betty Krumfutz or a Betty Krumfutz impostor at the quilt panel and the fact that Suter met his Mexican boyfriend, Jorge, through Alan McChesney, who had once been Mrs. Krumfutz's chief of staff and, following Bryant Ulmer's violent death, was now Burton Olds's.

I added nothing to this free-form speculation and pooh-poohed much of it. But I listened to and considered all of it. And by the time the conversation had concluded, I needed to ask Timmy for two of the aspirin he always carried with him—four tiny pills in a small plastic vial in the inner recesses of his jacket pocket, as if he were a spy on a dangerous mission deep inside enemy territory. I also tried to figure out who in the restaurant might be a D.C. plainclothes police officer watching us—and listening?—but I gave up after failing to narrow the field to fewer than seventeen possibilities.

# 15

A Names Project speaker at the start of the candlelight march on Friday night had termed it "a miracle" that the entire outdoor quilt-display weekend would be warm and dry, but Tuesday morning was unmiraculous and rainy. The tables outside the café with the excellent croissants were deserted, and we sat jammed inside the place, semimuscular thigh to semimuscular thigh with Capitol staffers jolting themselves with caffeine into states of wakefulness sufficient for conducting the nation's business.

Timmy read aloud from the *Post* while I nursed a double espresso and an imaginary cigarette. Dana Mosel had not yet filed her follow-up story on the Suter quilt panel—Dormer and Vicknicki had told us Mosel phoned them and they'd given her an earful on Suter's treatment of the legions of men in his life—but the paper had printed a brief update on Maynard's shooting and his improving condition. Ray Craig was quoted as saying that the police had no suspects but were pursuing "a number of leads."

"I wonder what 'a number of leads' means," Timmy said. "Is it a high number of leads or a low number of leads, and what are they?"

"That's just a thing police say to reporters," I told him. "It doesn't necessarily mean anything."

"I guess we're two of the leads if they're following us around."

I had relayed to Timmy the night before Chondelle's report to me on the D.C. Police Department's twenty-four-hour surveillance of the both of us, and he had received the news glumly.

"The other lead," I said, "is the two witnesses to the shooting saying two Mexicans did it."

"The police are not releasing that information to the press. I wonder why. That makes me nervous."

"I have to admit, Timothy, that I'm curious about that, too. Craig may actually know more about the shooter and his friend than Chondelle has been able to find out. And maybe whatever he knows has got this Captain Kingsley flying down to the Yucatán the same day I'm flying. It would seem unlikely that they'd assign a captain to follow me up and down the Western Hemisphere, so our travel dates could be pure coincidence. Although, it's also possible they scoured the airlines' reservation lists for my name, and when they spotted it, they saw it as an opportunity for a department big cheese to take a pleasant trip at taxpayers' expense while he keeps an eye on me. Or maybe they sincerely believe that I'm at the center of something important."

Timmy stared at me in amazement over what he obviously saw as my thickheadedness. "But, Don, obviously you *are* at the center of something important."

"Think so? We'll see."

Timmy just shook his head, then read more from the *Post*. Timmy told me that Bob Dole, numbers low and stagnant, was still predicting that the public would catch on to the ethically dubious Clintons before election day and virtue—i.e., Dole—would prevail.

I said, "Let's hope not."

Timmy said, "Clinton will win, but the voters will punish him for his endless parade of dreary misdemeanors by giving the House and the Senate to the Republicans again."

"No, people are sick of conflict and divided government. The party will not only retake both houses but Newt will even lose his own congressional seat. He'll abandon Georgia in a fit of pique and move to Absecon, where he'll finish out his career as a southern New Jersey late-night talk-radio host."

"Sure, and when John Sununu is on vacation, Newt will sub

for him on *Crossfire,* and his liberal antagonist on CNN's hollering contest will be Carmen LoBello doing G. Gordon Liddy Dole."

"I hope I can track down LoBello soon. He's as likely a candidate as anybody to be the Jim Suter quilt-maker. I'll bet he sews."

After our Thai dinner the night before with Martin Dormer and Peter Vicknicki, the two ex-Suter boyfriends had accompanied Timmy and me to Starkers, the Fourteenth Street gay club where Carmen LoBello had performed for several years. We located a number of LoBello's acquaintances there, but none had been in touch with him in recent months. And everyone who knew LoBello, including the club manager, described him as all but deranged by his brief affair with Jim Suter.

Soon after that romantic debacle, LoBello turned into G. Gordon Liddy Dole, a character unwanted by Starkers' customers, or by those in the few other D.C. drag venues where—as Hillary or Nancy or Judy Woodruff—LoBello might have been welcomed. We had struck out at Starkers, but my plan was to try to track LoBello down later that morning at his secretarial job at the Bureau of Mines.

"The thing I don't get," Timmy said, "is how Carmen LoBello could possibly be connected to Betty Krumfutz."

I said, "Maybe he isn't. There are connections so far either between or among Suter, Mrs. Krumfutz, Jorge the boyfriend, Alan McChesney, the dead Bryant Ulmer, probably Maynard, and maybe somebody in the D.C. Police Department. But so far LoBello is just another enraged Jim Suter dumpee."

"One of a cast of thousands apparently."

"There is a possible connection, of a sort, between LoBello and Mrs. Krumfutz. Which is, the Betty Krumfutz Maynard believes he saw at the quilt display on Saturday wasn't Mrs. Krumfutz at all. It was Carmen LoBello."

All in a fraction of a second, Timmy grinned, gasped, and winced. "Oh, good grief!"

"It makes sense."

"It does? I guess it could."

"Betty Krumfutz convincingly denied to me that she was anywhere near the quilt on Saturday. Nor is she, I think, a woman who goes around on a fall afternoon in Washington wearing shades and a trench coat, like some character out of Godard."

"She might if she wanted to examine the Jim Suter panel for whatever was typed on it about her, and she didn't want to be recognized."

"This is true. Still, I want to find out where Carmen LoBello was Saturday afternoon. And, if I can, what he was wearing."

Timmy was looking doubtful again. "But why would LoBello do that? What would he get out of it?"

"Good question. Maybe LoBello had spotted, or he had been told about, the Suter quilt panel—or he was the one responsible for getting the panel put into the quilt—and he wanted to hurt and embarrass Suter additionally by associating Jim's old employer and ideological cohort with this shocking fraud. Or LoBello could have had other strange reasons. Remember, by all accounts LoBello was driven pretty crazy by the collapse of his affair with Suter."

Timmy stirred his cappuccino thoughtfully. "I don't really understand that part—I mean, why LoBello was so traumatized by his breakup with Jim Suter that his life all but collapsed. Rejection is painful, yes, but this was not a ten-year relationship that fell apart overnight. It was a fling that had lasted a couple of weeks. No matter how shabbily they may have been treated, people tend to bounce back from disappointments of that limited magnitude. Whether or not he's responsible for the Suter quilt panel, and whether or not he did a Betty Krumfutz drag number at the quilt on Saturday, it's plain that LoBello did not recover normally from his affair with Suter. And I think knowing why would help us understand a lot of what's going on here."

"I think you're right, Timothy. Assuming, of course, that LoBello has anything at all to do with the quilt, or Mrs. Krumfutz, or any of the other awful events that we are currently so preoccupied with. Maybe Carmen LoBello has nothing to do with any of it."

Timmy grunted and glanced around the café. Ray Craig was nowhere in sight, so we assumed someone else from the DCPD was watching over us. Trying to pick out our minder had become a mordant game we played whenever we moved around Washington by cab or on the metro, and while we dined out or stopped for our morning coffee or a late-night beer.

Timmy had even brought up the possibility that our hotel room had been bugged. I considered that far-fetched. I did not go along with Timmy's request that we discuss my investigation and our respective plans only in the hotel bathroom with all the sink and bathtub faucets running loudly. Instead, I suggested that while in our hotel room we hold confidential conversations only when our voices were muffled and our words distorted by our lying on the bed with our pants down or off and with our mouths stuffed with each other's genitalia. Timmy said I wasn't taking our situation seriously enough.

# 16

The Bureau of Mines, now an office of the United States Department of the Interior, on C Street, NW, seemed like an unlikely spot for a terrorist attack. But after the Oklahoma City catastrophe, any U.S. government agency had to be considered fair game for ideological mad bombers, so the Interior building was well guarded. I never made it past the uniformed security detail in the lobby, but I was permitted the use of a phone to speak with the department's personnel office—"human resources" in the current puffed-up lingo of big government and big business.

Carmen LoBello was employed by the Bureau of Mines, I was told, but when I dialed LoBello's extension a woman answered and said Carmen wasn't in. He had taken a "personal day"—not yet labeled a "human needs day"—and he was expected back at work the next day, Wednesday. I'd be en route to the Yucatán then, but now, at any rate, I knew where to find LoBello when I got back, should I still think I needed to, after I had met with Jim Suter.

It was midmorning, and Timmy had taken the metro out to National Airport. He was to pick up my passport, carried down from Albany by a USAir flight attendant who was the boyfriend of a colleague of Timmy's at the legislature who had a key to our house. Then Timmy was headed over to GW, where he hoped Maynard would be in good enough shape for his first conversation since the shooting on Saturday night.

I was to meet two of Jim Suter's friends for lunch—the ones whose names I'd gotten from Bud Hively—with the hope that I might gather information about Suter's whereabouts in Mexico that was more specific than what I had pieced together from Hively and via Timmy's telephone trickery with Betty Krumfutz.

First, though, I figured I'd drop by Congressman Burton Olds's office and see what I could find out from another Suter ex-lover whose name kept cropping up, former Betty Krumfutz chief of staff Alan McChesney.

Unlike the Capitol and other nearby government edifices, the Sam Rayburn House Office Building wasn't so much monumental as monstrous. This big gray, graceless heap of marble slabs on Independence Avenue was about as welcoming as a federal penitentiary, and its immense, bleak corridors suggested not democratic representation but crude authority. I made it through the metal detectors and followed a guard's directions up to Congressman Burton Olds's suite of offices on the second floor, where, when I asked for Alan McChesney, the receptionist asked if he was expecting me.

I said no, but I thought Mr. McChesney would be interested in speaking with me about a missing person. The receptionist, an attractive green-eyed redhead who smelled of frangipani blossoms, spoke briefly on the phone. Then she said to me, "I'm sorry, but Mr. McChesney is with the congressman just now."

"Which one?"

"Which congressman is he with?"

"Right."

"With Congressman Olds," she said, and gave me an odd look.

"Do you have any idea how long he'll be in there? I'm sure everybody here is on a tight schedule, but I won't take more than five or ten minutes of Mr. McChesney's time."

"I can leave word that you stopped in, Mr. Strachey, and if you'd like to leave a phone number where we can reach you, we can probably set something up."

"I guess I'll hang around and hope for the best. If you mention Jim Suter's name, that should speed up the process. Would you mind giving that a try?"

The woman shifted uncomfortably—was I merely rude or a dangerous loony?—and then she got back on the phone. I studied the walls festooned with plaques and citations—from Illinois business and civic groups, from petroleum, chemical, and farm organizations. There were dozens of framed photos, in which Burton Olds, tall, muscular, and pinch-faced, was pictured with a variety of GOP present and former Illinois and national officeholders. Here he was with George and Barbara Bush, over there with Ron and Nancy in palmier days. In other shots Olds posed soberly alongside a grave-faced, bearded man I first thought might be the Reagan surgeon general C. Everett Koop, but who, on closer inspection, turned out to be the mechanical Abraham Lincoln at Disney World. Goofy was discernible in the dim background. There were also photos of Olds shaking hands with several foreign leaders, two of them Mexican: former president Carlos Salinas de Gortari and the current president, Ernesto Zedillo.

I seated myself and picked up a copy of *Time* just as a door opened and a beefy, square-faced man appeared. The receptionist indicated to him with a nod that I was the schedule interrupter.

"I understand you want to talk to Alan McChesney about Jim Suter." His tone wasn't hostile but it was far from friendly.

"Yes, if I may, please."

"Alan has a few minutes he can spare you. Follow me. I'm Ian Williamson."

I sensed that I was expected to know who Williamson was—as in "Hello, I'm Count Leo Tolstoy"—but neither his name nor his face was familiar.

I followed Williamson through a warren of cubicles and small offices and into a larger office with a window overlooking Independence Avenue and the Capitol grounds. Williamson rapped twice on a polished wooden door, which opened immediately, and a man strode out, quickly and quietly closing the door behind him. He brusquely indicated a straight-backed chair—the petitioner's seat—that directly faced the broad, heavy desk that he seated himself behind. Then he said to me coldly, "Is this some kind of shakedown?"

"Nope."

"I hope not."

"I'm a private investigator, not a criminal."

"I've met people who are both."

"So have I. But I'm not one of them."

"Mm-hmm."

McChesney gazed at me appraisingly while Williamson leaned against the doorframe, his thick arms folded. McChesney was forty-five or so with a chiseled face that was as hard and smooth as polished stone. His trim body had been carefully packaged in a black silk suit, and he wore a necktie with a subtle-hued, kaleidoscopic design that I suspected might reflect his personality as well as his politics.

"What makes you think I might have criminal designs?" I asked. "Have I got that reputation around the United States Capitol?"

"No," McChesney said, "you have no reputation whatever around the United States Capitol. But Jim Suter's name means trouble, and you bullied your way in here using Suter's name as an implied threat. I'd like to know what you meant by that. I haven't got much time to spare, so let's have it."

"I'm trying to locate Suter. I'm a private investigator, and a client, whose name I can't divulge, wants to contact Suter. It's rumored that he's in Mexico, and since you're reported to have introduced Jim to his current boyfriend, your friend Jorge Ramos, I thought you might know where the two of them are."

McChesney quickly shook his head and said, "You should go into politics, Strachey. 'It is rumored . . . you are reported . . .' You spew out this squid's-ink cloud of innuendo, and I'm supposed to tremble and gulp and confess all. Do you really think I'm that easy?"

"I hoped you might be."

"You're from—where?"

"Albany, New York."

"That's a grown-up political town. You should know better."

"Let's try this another way, then, that doesn't insult your intelligence, McChesney. You mentioned that Jim Suter's name means trouble. Which trouble did you have in mind?"

"Jim Suter is a sadist," McChesney said without hesitation. "He tortures men emotionally by seducing and abandoning them. He did it to me and hundreds of others, and if you meet him, he'll more than likely do it to you. I don't know if you're straight or gay, but either way he'll charm the pants off you—figuratively if you're heterosexual, literally if you're homosexual. Then, when you're hooked—and you will be, you will be—he'll turn his back on you and never take you seriously again, or ever speak to you again if he can get away with it. Jim is like some Christian-right caricature of a sick, cold-blooded, compulsively promiscuous American homosexual man. And if that's not trouble by any definition, I don't know what is."

Williamson, still leaning on the doorframe with his arms folded, looked a little sickened by McChesney's description of Suter, which left no room for sympathy for Suter's current alleged plight—which, in any case, I was still honor-bound not to mention.

I said, "I am gay, and I stand forewarned—by you and by others. But if Suter is so reprehensible, McChesney, how come you introduced him to your friend Jorge Ramos? That doesn't sound very nice."

"No, it wasn't nice," McChesney said icily. "Nor was it meant to be nice. I'll spare you the sordid details, but please take my word for it that Jorge Ramos and Jim Suter deserve each other. Getting them together wasn't as horrible a revenge as I've sometimes fantasized about for Jim. But for the time being it will have to do. Jorge and I, I should add, are no longer friends. I cut all my ties with Jorge months ago, when I discovered exactly what he was."

"Which was what?"

McChesney just looked at me.

"Was Jorge also an emotional sadist of some kind?"

"You could put it that way," McChesney said, and then his mouth clamped shut.

"Is it true that Suter is Mexico?"

"I wouldn't know because I haven't seen or been in touch with Jim Suter in months—a good year probably. But if Jorge got him down to Cancún and got his hooks in him, Jim may well have stayed. Even if after three days he and Jorge had had enough of each other, romantically speaking."

"What kind of hooks does Jorge have that he gets into people?"

"He's a hustler and a scam artist. Most of it's quasi-legitimate, but I suspect a lot of it's not—oversold vacation-condo time-share operations and the like. Drugs? Probably, once in a while, if a deal is foolproof. It's where the big easy money is made in Mexico. Every year forty billion dollars' worth of recreational narcotics passes through Mexico from South America to North America's fun-loving addicts and glamour seekers. And over half that forty billion ends up in the bank accounts of Mexican dealers and officials they've bought off. Jorge would not be one to let such an opportunity pass by, however cautiously he might go about it. He's always got money and easy access to the best of the good life on the Mexican Caribbean coast, and Jim Suter would go for that, I have reason to believe. Jim never made much as a writer, I don't think, so Jorge's lifestyle and circle of friends would be a definite draw for Jim—as it has been for so many men."

"Yourself included?"

McChesney didn't flinch at the insult. He just smiled a little sadly and said, "No, I was interested in Jorge's ass, not his expensive tastes."

"And he was interested in yours?"

"For a while, yes. Then his interests shifted and things got a little rough between us. Before I broke things off."

"Care to elaborate on that?"

"To you? No."

Williamson stood shaking his head with distaste, as if he

knew the McChesney-Jorge story, and he, too, found it too ugly to contemplate out loud.

I asked McChesney, "Where did you meet Jorge?"

"In Cancún."

"On vacation?"

"Yes, it's a gorgeous piece of Caribbean real estate. Have you been there?"

"I visited the Yucatán about ten years ago and enjoyed it. Does your boss go there, too? I saw his picture outside with some Mexican leaders."

"Those pictures were taken here in Washington. My former employer, Representative Krumfutz, is the real Mexico maven. She taught Spanish in the Log Heaven, Pennsylvania, high school before she ran for office, and she used to lead summer student tours of Mexico and during school vacations. She really knows the place and was the one who first got me interested in it, and I fell for Mexico the way a lot of people do—the quiet friendliness, the mix of traditional and modern cultures, the inexpensive comfort, the climate. My visits to the Yucatán, unhappily, have been curtailed since my falling out with Jorge. If you're tracking down Jim Suter, it looks as if you may be getting to Mexico well before I do, if that's where he is. And if, that is, your anonymous client is prepared to finance your trip to Cancún in search of Mr. Suter. What are you supposed to do when you find him? Shoot him?"

"No. Why do you ask that?"

"It's an impulse a lot of men have probably felt toward Jim Suter," McChesney said with no discernible emotion. "To take out a contract on him."

"I've no assassinations on my résumé."

"You're to be commended. Incidentally—or not so incidentally—I see that Jim made the news."

"That's right."

"Somebody put him in the AIDS quilt."

"Yes."

"What an insensitive thing to do. Not to Jim necessarily, but it sullies the quilt. A lot of dead friends of mine have panels in the quilt. So as much as I dislike Jim Suter, I think this is an extremely tasteless way for anybody to hurt him."

"I agree. I understand that you lost another friend last winter. Not to AIDS, but in a murder—Bryant Ulmer, your predecessor in this job. Or wasn't Ulmer a friend?"

"Bryant was not only a friend but a mentor. I'd been his deputy for two years. I miss Bryant very much, professionally and personally. I moved over here with Burton after Betty left office. Representative Krumfutz's career was fucked by her dim-witted husband, Nelson—and, I think, that ignorant cunt he's shacking up with in Engineville. Ever been up to Central Pennsylvania, Strachey?"

"Just passing through."

"It's beautiful country, but culturally it's a wasteland. If you're stuck up there for a month, as I was once, don't, say, go looking for tickets to the opera. Friday-night high school football, yes. The *Ring* cycle? Forget it."

"Unlike Washington, of course. Home of La Scala. Or is that someplace else?"

"We take the Metroliner to New York," McChesney said, and Williamson nodded. So these two were a couple?

"It's the same for us in Albany," I said, as if I'd ever set foot in the Metropolitan Opera more than twice. I hoped McChesney didn't start palavering about Wagner. What had happened to his tight schedule?

To my relief, he said, "I didn't like the way you bullied your way in here, Strachey, but I don't mind having been able to offer you my views on Jim Suter—unhelpful as I've been in locating him. I haven't got a current address for Jorge. I understand he's got some new place south of Cancún somewhere. So if Jim is with him, you'll have to find someone with more up-to-date information than I've got. But if I've added to your knowledge of Jim's foul history and rotten character, I'm happy to have been of assistance in that regard."

"Thank you."

"I've been far more forthcoming than anything I know about you suggests you deserve, Strachey. Now it's your turn. Who's your client?"

"I can't say."

"I could find out if I badly wanted to."

"How?"

"Ask around. I already knew you were in town looking for Jim."

"Well, go ahead. Ask around. That's up to you."

McChesney studied me for a moment, then said, "I might do that." Then he stood up, and as I stood, McChesney said, "If you go down to the Yucatán, I hope you have an enjoyable time, as you say you did ten years ago. But if you locate Jim Suter, the chances are, you won't. He's poison. And for Christ's sake, don't let him get you into bed. You wouldn't know what hit you. Not for the first week, I should say. That's bliss. But after a week or so, Jim Suter is Satan and life with him is life in hell."

I told McChesney I'd be extra careful. I thanked him and left. Williamson accompanied me to the corridor, and I made my own way out of the Rayburn Building and into a cool fall drizzle.

# 17

Who was my client, anyway? I wondered about that as I walked the four blocks back to the hotel—Ray Craig not visible but surely in the vicinity, for I caught a whiff of his nicotine spoor as I left the Rayburn Building.

Was Maynard my client? Timmy? Jim Suter, even though he hadn't asked me to be? I guessed it was Timmy, since he was planning on paying my expenses. In fact, I figured that he and I could split the costs of the investigation. That would make me my own co-client, and not for the first time either.

Luckily, I was solvent that month, having received a good bonus on top of my standard fee for tracking down the daughter of a commissioner in the Pataki administration and talking her into avoiding prosecution by returning to its owners the state police aircraft often used by the governor for official jaunts around New York State. The young aviatrix, who had only recently begun to suffer from emotional problems, had somehow made off with the plane at Albany County Airport and intended to follow Amelia Earhart's fatal 1937 route. The disturbed young woman had gotten only as far as Northampton, Massachusetts—not on Ms. Earhart's itinerary—when I caught up with her.

Did Alan McChesney really want to know who my client was? Or did he already know all or much of what there was to know of the past four days' events, and his alternating expressions of curiosity and pique were smoke-machine distractions? I was inclined not to trust him, but my mind was open.

I did plan on checking out McChesney's remarks in passing—if that's what they were—on Betty Krumfutz's Mexican connection as a high school Spanish teacher who, prior to her years in the Pennsylvania legislature and the U.S. Congress, could have taken part in illegalities—maybe Log Heaven schoolkids running drugs in their pencil boxes?—that Jim Suter later got wind of or was somehow involved in. But if Mrs. Krumfutz was knowingly connected to Jim Suter's danger—and Maynard's shooting and the ransacking of his house—she certainly had not betrayed any of that to me during our Log Heaven encounter. She had, on the contrary, seemed genuinely surprised that Jim might be in trouble. Or was that all an act put on by an experienced pathological liar? I'd run into that before.

Soon, I hoped to meet the actual Jim Suter. Then I would know if Mrs. Krumfutz was up to her neck in "it," or Nelson Krumfutz was or Tammy Pam Jameson or Alan McChesney or Carmen LoBello or any of Suter's other angry ex-lovers or his mother or brother or Ray Craig, or any other person or persons I had yet to meet from Jim's personal or professional life who had a reason, they believed, to threaten and badly frighten Suter and to try to kill Maynard Sudbury.

The only thing I was sure of was, it was Jim Suter who held the answers to all my questions. And, of course, I also knew that Suter was the Gay Male Siren of the Decade, the great sex bomb who had lured Washington's strongest gay men onto his irresistible shoals, where all were wrecked and some sank. I'd always thought of myself as being immune to the obvious—it was subtlety that could dampen my palms—but I was certainly interested in seeing for myself what all the excitement was about.

Back at the hotel, Timmy had left a message for me at the desk, saying that Maynard was doing well and Timmy expected to speak with him over the lunch hour. Timmy said he'd be back at the hotel by late afternoon.

Another message had been left by Chondelle Dolan: "Ray and Filbert switched." That was all. Officer Filbert Furlong, it seemed, was now following Timmy, and Ray Craig was trailing me around. I'd guessed that was the case—Craig's sour scent was often in the air around me. And the question remained, was I such a criminal, or potentially criminal, big cheese that the D.C. Police Department believed it needed to send a detective lieutenant out to keep watch on me? Or was Craig involved in some unofficial rogue operation—the grotesque conspiracy that had seized Timmy's imagination and made his skin crawl even when he had no idea at all as to what it might be about? Again, Jim Suter was the man with the answers.

# 18

At twelve-thirty I met Red Heckinger and Malcolm Sweet in a restaurant at the Hyatt Regency just north of the Capitol. These were the two friends of Jim Suter's that Bud Hively had told Dana Mosel about and I'd tracked them down. They were a couple, it turned out, and neither had been at all reluctant to meet with me, despite my vague description to them of my professional identity and my current role. As we sat down, the reasons for their willingness to have a word with me became all too plain.

"Jim Suter knows you're looking for him," Heckinger said, "and he wants you to *stop* looking. *Now.*"

"Do not pass go," Sweet added. "Do not collect two hundred dollars. Or, if you feel you must, *do* collect two hundred dollars from anybody you think might provide that sum. That's up to you. Just don't go looking for Jim Suter. Do you understand what we are saying? That way, no one will have to go looking for you."

I sat for a moment and considered this new wrinkle. Heckinger and Sweet watched me and waited. Both men were in their forties, in the mandatory dark-suit/bright-tie get up, and loafers that shone as bright as a thousand suns. Heckinger, with thinning, pale orange hair, was a slight man with a little face and big words that came out of it in a voice that sounded as if he were forcing it down an octave or two. Sweet was bigger and thicker, with a muscular neck, a nose like a shoehorn, and a sandy-colored brush cut that looked as if it could shred a turnip with a couple of swipes. Sweet had a big mouth that had smiled broadly when I introduced myself, but now neither Sweet nor Heckinger looked congenial at all.

"Care for a drink while you're deciding?" A waitress dressed like somebody's idea of a mod Dolley Madison had appeared. Heckinger asked for the house Chablis, Sweet a Sam Adams, and I decided a Molson might provide some welcome false reassurance.

Then I said to Heckinger and Sweet, "I detect a note of threat in your words. Or is my inference unwarranted?"

Sweet looked at me and said, "Bite my ass."

"My inference was correct then, I see."

Heckinger had lowered his head and was shaking it with regret tinged with disgust. "Strachey, Strachey, Strachey." He sighed.

I said, "Yo, bro."

"Don't you understand, Strachey, that this is bigger than you are?" Heckinger said, and it was all I could do to keep from guffawing.

"Are you guys for real?"

They both glared, and Sweet said tightly, "Do you know who we are? If you did, you wouldn't be so fucking . . . so fucking soigné."

Soigné? "I haven't the foggiest idea who you are. Are you escapees from some Lawrence Sanders Washington potboiler? That's what you talk like. When I walked in here today, I was under the impression I was experiencing actual human life. Now I'm not so sure."

Heckinger sneered. "Malcolm and I represent a consortium of interests. A consortium of powerful interests. Let's just leave it at that. Is that real enough for you?"

"A consortium of powerful interests. Heavens. Everybody stand back, for I'm starting to feel somewhat less soigné."

"Maynard Sudbury isn't feeling too soigné," Sweet said expressionlessly. "Is he?"

I said, "No, he isn't."

They watched me and said nothing.

"Did you have Maynard shot?" I asked.

Heckinger leaned toward me, sighed, and shook his head. "No, of course we didn't have Maynard shot. Malcolm shouldn't have said that. We don't know who shot Maynard. He's a nice guy—Malcolm and I have known Maynard for years. I'm sorry he got dragged into this, and Jim is very sorry about Maynard, and we're all relieved that he seems to be recovering well. Malcolm was just trying out a bit of shock treatment on you, Strachey, when he said that. But he didn't mean anything besides emphasizing the point we're making. On Jim's behalf, we're simply trying to get your attention, basically, and to convince you to stay away from Jim. That's all we want from you. And that's what Jim wants. *Comprende, amigo?"*

*"Yo comprendo.* And it's also what your powerful consortium of interests wants?"

"That's part of the picture, yes."

"To me, that part of the picture is still awfully blurry. Once it's clear, then I'll see what I'll do. I'll bet you fellows are in a position to help me out in that regard, no?" They sat tight-lipped and I went on, "Here are some questions I'll need comprehensive answers to before I'll even begin to consider backing off. Ready to take some mental notes? Got your thinking caps on?"

They glowered.

I said, "Which powerful interests do you represent? Where exactly is Suter, and why is he hiding? Is he in Mexico? Is he in danger there? Are others in danger there or here? Who shot Maynard and ransacked his house, and why?

"Are drugs involved? Have there been other illegal activities Jim's involved in? What is Betty Krumfutz's connection to whatever is going on here, if any? Does Betty's husband fit in? Does Tammy Pam Jameson? What about Jim's ex-lovers, such as Carmen LoBello and/or Alan McChesney? And Jim's mother and brother—what's the deal with them anyway? Is Bryant Ulmer's murder related to any of this? Why was a panel with Jim's name on it placed in the AIDS quilt, and why was the panel vandalized late Saturday afternoon and portions of Jim's Betty Krumfutz campaign biography taken?

"Answer these questions clearly and concisely, if you can, guys, and then I'll begin to think about winding up my investigation. But not before then." I didn't ask about Ray Craig, who was nowhere to be seen but whose distinctive scent I'd been aware of less than a minute after my arrival in the restaurant.

Heckinger and Sweet sat glaring at me. Neither could see the sweat trickling down my sides nor the muscular twitch on the back of my left calf. No one spoke for a moment, then Heckinger said, "You must be quite the conspiracy buff, Strachey, to imagine that all those persons and all those events that you enumerated could possibly be interrelated."

"Nope. Not at all."

"No?"

Dolley Madison reappeared with our drinks and said, "Ready to order yet?"

"Not yet," Sweet snapped without looking at the waitress, who, apparently experienced in her line of work, was unruffled by bad manners, and away she flew.

Heckinger said to me, "You're not among the sizable percentage of the American public who believe that Vince Foster was murdered at the White House and the U.S. Park Police, under Hillary Clinton's direction, dumped Foster's body in a Virginia glade with a gun in his hand, and then moved a truckload of incriminating Whitewater and other documents out of Foster's office and into the Lincoln bedroom, where the papers were shredded and flushed down Mary Todd Lincoln's bidet?"

"No," I said. "I doubt anything like that happened."

"Then you're very naive," Heckinger said. "Minus the embellishments that I added for my own amusement, something very much like what I just described is very probably what happened to the unfortunate Mr. Foster—a man who knew too much and may have been wavering in his loyalty to the extremely powerful people he knew it about."

I waited for Heckinger to break into a sly grin and then maybe give me an affectionate noogie, but both he and Sweet continued to regard me gravely. They believed that hooey?

I said, "My opinion, based on the results of several federal investigations and on the thorough reporting in an excellent daily newspaper, the *New York Times,* is that you are incorrect."

They both snorted, dismissing both the national law enforcement establishment and the Sulzbergers as, I guessed, either patsies or coconspirators in the Vince Foster plot.

I went on, "It's not that I believe conspiracies never happen. They do, obviously. There were all those CIA plots to overthrow governments in Guatemala and Iran and Guyana and the Congo, and of course, Hoover trying to ruin Martin Luther King or drive him to suicide. And the King assassination itself I also wonder about—James Earl Ray came out of a rat's nest of racist crazies, and King's murder could easily have been a plot hatched in the back of a Southern barroom.

"On the other hand, Sirhan Sirhan pretty clearly acted alone when he shot Bobby Kennedy. And I've never seen any really good evidence that the JFK assassination was the work of—to use your terminology—'a consortium of powerful interests,' including, in the popular Oliver Stone version, the CIA, the Joint Chiefs of Staff, Lyndon Johnson, the mob, and the board of directors of the Marriott Corporation. I think Oswald did it himself because he was a pathetic schmo with some confused leftist ideas who thought he'd knock off the suave, good-looking rich guy who was the president of the capitalist United States, and damned if he didn't somehow pull it off. People can't stand to think that a dork like Oswald could turn history upside down, so they look for some larger, darker, more sensationally evil explanation. But there probably isn't any.

"In fact, the Lee Harvey Oswalds are the source of most of the evil in the world, I think. Individual persons who are mad at the world, or mad at their wives, or just mad, or just weak and mixed up—they gradually or suddenly lose it, and then they rape or rob or commit murder. There *are* criminal conspiracies, sure—mob racketeering, drug smuggling, savings-and-loan rip-offs, and other organizational crimes. Sometimes angry, disturbed people do commit their crimes in groups—I know that—ordinarily for reasons of greed. There's violent mass folly, too, like Vietnam or Bosnia, but that's another story. By far, most of the people who inhabit the jails around the world, or ought to, are people whose folly is only personal. For reasons of their own, they are impelled to do the wrong thing, maybe a very wrong thing, and somebody else gets hurt.

"That's what I am inclined to think has happened to Maynard Sudbury. He was the victim of a few people doing the wrong thing in concert with one another, probably in order to make a fast buck. But a monstrous mass conspiracy? Something 'bigger than you are, Strachey,' as you guys so melodramatically put it? I don't think so. My question about all those people I listed is not how are they all interrelated? It's which one put Jim Suter's name in the AIDS quilt, and who's the asshole who had Maynard Sudbury shot?"

Heckinger and Sweet regarded me dully throughout this second oration of the early afternoon. When I had wound down, Heckinger sipped from his wineglass and said, "You're awfully old-fashioned, aren't you, Strachey?"

"Old-fashioned? I don't hear that one often. Can I get a signed affidavit to that effect to show to my boyfriend?"

Sweet shot me the hairy eyeball and snarled, "I'll give you an affidavit to think about!"

Then the waitress was back. "You gentlemen ready to order? Or do you need a few more minutes?"

"I'll have the ham club on wheat toast. This one," I said, indicating Sweet, "would probably enjoy the thumbtack salad with croutons of gypsum and a tapénade of ground glass."

The waitress chortled, then glanced at Sweet and saw the look on his face. She said, "If you'd like a little more time to think it over, I'll come back in a few minutes. Take your time." Instantly, she was gone again.

Ignoring Sweet, I looked at Heckinger and said, "So, how about spitting it out? You're a friend of Jim's—that I know—and you say he doesn't want to talk to me. Why?"

"Because if he talks to anyone," Heckinger said mildly, "he may be killed."

"Please explain that."

"I can't."

"Why?"

"I can't tell you that."

"But he talked to you, and you're alive."

Heckinger and Sweet glanced at each other and shared a moment of amusement over this. "Yes, we are alive," Heckinger said. "Indeed we are."

"Why are you threatening me?" I said. "Are you with the people who are threatening Suter? Is that what you do? Is the consortium of interests you say you represent an organization that, as part of its normal operating procedures, routinely threatens people?"

Heckinger said mildly, "That pretty much describes it."

So what were they then? They came across as a couple of unemployed bad actors, hired down at the union hall for an afternoon of impersonating thugs. But since actual thugs, more than they used to, pick up their styles and techniques from popcorn movies and TV series, maybe these two were authentic—what? Mobsters? CIA? KGB? Agents of the National Realtors Association?

I said, "Whoever you are, there is one question you can answer for me without violating your instructions. Give me this much. Is Jim, in fact, in Mexico?"

"He is, actually," Heckinger said.

"Where?"

He looked at me levelly. "I've told you all I can tell you, Strachey, and that is all the farther I can go. Don't go down there. That is Jim's wish and that is his instruction to you. If you get near him, you could get him killed. Now, *there* is potential folly for you, some human anger and confusion, and a resulting distinct evil."

*All the farther I can go?* This, I knew, was a Pennsylvania Dutch construction—German actually—meaning "as far as I can go." I hadn't heard it since my college affair at Rutgers with Kenny Womeldorf, of Lancaster, Pennsylvania. Kenny occasionally came out with these peculiar locutions that the Amish and German Mennonites had, over the years, deposited in the otherwise Mid-Atlantic Standard English of rural and small-town southeastern and Central Pennsylvania.

I took a leap and said, "Look, let's quit playing games here. You seem to know a lot about me and my current activities, and the fact is, I know a lot about the two of you. I know, for example, that despite your amateurish goonish threats, you work for neither the CIA nor the Mafia. You work for one or both of the Krumfutzes."

Heckinger and Sweet both got very busy now not reacting at all. "Oh, you know that?" Heckinger said tightly. Heckinger's face was red and Sweet's was white.

"Uh-huh."

"Well, I do believe you have been misinformed."

"Nope."

They stared at me.

"Moreover, additional disturbing information I have obtained concerning you and your colleagues up in the Keystone State has been handed over to reliable outside individuals. And if anything bad happens to Jim Suter or to me or to Timothy Callahan, or if anything else bad happens to Maynard Sudbury, that information will move swiftly to *(a)* the *Washington Post* and *(b)* the U.S. attorney's offices in both Philadelphia and Washington."

Heckinger and Sweet both sat stone-faced and silent. Just then the waitress showed up and made another tentative foray. "Ready now?"

Heckinger gestured to Sweet, and the two of them stood up

abruptly and walked out of the restaurant. I made a mental note to bill them later for the wine and the Sam Adams.

After lunch, I found a pay phone in the hotel lobby and tracked down Chondelle Dolan again.

"I had a quick look," she told me, "at the case file on the Bryant Ulmer homicide. On the night the crime occurred last January the eighth, it did look to be a robbery. Ulmer's expensive watch was taken, and his wallet with cash and credit cards. But there was something a little bit different about this robbery that made the investigating detectives wonder about it. Ulmer was shot six times—a lot for a perpetrator who wants to gather up his loot and start running away with it. And the gun that killed Ulmer wasn't an MP-25 or some other piece of street junk. Ulmer was killed with a Cobray M-11. This is a mean nine-millimeter firearm that's rare among everyday street thugs in Washington. Only the serious drug professionals carry M-11s—usually just to terrorize people they want to keep in line. And you know what else, Strachey?"

"What else?"

"I checked Ray's case file on the shooting of Maynard Sudbury. Your pal Maynard was shot with the same type of weapon."

"Does Ray know this? Is he having forensic comparisons done on the bullets in the two shootings?"

"If he is, there's nothing in his file on it."

"I wonder why."

"Me, too."

# 19

In the icy depths of an abnormally frigid Northeastern winter in the mid-1980s, Timmy and I had fled Albany for the tropics and ended up spending ten mostly happy days exploring Mayan ruins on the Yucatán peninsula. We observed the cliché of tourism in Mexico and got sick. But that hadn't lasted, and as refugees from the glaciated Hudson valley, we found the Yucatán heat and dust as therapeutic as thc sober hospitality of the Yucatecan people.

Now I was on a plane on my way back. I was eager to revisit the big, flat limestone shelf that had been home to a pre-Columbian civilization that worshiped a rain god, ripped the hearts out of its enemies, excelled in stone architecture and astronomy, and understood the concept of zero when the Europeans, apparently working backward from ninety-nine, were still stuck at about six. The Yucatecan Caribbean coast had only in recent years been developed, and it lacked the charm of the inland colonial-era population centers such as Mérida and Valladolid. But except for Cancún, a teeming monument to soulless industrial tourism, the coastal strip down to Tulum was still relatively un-Hyattized, I'd been told. And most of the beaches were so pure and sparsely trod upon that it was possible to imagine this turquoise coast as wild-eyed Cortés had first viewed it in 1519. I hoped my visit would be more congenial than his had been, and briefer.

I had in my possession on the flight from National to Miami, and then on to Cancún, directions to Los Pájaros, the small town where Betty Krumfutz had told Timmy that Jim Suter was living with his boyfriend Jorge. I also had a photo of Suter that Peter Vicknicki had provided, and a bathing suit, T-shirts, and sandals I'd picked up at a mall near the airport. Otherwise, I was traveling lighter than light.

The information from Betty Krumfutz was now suspect, of course. Why would she tell anyone where Jim Suter might be found if her thuggish employees Heckinger and Sweet (assuming they were Mrs. Krumfutz's agents) adamantly refused to do so? So I was as uncertain as ever what to expect in Los Pájaros, which in Spanish meant "the birds."

I wondered if, avianly speaking, I was in for some Audubon or Aristophanes or Hitchcock. I hoped it was Audubon. I knew Los Pájaros existed—I'd found it on the Yucatán road map I'd brought along—but I did not know if, when I arrived there, anyone would have heard of Jim Suter or Jorge Ramos. Before flying out early Wednesday morning, I asked Timmy to do some digging while I was gone on Heckinger and Sweet and to learn, if he could, from Maynard or Bud Hively or from Vicknicki and Dormer, who these two characters were, what they did for a living, and who they did it for. Timmy also planned on contacting Carmen LoBello at the Bureau of Mines and feeling him out on the quilt panel and the panel vandalism.

As the American Airlines 737 bumped across the top of some Gulf of Mexico fall thunderstorms, I got out the photo of Suter and studied his face. It was not hard to memorize. As had been widely attested to, Suter was a looker. In the head-and-shirtless-torso shot Vicknicki had lent me, Suter was muscular and trim in an appealingly natural way—both gym-slave obsessiveness and pectoral implants seemed unlikely—and he had a subtly sculpted Botticelli face topped with the notorious golden curls.

Maynard had referred to Suter's looks as those of a sensual Harpo Marx, and while I saw in his face the logic of the comparison—the gold, the glow, the obvious capacity for worldly delight—there was nothing shy about Suter's look, and no hint that, like Harpo, Suter might choose to express himself chiefly with a musical instrument or by honking a horn. Suter's gaze was direct and inviting, and in the photo his mouth was open slightly, as if he were about to tell you something you very much wanted to hear. What I wanted Suter to tell me was the truth, but I could not read in this single photograph whether I was likely to hear it from him or not.

The Yucatán's summer-fall rain-and-occasional-hurricane season was largely spent by mid-October, and as the plane came in low over the resort island of Isla Mujeres, the early-afternoon, mile-high, billowing clouds had spread apart and the sun was streaming through. This was off-season for tourism in the Yucatán, and the plane was less than half-filled. As the sixty or eighty passengers filed off at Cancún airport, I tried to spot Milton Kingsley, the D.C. police captain Chondelle said was traveling to Cancún around the same time I was.

I saw no onc fitting Chondelle's description of Kingsley—"George Foreman underneath a toupee that looks like a sleeping hamster"—and if Ray Craig had anyone else tailing me, there was no way of my knowing who on the flight it could have been. I half expected to detect Craig's scent in the airport, but had he been there, his odor would have been masked by the tobacco smoke in the poorly ventilated building, which could have been doubling as an air terminal and a Government of Mexico Ministry of Health emphysema research project.

I bought five hundred dollars' worth of the depressed local currency—NAFTA, a net plus for Mexican business, had not saved the peso from one of its periodic bungee jumps (the cord being the U.S. Treasury)—and stuffed the wad in my pocket. I picked up the rental car I'd reserved, a GM maquiladora assembly-plant product called, I think, a Chevy Outtie, and turned south. Making my way through the unmarked, chaotic road-construction area below the airport—driving in Mexico, as in Italy, Nigeria, and Boston, was not for the faint of heart—I headed down the Caribbean coast.

The air was heavy and hot, and my heart swelled with pleasure over being back in the tropics. Before I'd met Timmy in un-tropical Albany, two of my best love affairs had been with men in cities well south of the tropic of Cancer. The first was with sweet and exuberant Mike Akenjemi in Lagos, during a summer work-study program after my junior year at Rutgers. Two years later it was Ted Metzger, in that period when my government announced that it needed me and I concluded that two dangerous years in Saigon were preferable to any kind of a lifetime in Winnipeg.

I later heard from a decent and conscience-stricken friend who went there that summers on the Canadian plains were fiercely hot, too. But for me a hot climate was not a cultural advantage, just a circumstance under which I had twice somehow found romance and sweaty erotic joy.

None of that was about to be repeated, I was sure. For Jim Suter, despite his famous physical allure, sounded to me like a deeply problematical piece of work. Also, I had long since ceased sexual meandering, much to Timmy's relief. Both of our rare extramonogamous erotic adventures consisted of two-or-three-times-a-year, joint visits to far-from-home gay bathhouses—in Paris, Amsterdam, San Francisco—for some no-exchange-of-fluids, happy carnal comingling with others that was as harmful as a couple of farm boys in 1927 attending the hootchie-kootchie show at the Nebraska state agricultural fair, and far more wholesome. Those excursions pretty much satisfied the urges in both of us for sexual variety. So, the Yucatecan jungle heat notwithstanding, I expected that in the department of erotic temptation, my meeting with the allegedly irresistible Jim Suter would be—in the words of a droll Mexican I'd once met who liked to imitate the speech of gringo tourists—*no problemo.*

About halfway between Playa del Carmen and Tulum, just north of the resort complex at Akumal, I saw the road sign for Los Pájaros. It directed me off Route 307, the two-lane blacktop that ran the length of the coast from Cancún down to Chetumal on the border with Belize.

A third of a mile off the highway, behind a strip of jungle

thicket, Los Pájaros consisted of an assortment of perhaps a hundred small houses along a scraggly network of muddy streets. Most of the houses were cement, but there were a couple of traditional Mayan *palapas,* too, made of sticks and palmetto thatch, and it was the *palapas* that looked the most inviting in the midafternoon wet heat. Few people were out and about, just some kids kicking a soccer ball around the grassy town square and a woman in a white Mayan *huipil* toting what I guessed was a bucket of cornmeal down the main street. A cow was tethered under a shady scrub oak in front of one house, and a skinny dog that looked as if it might have been the source of the term *hangdog expression* sniffed at some trash in a front yard.

The few remaining older towns on the coast had Mayan names—Muchi, Pamul, Chemuyil—and I figured that the newer Los Pájaros had been built to house workers at the same time the nearby beachfront resorts went up. The central plaza had nothing identifiable as a Catholic church, just a one-story community center with a ramshackle arcade and some faded endorsements by the PRI, the forever-dominant Mexican political party, of former presidents who now were dead, fled, or under indictment somewhere.

Away from the highway, the only sounds in Los Pájaros were of the soccer-playing kids exclaiming in an unfamiliar language I took to be Mayan, and the recorded hymns, in Spanish, coming out of the front of the Seventh-Day Adventist meetinghouse. I recognized "Onward, Christian Soldiers," although on this torpid Wednesday afternoon no one in Los Pájaros was marching as to anything.

I had a hard time envisioning the scintillating Jim Suter in this place and wondered if maybe Timmy hadn't been misinformed by a wily Betty Krumfutz. I found a small *tienda* that was open, and using my combination of phrase-book and hazily remembered high school Spanish, I asked the elderly proprietress where I might find the *norteamericano* Jim Suter.

*"La playa,"* the old woman replied.

I asked her if she was acquainted with Señor Suter, and she gestured vaguely in an easterly direction and repeated, *"En la playa."* I took this to mean that she did not know Suter personally but that all the North Americans in Los Pájaros lived over by the beach and not here in the village. She explained to me where to find the beach road. I bought a two-liter bottle of *agua purificada* and swigged from it as I drove another mile down the main highway and then turned onto a road marked by a small sign that read *Playa.*

So as not to damage my Outtie's tender underbelly, I drove slowly and carefully down a potholed muddy road with thick, low jungle on either side of it for half a mile. Then the thicket ended and the road swung sharply left and ran parallel to the beach. The first house I came to was a big, two-story, L-shaped, white stucco job, between me and the sea, with terraces on either side of it, a terra-cotta-tile roof, and lots of big, louvered windows thrown open. A small satellite dish pointed skyward from the roof, although I saw no electrical lines and I wondered what the house's power source was.

A chest-high stucco wall crawling with vermilion bougainvillea wound around the house on three sides. It was interrupted by a gravel driveway that led up to a two-car garage and a smaller outbuilding. The only vehicle visible was a blue Chevy Suburban with muddy fenders. From my vantage point, some flowering trees obscured the front door, so I pulled my tiny Chevy up alongside the big one and climbed out into the bright heat. As I shut the car door, a couple of grass-green parrots shot out of the flame tree next to the garage and careened into the jungle squawking. So here were some actual *pájaros.*

Then the afternoon air was quiet again except for the sound of the light surf beyond the house. Off to my left the beach road continued on northward with other similar large, nicely designed stucco houses along it every twenty-five yards or so. I meant to ask at this house where Jim Suter was staying. But that wasn't necessary, for when I walked around the trees and approached the front door, it was already open and a man in cream-colored running shorts and a powder-blue tank top was standing just inside the doorframe grinning out at me.

"Don Strachey?"

"I am he."

"God, where have *you* been all my life?"

"That's an awfully tired line, Suter."

"It sounds as fresh to me as it did the first time I uttered it more than twenty years ago. It must be you who's jaded, Strachey."

"Not jaded, just well informed—about you and your habit of seducing and abandoning men."

"Oh, and you're too frail for that?"

"Not frail, just not interested." He was radiant, and now I saw why otherwise rational men had lost their senses in Suter's presence. Trying hard to keep my voice steady, I said, "Anyway, we've got more urgent matters to discuss, no?"

Suter gazed at me, his mouth open slightly, for a long moment, before indicating with a little toss of his golden locks that I should follow him into the house. He turned then and shut the door behind us. He said, "I take it you came alone. There are people who want me out of the way, as I know you know."

"I know that that's what you said in your letter to Maynard."

"Right. God, I am so, so sorry about what happened to Maynard. I hope you can believe that."

"He's lucky to be alive. And you're lucky he's alive, Suter."

"I know. You're right. Poor Manes. He was just in the wrongest possible place at the wrongest possible time. That poor guy has been to Beirut and back, and what does he do but get shot in the gut on E Street. Talk about unfair."

"Yes, it was unfair. Who shot him?"

"I don't know," Suter said, shrugging. "Honestly I don't. You're going to have to go back to Log Heaven, Pennsylvania, for the answer to that question. Log Heaven or Engineville. But I'm confident that after you hear what little I can tell you about all of these recent disturbing occurrences, you'll decide on the spot to dig no further and concentrate instead on doing the one thing you can do safely, and that's helping Maynard get back on his feet. And don't worry, he won't be in any danger from here on out. His getting shot was nothing more than an absurd misunderstanding."

"So you're telling me that the Krumfutzes were involved?"

"We can talk about that," Suter said with a little shake of his ringlets. "There's a lot you're not going to hear from me because there's no way in hell I can get away with telling you or anybody else. You're just going to have to take my word on that score. But I will tell you what I think I can, and then you can decide where you want to take it from there. I'm confident that you won't want to take it anywhere at all. Meanwhile, Strachey, why not bring your bag in and plan to spend the night? As you can see, we've got plenty of room. You won't have to share a bed with me if you decide not to."

"A lot of people know I was headed here. If anything happened to me, they would know where to look."

He started to crack a smile, then didn't. "So, what do you think might happen? Are you afraid you might have your heart ripped out, old Mayan style, and your body tossed down a *cenote*—either actually or metaphorically? Believe me, for you the greatest danger is of the latter."

"Of getting thrown down a sinkhole?"

"No, of having both happen, but only figuratively speaking."

"Jesus, Suter, you just don't know when to quit, do you?"

He grinned again, showing me his perfect teeth.

# 20

The interior of the Ramos house contained a mix of heavy Spanish-colonial, dark-wood furnishings that looked unused, more casual stainless-steel-tube-and-leather chairs, and lots of shelves displaying good crafts from all over Mexico: pottery, figurines, tinwork, and brightly painted wooden animal and human carvings from Oaxaca and Toluca, I thought, and I wasn't sure where else. The crafts collection looked all new, as if someone had walked into the gift shop at the Cancún Sheraton, glanced around, and said, "I'll take two thousand dollars' worth of this stuff."

Only Suter's airy room on the second floor, overlooking the water, next to the one where I deposited my bag, appeared to be lived in by anyone with a life. He had his computer there, and the beginning of a collection of books, in English and Spanish, that looked read. Suter had insisted that I come into his room to see his computer with its new Beta DVD. While he was there, he decided also to change his shorts for no apparent reason. He slipped out of the cream-colored pair, retrieved a Nantucket-red pair from a dresser drawer, then stood there for a minute, which grew longer and longer, holding the clean shorts, naked from the navel down, as he described his gigabitage.

I finally said, "Look, if you expect me to notice your bare ass, now I have. It is excellent. Now quit wasting your time and mine."

Suter laughed and stepped into his fresh shorts. "I have to be crass. I can't waste time. I'm forty."

"Don't you have a boyfriend here?"

"Sure, this is Jorge's house. But he's in Mérida for a few days. Anyway, who do you think we are, Jimmy and Rosalynn Carter? I'm married, but I'm not dead." Leading me out of the bedroom, Suter added, "You're probably amazed by both. I know I am."

I ignored that, and as we headed down the tiled staircase, I said, "How did you know I was looking for you, and how did you know I had located you and that I would arrive this afternoon?"

"Let's have a drink. It's too darn hot." Suter led me into the kitchen. He retrieved two bottles of Dos Equis from the refrigerator and proceeded out onto the tiled terrace overlooking the beach. As I followed Suter, it hit me again how beautifully formed he was, and I knew he knew I was studying him and that the erotic tension in the air was not entirely of his cynical manufacture. His bronzed skin was as aglow as his hair, and he smelled faintly of whatever he had had for lunch—ham? papaya? ripe cheese?

I said, "Where does the electricity come from? For powering the refrigerator and the other appliances."

"Wind and passive solar from a house up the beach. The lines run underground. Each place has a backup generator, but none of these houses uses much power, so we rarely need the backup system."

"So all of the houses along here are owned by Jorge?"

"No, but his family built them all at the same time." We seated ourselves at a wrought-iron table in the shade of the big house. "Señor Ramos is a developer and sold off the other houses almost immediately a couple of years ago. This coast is one of the last choice, unspoiled spots left on the Caribbean. Most of the islands are sinking under the weight of development, but the Yucatán still has a long way to go. At one point, O.J. was looking at a place not far from here. This was back during his first trial. Did you know that?"

"Would his presence have lowered the tone of the neighborhood or elevated it?"

Suter frowned, swigged some beer, and said, "You think I'm a piece of shit, I know. But I'm not as bad as you imagine, Strachey."

"Uh-huh."

"I'll admit, I do have some problems with what some people like to call intimacy issues."

"That sounds far more passive than what's been described to me." The beer was icy and fresh, and I kicked off my sandals and leaned back in my cushioned chair. I'd been up since five to catch my early-morning flight, and despite the problematical company, I was enjoying the sea breeze and the sight of the uninterrupted expanse of water, turquoise near the beach, dark blue-green farther out.

"Who did you talk to about me?" Suter said. "I know you went out to Silver Spring and harassed my mother and brother. They didn't believe for a minute that you were a reporter for the *Sun,* by the way. You weren't frantic and you weren't rude enough to be a newspaperman, Mother said. She was worried about who you might actually have been. Until, that is, I received another call from a friend explaining who you were, and that you meant no harm. Then I was able to reassure Mother. She was relieved."

"Who called you and told you who I really was?"

Suter looked at me with his big green Botticelli eyes. "You should know better than to ask me that."

"Was it the person who shot Maynard? Or arranged to have him shot?"

"No. Not that I know of, I guess I should say. I actually have no idea who shot Maynard. I only know of the general circumstances."

"And have you notified the D.C. cops of those general circumstances?"

Suter gave a little shudder. "Nope. Can't do that."

"You said in your letter to Maynard that he must not let the D.C. cops know where you are. Why?"

He said ruefully, "I'm sorry to disappoint you, Strachey. I am, truly. But there's just no way I can go into any of that."

"You can't seem to go into much of anything."

"No."

"Who's trying to kill you because you know too much about them, or because they think you know too much about them?"

"Sorry. Can't say."

"Uh-huh." I watched him and waited.

Suter studied the horizon thoughtfully. After a moment he said, "I've decided that there is some background I can give you that will put things into perspective. In fact, when I heard that you might show up here, it became obvious that I'd have to explain a couple of things about the Krumfutzes in order to get you off my back, as well as for your personal safety and your boyfriend's."

I waited.

"It's about drugs," Suter said.

"Drugs and the Krumfutzes? That sounds unlikely."

"Not Betty, just Nelson. If you knew this man, you wouldn't find any of what I'm about to tell you surprising at all."

"Fill me in."

Suter sighed. "Here's the situation. The situation is, it all has to do with a drug operation, and drug-money laundering, and Nelson's greed, and Hugh Myers, a Log Heaven businessman who put a lot of money into Betty's first congressional campaign. There's no way I can tell you or anybody else what I know—or what some people think I might know—about the Mexican end of the operation. But I can tell you that Nelson Krumfutz is a very bad and dangerous man."

When I didn't react to this and just sat watching him, Suter went on, "Okay, here's the deal. The deal is, when the Log Heaven furniture factories folded up about ten years ago, the GM dealership Nelson owned with Hugh Myers nearly went belly-up. Hugh had other investments to fall back on, but Nelson was in deep shit financially. Betty was still teaching high school Spanish at the time, and Nelson went with her on one of the Spanish club's spring-break trips to Mexico. Nelson met some people down here who saw the shipment of GM products from the Chihuahua assembly plants to U.S. dealerships as a means for smuggling coke. The deal saved Nelson's ass. He didn't actually have to make a profit on all those cars he brought into Central Pennsylvania. He just had to disassemble and remove the packages sealed into the seat backs. It wouldn't surprise me if the entire eight-mile-long Log Heaven dike-levee system is stuffed with new Buicks and Chevies that Nelson didn't need to sell."

Suter watched for my reaction to this story, which was, "Hmm."

"Quite a production, wasn't it?"

"Remarkable."

"So the point is," Suter went on, "Nelson got nailed by the feds not for the drug operation, which they don't know about, and which Nelson and Hugh Myers have since sold to another GM dealer in Wilkes-Barre, but for pocketing a quarter of a mil of Hugh's and a couple of other guys' campaign money—all of which was part of some crazy-ass scheme Nelson and Hugh developed for laundering the drug profits. If you really want to know how it worked, you'd have to ask Nelson. But of course if you did that, then he would tell the Mexicans you know about him—and them—and they would kill you. That's what they do. With no hesitation whatever, they kill you. So now do you understand what your problem is with this thing, Strachey? And mine?"

"I'm starting to. If you're telling me the truth, Suter."

He laughed once. "Do you really think I could have made that up? I've never been big on conspiracy theories to explain evil in the world. So my mind just doesn't work that way."

"So Betty wasn't in on this . . . this drug-running operation?"

"No. I don't think she ever even suspected. Betty is ripshit over Tammy Pam Jameson, but that's something else. Nelson not only ruined Betty's political career, but then he moved in with Tammy Pam, who he'd been keeping on the side up in Engineville for ten years. Not that Betty doesn't have her own romantic idiosyncrasies. She likes to pretend that she's the first queen of the Mayas, and she hires Mexican guys to fuck her and then kneel at her feet while she rips their hearts out for breaking warrior training. She doesn't rip their real hearts out naturally. Betty's a good egg. She uses beef hearts that she picks up when they're on sale at the Log Heaven A and P."

I remembered the scene I had briefly witnessed through Mrs. Krumfutz's back window, which added to the plausibility of Suter's lurid tale. "That's pretty wild, Suter. How do you know about Mrs. Krumfutz's playacting habits?"

"Alan McChesney told me. He used to be on Betty's congressional staff. He caught her at it once, and anyway word got around among the Central Pennsylvania illegals on how to pick up a couple of extra bucks. Of course, she made them do yard work, too. If George Bush had been reelected, Betty would probably have been his second-term ambassador to Mexico. That's the job she was after, and she certainly would have livened up the U.S. embassy in Mexico City. It's a stodgy place, from what I hear."

A sudden motion off to the left of the terrace caught my eye, and I glanced over in time to see not a drug-gang assassin with an automatic weapon aimed at Suter and me, but a plump iguana disappearing into a crevice in the rocks.

I said, "So it's your opinion, if I've got this right, that my approaching Nelson Krumfutz would be not only highly dangerous but redundant, since he'll probably go to prison anyway?"

"Of course. Nelson is fucked no matter how you cut it. And nobody is going to lay a glove on the Mexicans anyway. So why should you or anyone else risk your lives for nothing?"

"You might as well tell me what happened to Maynard. Was it the quilt panel? Did someone think Maynard spotted something on the quilt panel with your Krumfutz manuscript on it? *Did* you put something incriminating in the manuscript? Something that might be discovered if you were killed?"

Suter gazed at me with a look of fright, which, at the time, I interpreted as a man confronting a dramatic sign of his own mortality. "Yeah, something like that."

"Who put the panel with your name on it in the quilt?"

"I honestly don't know. But I'm sure it was meant to intimidate me. Which, when I heard about it, it sure as hell did."

"And Maynard was shot and his house ransacked both as a way of eliminating him as a source of information on the Mexican end of the drug operation, and as a warning to me or my boyfriend, Timothy Callahan, or anyone else Maynard may have spoken to about—about this thing Maynard actually knew nothing about?"

Suter slowly nodded. "Yeah . . . yeah."

"If that's true, it's disgusting."

"I know it is. I know."

"And what about Red Heckinger and Malcolm Sweet? Who sent those two buffoons to scare me off? You or the drug cartel?"

Suter gave me a droll little grin. "They're friends of mine who used to work for Betty. They're harmless. Red and Malcolm don't even know about the drug operation. I told them you had a lot of wrong ideas about me, and would they help me get you off my back? I also wanted to save you the trouble of coming down here only to be convinced that there was nothing you needed to do to apprehend the North American who was once directly involved in the drug scam, since the law had already gotten its meaty paws around Nelson Krumfutz's skinny neck. But I guess Red and Malcolm weren't as convincing as they could have been as mob enforcers."

"No. They were just a couple of putzes."

"You could have saved yourself the airfare, Strachey. Not that I'm not enjoying your company. I am. You're an extremely attractive man. You come across as a kind of straight Tom Selleck. That's one of my favorite types."

"I believe you mean one of your several hundred favorite types. So, what's the deal with Jorge? You've never stayed with one man this long before. Is he not really your boyfriend? In your letter to Maynard, you described yourself as still unlucky in love. Is Jorge's father the head of the drug cartel, and is Jorge really your jailer?"

Suter reddened under his tan. He took a long swig of beer and swallowed it. He looked at me and said, "He's both."

"Your boyfriend and your jailer?"

"If he were only my jailer," Suter said impatiently, "what would the point be? To silence me, they could just kill me. Like they tried to kill Maynard. The reason they *don't* kill me is that Jorge is my boyfriend. His father would prefer to kill me, but he lets me live because Mrs. Ramos, Jorge's mother, considers me her son-in-law. To her I'm family. To Señor Ramos I am an embarrassment and a dangerous pain in the ass. And to Jorge I'm his lover and his prisoner. I'm his love slave, like in the popular song. Except this one is not much fun to dance to.

"And, of course, to other higher-ups in the drug operation, I'm a potential witness against them in court. That's the reason I fear for my life. I don't really know that much about the actual operation, of course. Not the incriminating particulars. But there are people down here who think I know more than I actually know, and they have let me know that they would feel more secure if they were to gouge my eyes out.

"So, you see, Strachey, I've learned to take care who I talk to and who I'm seen with. That's why I panicked and ignored Maynard in Mérida last month. What's ironic, of course, is that I first learned about this sordid shit the first night I went to bed with Jorge. Alan McChesney introduced us, and I thought wouldn't it be fun to have a quick tumble with this cute Mexican who was probably one of Betty Krumfutz's love slaves? And what happened instead? I became his love slave—for life, it appears."

"Jesus, Suter."

"Now you know all the essentials," Suter said wearily. "Hey, how did that happen? I guess you used your wiles on me, Strachey. This keeps happening lately. I mean to be the fucker and end up the fuckee. The royal fuckee, it seems."

"I feel bad for you, Suter," I said, and meant it. "I wouldn't have thought that was possible. Not after I heard what a contemptible creep you've been with the many men in your life. But what you have described to me is poetic justice of a rather severe variety. You can't redeem yourself because you can't free yourself. You're trapped in a kind of eternal, awful reversal of fate."

"You put it ever so vividly."

"The lines of your dramatic narrative emerge boldly on your own."

"Since you feel so bad for me, will you go to bed with me? That would cheer me up, and I know you'd enjoy it hugely, too."

"No, of course I won't go to bed with you. Don't be absurd."

He put down his beer. "Let's go for a swim then and have a lovely dinner instead. You might as well get something satisfying out of your visit to this tropical paradise." Then Suter flung off his shorts and shirt and ran naked toward the surf. I figured there was no harm in that and did the same.

# 21

"Do you know a D.C. cop named Ray Craig?" I asked Suter.

"No, who's he?"

"How about a Captain Milton Kingsley?"

"I don't recognize the name."

We were on the southern terrace of the house now, watching one of the sunsets that must have been an inspiration for those big Mexican oil paintings that are full of Spanish-conquest blood and gore—another inspiration being the Spanish-conquest blood and gore itself.

After our swim, Suter and I had put our shorts on and walked up the beach a mile and then back. The houses we passed, built by Jorge's father, were even bigger and more opulent than Jorge's. They were owned, Suter said, by wealthy North Americans, many of whom spent little time in their tile-and-stucco palaces. We walked by an occasional well-tanned bather or sunbather, many of them nude. Most seemed to be foreigners. I heard mainly North American accents, as well as a few German and Italian speakers. The scattering of Mexicans on the beach tended to be families, in bathing suits or fully clothed. Suter said the Mexicans considered the nudism shameful but that they are an almost endlessly tolerant people. Also, Mexican men who otherwise were not necessarily nature lovers liked strolling on the beach and staring at the bare-breasted European women, quite the erotic spectacle in a society where only the men were allowed to be lewd.

We also passed a beautiful young Mexican woman in a white, one-piece bathing suit in the company of a man I recognized as a well-known U.S. congressman from a Midwestern state. Suter greeted them both, and then told me that the congressman, Lawrence Grandchamps, was a frequent visitor to a house owned by a Mexican cement tycoon whose exports to the south-central United States increased by roughly 1,000 percent after the North American Free Trade Agreement was passed and signed. Suter laughed and said he was sure the two men's deep friendship was based on a love of scuba diving out by the reef and not on a love of cement profits.

Back at Suter's house, he was stretched out on a chaise with another Dos Equis in his hand, and I shoved myself back and forth in the string hammock that hung between two coconut palms alongside the tile terrace. When he told me he didn't recognize the names Ray Craig or Milton Kingsley, I asked Suter again why he was so anxious that the D.C. Police Department not know where he was.

"Unpaid parking tickets."

"I don't think so."

"Well, then—here's the actual thing," Suter said, sucking in air. Then he didn't go on.

"Yes? And?"

He sighed again and said, "I'm being sued. There's a summons going around looking for me, I'm told."

"Oh? Sued for what?"

"I don't want to go into it. It's a professional thing that has no bearing on the Krumfutzes or Jorge or why I'm down here."

"Is the dispute with a publisher?"

"No."

"Anyway, what have the cops got to do with a civil suit? The plaintiff's lawyers will go after you, or maybe a process server will. But cops only deal with criminal matters."

"This situation is a little more complicated than that."

"Complicated. Uh-huh."

I waited, and when it was plain that Suter had nothing more to offer on the lawsuit against him, I said, "I'm sure the D.C. cops know where you are. If I found you, they could do it. I knew from your letter to Maynard that you were in the Yucatán, and my partner, Timothy Callahan, extracted from Betty Krumfutz the name of the town where you were most likely to turn up. Ray Craig is investigating Maynard's shooting and made his first Mexican connection when two eyewitnesses described the shooter. He knows, too, that Maynard was down here in September. Craig has been investigating me, so he undoubtedly knows by now that I'm investigating you."

"Thanks for nothing," Suter said sourly.

"Milton Kingsley is a D.C. police captain who, according to a source of mine in the department, was set to travel down here around the same time I came."

"Well," Suter said, "thanks to Jorge's father, this cop would have a very hard time finding a Mexican judge or any other Mexican official who would agree to have me extradited. Anyway, this awkward situation is not criminal, which means I can't be extradited. It's just that I'd prefer to avoid the hassle of having to deal with the suit right now. I need peace and quiet and the chance to concentrate. The thing is, I'm working on a novel." His eyes shone brightly.

"Ah. Working on a novel." So was the weekend weatherman on Channel 8 in Albany. And Timmy's aunt Moira. And six or eight of Timmy's colleagues in the New York State legislature. And Kathie Lee Gifford probably. And Radovan Karadzic. I said, "But the novel is dead. Why aren't you writing a screenplay?"

"I am. I'm doing the novel and the screenplay simultaneously."

"You're quite efficient."

"Yeah, I am. Even though I don't have to be. I've got nothing but time on my hands down here."

Fools rush in. "What's the novel about?"

Suter smiled ruefully. "It's about an exceptionally charming and attractive man with intimacy issues. Sound familiar? I confess. The novel is autobiographical."

"Oh, well. 'Intimacy issues.' I'm glad to hear you're writer enough to tackle one of the great literary themes."

"You're ridiculing me."

"You bet."

"Why? Why should you make fun of me?"

"Because you talk about yourself in vague, psychobabbly euphemisms. You don't have 'issues,' Suter. You have a history of playing with gay men cruelly. What it is, is acting like a total asshole. In fact, there's a title for you: *The Autobiography of an Asshole.*"

Suter stared at the blackening sunset and said nothing.

"I feel sorry for you," I said, "because for whatever reason, you can't seem to help yourself. You do have some shallow understanding of your weaknesses and their cruel effect on others. But some critical part of what ought to be your moral ballast is missing, so you minimize what you do to people. You call it 'issues,' when it's actually psychological sadism. I'm sorry that you're deluded, and I'm sorry that you met a man who apparently is even more sadistic than you are. I think you deserve to be socked in the jaw, figuratively or actually. But I don't believe you deserve a lifetime of Jorge. He sounds grotesque."

Suter lay very still on his chaise through this. Then he said, without much emotion, "It won't be a long lifetime, however. My looks will soon fade, and Jorge will lose interest. He'll find another, younger, beautiful slave. His mother will die, I'll lose my protector, and then I'll be killed."

I thought of Timmy back in Washington and his conviction that Maynard's shooting was one of the events flowing from a vast and terrible conspiracy, and then I thought of my own belief that surely all these gruesome events flowed instead from more mundane examples of human weakness and folly, and I told myself with no satisfaction whatsoever that I was right and Timmy was wrong. A drug gang—even one that reached from

Mexico into small-town new-car dealerships in Central Pennsylvania—was brutal, but it was also contained and, in the United States of the 1990s, such things bordered on the banal. And Jim Suter? Here was individual-human folly personified.

I said, "But you don't have to be killed, Suter. Before Jorge finished with you, you could go to the feds. You've got the goods on Jorge, his father, Nelson Krumfutz, Hugh Myers, and, I'll bet, others in the organization. You must know enough to buy your way into the Witness Protection Program. No?"

"All I really know is what Jorge told me. None of the threats I've received from Señor Ramos or his business associates, as he calls them, were in writing, or even that direct. I know the outlines of the drug operation but not enough of the specifics to be of much help. I doubt, honestly, that I'd have all that much to offer."

"You've got plenty to bargain with, including the fact that large quantities of coke are being smuggled into the United States inside the seat backs of cars assembled at the plant that supplies GM products to Central Pennsylvania. That will make for a well-attended news conference and thirty or forty promotions at the DEA. If you walked into the U.S. attorney's office tomorrow, Suter, I'll bet you could name your price for the information you've got inside your head."

Suter watched the sun disappear and seemed to mull this over. After a moment he said, "If I went into the Witness Protection Program, would they have to change my appearance?"

What a vain fool he was. "Not significantly, I think. Maybe a mustache or something. I doubt you'd have to have your nose bent sideways or your head shaved." After our walk up the beach, Suter had showered and shampooed his locks, which shone dark orange now in the last light of the day.

"My looks aren't going to last anyway," he said matter-of-factly. "I'm getting crow's-feet and my teeth are yellowing. And if I eat more than one flan a week, my skin breaks out like an adolescent's. This week I've got a zit on my upper lip and one on my butt." I had noticed both, in fact, and thought they only lent a touch of becoming vulnerability to Suter's otherwise flawless appearance.

I said glibly, as if normal bodily deterioration were of scant concern to me, "I'm sure you'll be nicely presentable toward the middle of the next century, Suter. Meanwhile, you've got more urgent matters to consider, such as making sure you're still alive at the end of this one."

"I know that," he said, and shuddered. "By the way, you would not take it upon yourself, I hope, to talk to the feds on your own, and to get them breathing down my neck? That might just get me killed within a matter of hours."

"No," I said, and meant it. I believed that Suter had to get out of the box he was in on his own. "I'm not going to put you at immediate risk—or myself or Timmy or Maynard or anybody else. I am going to check out some parts of your story discreetly. But I won't go to the cops or the feds with any part of this thing without your permission. I wouldn't mind seeing you punished, Suter, for the way you have toyed with people's emotions—a good spanking might be in order—but I certainly don't want to see you killed, and neither does Maynard."

Suter sighed. "Dear, sweet old Manes. That man was one I could have stuck around a lot longer if we'd both been a little differently put together. It was just too bad he was such a bleeding heart. I tend to go for more tough-minded men, for men who are realists, with no illusions about the nature of the human beast. Men such as yourself, for example. But then you already know that. I keep repeating myself in that regard."

I ignored the continuing come-on, which was far too crude for my tastes, and I said, "As I understand it, you broke up with Maynard not just because of your clashing political philosophies but because he refused to play your psychological S-and-M games. When your romance was hot and you suddenly turned cold, he was disappointed but he just let it go. And you couldn't stand that, so you lured him back. Then you did it again—froze him out—and Maynard concluded in his Midwestern way that you were ill-mannered—an extremely serious matter in Southern Illinois—and that was the end of that. Not true?"

Suter said simply, "Maynard is a strong individual. Don't get the idea I never appreciated him or didn't know what I was losing." He smiled weakly and added, "But the problem is, of course, that I have . . . can I say 'psychological sadism issues'? Is that an honest enough description for you?"

"Almost."

He laughed once, pulled himself off his chaise, and said, "Let's eat."

Suter drove me in his big Chevy back to the main highway, then south five miles to a resort-hotel complex near Chemuyil. The *palapa*-roofed restaurant where we ate was not at all crowded—Christmas to early April was the tourist season here—and it served a nice slab of grouper with grilled onions, tomatoes, and peppers. The dessert flan was good, too. The after-dinner coffee was the characteristic Mexican cup of tepid water, served with a jar of Nescafé and a sticky spoon—a well-loved old Aztec ritual apparently.

During dinner, Suter told me he would consider my suggestion that he throw himself on the mercy of the U.S. narcs and attempt to enter the federal Witness Protection Program. He said any such exercise would have to be swiftly and expertly carried out, and I agreed. He said he had never really thought of this as a possibility for his salvation from Jorge and the Ramos family, and the idea of it was both intriguing and terrifying. He said if he decided to do it, he would like my help in making the arrangements. I said, whenever he was ready.

Back at the house, I tried to reach Timmy on Suter's phone for an update on Maynard's condition. But Timmy wasn't yet in our room at the hotel, so I left word for him at the desk that I had arrived safely at my destination and that I was finding my visit useful.

Suter and I sat for a while longer on the terrace talking mainly about Mexican history and politics—his knowledge was wide and deep—and looking up at the moon and stars. A warm breeze off the water kept the insects at bay and felt lovely against my skin. I wished Timmy were with me, and I resolved to plan a vacation with him on this sensuous tropical coast early in the wintery New Year.

I was in bed and dozing off by midnight. Soon after, there were bare footsteps on the tile floor and I felt Suter lift my sheet and ease in next to me. As he kissed me, I looked into that face, moonlit now, and ran a hand through the famous curls. But otherwise I was more efficient than passionate, and when I dropped into a deep sleep no more than ten minutes later, I sensed that Suter's predominant reaction to our encounter had been, like mine, exhaustion.

# 22

Timmy's first words, when I stepped off the plane at National Airport Thursday night, were "That was fast."

"You have no idea."

"I'm so relieved you're back."

"And I'm so happy to look into your guileless eyes."

"Did Suter get you into bed?"

"Something like that."

"And you liked 'it,' probably, but you didn't like him."

"I wouldn't even go so far as to say I liked 'it,' fleeting as it was. God knows what it was like for Suter. He had to prove to himself that he could at least get that far with me, and he did. But for me it was almost entirely aesthetic."

"Do you mean like visiting the Uffizi?"

"Yes, except with a shorter queue to get in. That was the case last night anyway."

"And there was no risk to anybody's health?"

"There was barely any risk to the bed linen."

"Even so, do not do that again, please." His look said he meant it.

"Okay. I won't."

During the cab ride from Alexandria into Washington, I tried to give Timmy an account of my under twenty-four hours with Jim Suter in Los Pájaros and of the dramatic and complex story he had told me. Timmy kept indicating the cabdriver with his eyes, as if Mulugeta Fessahazion might be more than passingly interested. So I gave up on the Suter narrative and instead described physical developments along the Yucatán

Caribbean coast since Timmy and I had vacationed there in the mid-eighties. We planned another trip together in January or February—not to include, Timmy suggested, Los Pájaros. "It sounds as if it's not our style," he said.

Timmy did tell me during the cab ride that Maynard was still weak but recovering from his wounds and that he was alert and bordering on the garrulous. I asked if he had told Timmy anything useful to my investigation about Suter or anyone else. But Timmy raised an eyebrow in the direction of Mulugeta, locked his lips, and threw away the key.

Back on Capitol Hill, something pungent was in the late-evening autumn air. It wasn't burning leaves, just Ray Craig, who stepped out of the shadows near the hotel entrance as we climbed out of our cab.

*"Buenas tardes,"* Craig said to me, sneering.

"Yo, Ray."

"Been south of the border, Strachey?"

"Could be."

"I guess going down is nothing new for you." Craig snorted with satisfaction over his witticism.

"Did you follow me all the way to Argentina?"

"You weren't in Argentina. You were in Mexico."

"Oh, I guess you're right about that."

"Calling on Jim Suter."

"Was I?"

"The question is, why?"

"No, that is the answer, Ray. But what is the question?"

He glowered at me for a long time. Timmy stood nearby sending ESP messages my way: Don't irritate him, just get rid of him.

Craig finally said, "The question is, when am I going to bust your ass, Strachey, on a narcotics charge?"

"Not ever, Ray. Because I'm involved in no such thing, and you know I'm involved in no such thing."

"Do I? And do I know that Maynard Sudbury was never involved in smuggling controlled substances from Mexico?"

I sensed Timmy stiffen. "I think you know that, yes," I said.

"Then why," Craig said, giving me the beady eye, "did my two eyewitnesses to the E Street shooting pick Reynaldo Reyes out of a mug book of violent offenders with known drug-gang connections? The witnesses had gotten a good look at the shooter as he passed under a streetlight, and each witness independently ID-ed Reyes yesterday afternoon. We'll put Reyes in a lineup when we find him and pick him up. Suddenly he's either out of the country or he's under a rock over in the Alexandria barrio. Now, why would this lowlife want to shoot your buddy, who had traveled to Mexico just a couple of weeks earlier for travel writing, you say, if they weren't both involved in the same degenerate occupation? You tell me, Strachey."

Telling Craig what Jim Suter had told me would have explained Maynard's innocent involvement in the affair, but I couldn't do that. I said, "I can't answer that. But Timothy and I know Maynard Sudbury well enough to know that he's about as likely to be involved in drug dealing as Newt Gingrich is. Less probably. Sudbury is one of those ex–Peace Corps, liberal, dilettante types with no particular interest in accumulating money. They're all in the arts and journalism and social services and education. The profit motive seems alien to these people, and I'm not sure how so many of them seem to survive in post-Reagan America, but they do. Without becoming criminals even. Ray, this is strange but true."

Timmy was shifting from foot to foot. Not only had he to put up with Craig, he had also to endure my joshing on the subject of his dearest friends, the ex–Peace Corps mob. But he knew when to keep his mouth shut, and now was one of those times.

Craig said, "I hope for your sake that what you're telling me about Maynard Sudbury is the truth, Strachey. If it's not, you'll have me to answer to. What did you find out from Jim Suter?"

"You still haven't explained," I said, "why you think I went to Mexico to see someone you keep referring to as Jim Suter."

"Skip the bullshit game-playing. If you knew your ass from your left nut, you'd know that I've talked to Suter's mother and to six other people, most of them admitted homosexuals, that you've interviewed about Suter. What's Suter's connection to Sudbury? Is Suter Sudbury's drug connection in the Yucatán?"

"No, Ray. Suter and Sudbury were once boyfriends, and I'm talking to all of Maynard's ex-lovers trying to develop a lead on the shooting. You're hung up on this drug thing, and that's a nonstarter. In order to see that Timothy's and my friend's attacker is brought to justice, I'm simply doing your job the way it ought to be done. Instead of ragging me and having me followed everywhere I go, you ought to be cooperative. Grateful even."

At that, Craig spat a wad of tobacco-y phlegm at my feet and said, "What a bullshitter you are."

I said, "Tell me about Suter's lawsuit."

"His what?"

"Somebody is suing him, he says. Suter convinced me he knows nothing about the Sudbury shooting. But he said there's a lawsuit against him here in D.C., and the cops are involved in it somehow. What's that about?"

Craig said, "It's chilly out here. Let's go up to your room. We can sit down where it's comfortable, maybe throw back a couple of brews, and have an exchange of information."

Timmy said, "It's getting late. What about tomorrow? Could you have your exchange of information tomorrow?"

"Let's have an exchange of information here and now," I said. "Why wait? Ray, why don't you light up a butt and relax? Timmy, if you want to take a load off your feet, you go on up. But I'm going to tell Ray right now that Jim Suter has two connections to Maynard, and both, I discovered, apparently have nothing to do with the shooting.

"One connection is, many years ago Suter and Sudbury were lovers for a short time. The other connection is, a panel with Suter's name on it appeared in the AIDS quilt on Saturday, and Maynard recognized this and notified the Names Project of this strange occurrence the day he was shot. The Names Project is where I plan to concentrate my investigation next, Ray. And if you were smarter than I'm afraid you might be, that's where you'd start asking questions, too."

Craig was sucking in the carbon monoxide, etc., from a Camel Light now, probably reducing the chances that in the throes of withdrawal he would suddenly yank out a service revolver and slam hot lead into our chests. I hated to sic him onto the Names Project—these people deserved better—but I needed time to check out Suter's wild tale of drug gangs in Central Pennsylvania and then to talk him into the Witness Protection Program and save him from his lover-jailer Jorge and the Mexican drug cartel killers.

Craig said calmly, "I already am in touch with the AIDS quilt organization."

"Hey, good."

"They faxed me a copy of the form that came in with Suter's panel. The panel was submitted in April by a David Phipps, but the name seems to be phony. He used a Mailboxes, Etcetera drop, and now I gotta get a fucking court order to find out who rented the box. I'm working on it. Am I conducting my investigation to your satisfaction, Strachey?"

"Nice work, Ray. Now tell me this. Who is Captain Milton Kingsley, and why did he follow me to Cancún? I know that a couple of your junior officers have been tailing me around D.C. since Sunday morning. But am I such a criminal celebrity in your department that I merit a captain to keep tabs on me?"

In middrag, Craig went very still. "You spotted Kingsley? Tailing you? In Mexico?"

There was no way I could have blabbed to Craig that a pal of Chondelle's in the department had been the source of Captain Kingsley's travel plans. "I spotted him, yeah."

"How do you know Kingsley?" Craig said grimly. "How did you recognize him?"

"Suter recognized him. He knew him from a piece he once wrote for *Washingtonian* magazine."

Craig dragged deeply on his cigarette and said nothing more.

I asked him, "What about the lawsuit? Suter wouldn't tell me what that was about. He seemed embarrassed by whatever it was."

Craig still stood looking pensive, disturbed even, apparently over my report that I had spotted Milton Kingsley in Cancún. Finally Craig said, "I ran Suter's name. It came up once. He was charged with assault last year. The judge threw out the assault charge. But the court record says the victim told the judge that he planned on pursuing a civil action. I've got somebody checking to find out if that was done."

"Who brought the charge, and what was the nature of the assault?"

"The alleged victim was a Carmen LoBello. LoBello is a man who used to do a drag act, pretending to be Mrs. Liddy Dole. The so-called assault was this: Suter gave LoBello herpes, LoBello claims, and now LoBello's got a big cold sore on his upper lip half the time. LoBello can only do G. Gordon Liddy Dole, with a big mustache that covers up the cold sore. Except, nobody wants to go see a drag act with somebody called G. Gordon Liddy Dole. So LoBello is up shit creek. You queers sure pick up some interesting ways to get yourself in trouble," Craig said, and I had to agree with that.

# 23

Of *course* I'm going to sue that evil man!" LoBello spat out. "Because of Jim Suter my career is in ruins! Until I kissed Jim Suter, I was a star! God, I was fabulous. I did Hillary to a tee, my Jamie Gorelick was dead-on, and I had Dianne Feinstein nailed, and Barbara Bush and Maxine Waters, and—God, can you imagine what the demand would be for my smarmy-marmy Liddy Dole now that that nine-faced Southern bitch is all over the tube, doing her white-bread Oprah routine at the Republican convention! I'd be doing Liddy on *Jay,* on *Letterman,* on *Nightline.* Instead, I'm still pushing mine-acid reports around, and it's all because of that lying, manipulative, vicious, evil rodent Jim Suter. Oh, I'm suing him, all right. I'll sue his ass from Dupont Circle to the Supreme Court! When I catch up with Mr. Pretty-head-herpes-mouth Jim Suter, just you watch the subpoenas fly!"

The three of us were seated around a small outside table at the café with the excellent croissants on Second Street, SE. The early-morning Capitol Hill before-work crowd had been arriving for some time, and those seated closest to us must have been having trouble concentrating on their *Posts* and *Timeses* and lattes. LoBello was a strikingly attractive man, with the womanly—as opposed to effeminate—manner of the best drag queens. He had longish, swept-back, perfectly groomed dark hair in the style of an Italian maestro, and a fine-boned face that could have been out of *La Dolce Vita* except for the spectacularly large cold sore that took up about a quarter of his nicely shaped upper lip. The mustache LoBello had grown for his G. Gordon

Liddy Dole act, and to cover up the sore, was gone now, as was the fat cigar.

Timmy had set up the meeting with LoBello while I was in Mexico. We had known that LoBello was a disgruntled former boyfriend of Suter's who, we figured, might have quilt-panel sewing ability. This was before Suter theorized to me that the panel had in fact been a warning to him from the drug gang, but also before Ray Craig had come up with the news that LoBello had once charged Suter with assault—assault to the upper lip with an ugly virus.

I said to LoBello, "I guess you don't know where Jim Suter is. Otherwise you would have launched your suit against him."

"I haven't got a clue where Jim is. Wherever he is, I'm sure the place has turned into Chernobyl just from his presence. I could probably just keep my eyes peeled for emotional mushroom clouds rising. Meanwhile, I was thinking of hiring a private detective to locate the elusive Jimmy. And Timothy tells me you're a dick. Since you're looking for him anyway, perhaps you would do me the kindness when you locate Jim to give me or my attorney a jingle. You can bill me for whatever you want—up to twenty dollars, if you don't mind."

"Okay."

"I've done everything I could think of to smoke Suter out. But he's gone. His phone's disconnected, and I've waited outside his building dozens of times, sometimes for hours, just sitting on the curb nursing my rage. But he never goes in and he never goes out. It's hard to imagine that Jim Suter could stay away from Washington for long. This town is where he's a star—a big, big star. Jim's the Jane Fonda—I used to do her, too, by the way—he's the Jane Fonda of backroom, right-wing-political Washington, is what he is—as Jim will be the first to let you know."

"Suter may be a star," Timmy said, "but he seems not to be a well-loved star."

"No, Mary Tillotson, Jimmy is not." LoBello dabbed at the filmy latte mustache that didn't begin to camouflage his large cold sore. "There's a good chance, of course, that he's here in town and he's hiding out. There are probably dozens of Washington men looking for his ass so they can take legal action. Either on grounds of mental cruelty—which won't get them far in one of the local homophobic courts of law—or for passing his hideous herpes around, as in my unhappy case. My attorney has advised me that anybody whose livelihood is dependent on their physical appearance—and let's face it, whose isn't?—could make an airtight legal case against any person who ruined that physical appearance. Legally, it's disfigurement."

"You're still quite lovely, Carmen," I said sincerely.

"Thanks, but I'll never be Liddy Dole again. Do you think Liddy Dole would leave her apartment looking like this? Oh, no. 'No. Thanks,' the great lady of the Red Cross would say, 'but no thanks.' I mean, did Clara Barton have herpes? I don't believe so."

"Don't cold sores tend to come and go?" Timmy said. "I know people with herpes of that type, and they'll sometimes go for months without a sore breaking out."

LoBello gave Timmy a duh look and said, "Timothy, honey, do you know what makes cold sores break out?"

"I've heard fatigue can do it. And of course stress."

LoBello grimaced theatrically and said, "Say no more. Also, it's not just that Suter gave me herpes. It's that, like everything else, he *lied* about the sore on his lip when we went to bed. He said it was just some dumb zit. I told him, 'Honey, you better stay away from those candy bars.' Later, when I broke out with this grotesque thing on my lip, and I caught up with Jim and made him admit to the truth, he not only confessed. He admitted to me that he himself had picked up the virus from rimming some closeted right-wing queen on Jesse Helms's staff who had anal herpes. God, if I ever run into Helms, I'd love to plant a big, wet one on that ugly kisser of *his.*"

Timmy was staring at my mouth. I said, "I can appreciate, Carmen, why you might be upset about this."

"Upset? That hardly describes how I feel about James Suter."

"And I can see why you're determined to track Jim down."

“My latest tactic,” LoBello said, leaning closer to me and lowering his voice, “has been trying to smoke Jim out by using what I have to admit is a kind of tasteless stunt.” He glanced quickly around the café and, his face flushed, said, “I know you know about a panel in the AIDS quilt with Jim’s name on it, even though as far as I know he’s not dead. He doesn’t even have AIDS or HIV.”

“We’re aware of the quilt panel,” I said.

“I know you are. I saw you looking at it on Saturday.”

“Uh-huh.”

“Well—I did it. I made and submitted the quilt panel in memory of Mr. Suter.” LoBello grinned nervously and fluttered his eyelashes.

“You did this to smoke Jim out?”

“Yes, and it’s been all over the media. I thought, if I can’t find Jim, maybe the press can. Although they haven’t so far apparently. Anyway, I knew he’d hear about it, and it was a way of telling Jim exactly what I thought of him. I’m sure he knows who did it.”

I said, “Why is that, Carmen?”

“Because I took one of his old manuscripts out of his apartment the last time I was in it, and I kept it, and in May I sewed pages from the manuscript into the quilt panel. I took the manuscript in the first place because I thought there was some dirt in it that I could use against Jim, though it turned out there wasn’t. It was just his Betty Krumfutz campaign biography—a piece of cheap political hackery. But I stuck it on the quilt panel to humiliate Jim—and maybe to fuck him up professionally, the way he did me—and to lower him in the eyes of his good pal and onetime employer, that obnoxious right-wing Republican witch, Betty Krumfutz.”

With a feeling that was not yet sinking but was poised to descend, I began to wonder why Suter had told me thirty-six hours earlier that he guessed the quilt panel had been a menacing stunt perpetrated by the drug gang to keep him in line. If he knew LoBello had possession of his Krumfutz campaign-bio manuscript, and Sweet and Heckinger were keeping him up-to-date on Washington developments, he would surely have fingered LoBello, the angry ex-lover with sewing skills who wanted to sue him, as the quilt-panel creep. Yet Suter had apparently lied to me about the quilt panel and what he must have known about it.

I asked LoBello, "What made you think the Krumfutz manuscript might have had dirt in it that you could use against Jim? What kind of dirt?"

LoBello smirked, but uneasily. "This is quite intimate. It involves pillow talk between me and Jim. Can you take it?"

"Mm-hm."

"Right after Jim and I met," LoBello said, lowering his voice again, "when things were hot and heavy between us, we were in bed sharing a joint one night while I was running my fingers through that gorgeous head of hair of Jimmy's. Jim started to tell me how much our relationship meant to him because it took his mind off something big and important in his life that had been gnawing at him. He dumped me two weeks later—the big puddle of puke—but that night I had brought peace to his soul, Jim told me, and I helped him get centered at a time when he needed that more than ever. Jim said he knew things about certain well-known people that would rock Washington and rock the country. That's how he put it: 'rock Washington and rock the whole country.' "

LoBello sipped his latte, dabbed his lips with a napkin, and as Timmy and I watched and listened with mounting interest, he continued, "Naturally, I asked Jim, what's this thing that's so earthshaking? But he wouldn't tell me. Which was unusual. Jim loved dropping names and dishing people on the Hill—who's fucking whom, metaphorically and actually and whatnot. This big thing was a Hill thing, he said, that might have changed the outcome of the '94 congressional elections if it had gotten out.

"I could tell that Jim was actually quite scared of this big, scandalous whatever it was, and he never brought it up again. But when I suddenly realized one night a couple of weeks later that it was my turn to get dumped on my ass by Jim Suter, I remembered this conversation, and as I was on my way out, I grabbed the first thing on Jim's desk that looked like some kind of Hill papers, and I stuffed it in my bag. I went over the damn thing with a fine-tooth comb, and all it was, was the stupid campaign-bio manuscript. What a waste of time, and what a bore. But I kept the thing, even after Jim called all irritated and indignant and demanded that I mail it back to him, and then in May I sewed a chunk of the stupid thing on the quilt panel. So I got to use it to stick Jim and give the knife a twist after all."

I said, "When did this conversation about the scandalous situation take place?"

"In January of this year. Around the tenth or twelfth, it would have been. On the twenty-seventh I became another of Jim's ex-lover nonpersons. I guess you've heard about that category. There are hundreds of us. Thousands maybe."

"Did Jim give you any idea of when the shocking event, or events, actually took place?" I asked.

"Not really. Only that it was on his mind at the time, and he said he'd be lucky if he didn't come out of this one with an ulcer."

"You said, Carmen, that you were sharing a joint when this thing came up. Is it possible that drugs were involved in the scandalous circumstances? And that your smoking marijuana somehow triggered Jim's discussion of this large matter that was eating at him?"

LoBello gave me a don't-be-ridiculous look. "Honey, we shared a joint just about every night. Both before and after we made love. And making love with Jim Suter is about as good as making sweet love gets. You can take my word for that and put it in the bank. It's just too bad Jim was also a liar, an emotional sadist, and a morally empty shell. Except for those, he was the best. But he *was* all of the above, and worse. And for doing what he did to me, Miss LoBello regrets to say, Mr. Suter is going to have to pay. He's going to have to pay very dearly."

I said, "Carmen, among the Washington power-women you

impersonated in your drag act—and impersonated quite brilliantly, by all accounts—was one of them Betty Krumfutz?"

LoBello affected a poker face and said, "Oh, yes. I did Betty." He was both trying hard not to grin and obviously enjoying letting us know that he was trying hard not to grin.

"And did you reprise your Betty Krumfutz routine Saturday afternoon at the AIDS quilt display? Maybe to draw extra attention to the Suter quilt panel you sewed and submitted to the Names Project in order to embarrass Jim among his Capitol Hill friends, acquaintances, and colleagues?"

LoBello beamed. "Am I good, or am I good?"

Timmy and I looked at each other. I thought, yes, LoBello is an accomplished actor—as is Jim Suter.

# 24

I needed to speak with Betty Krumfutz fast. I called her office at the Glenn Beale Foundation and was told that she had left Washington Thursday night for Log Heaven and would not be back in her office until Monday morning. I could have phoned her in Pennsylvania, but a face-to-face meeting was what I wanted. I needed to question her in depth, if I could, on whatever it was that she had on her husband, Nelson, that would put him away "for the rest of his life," as she had worded it to me during my visit to Log Heaven, but which she had held back at his trial.

Did Mrs. Krumfutz hold incriminating evidence of the car-dealer-drug-smuggling scheme? If she knew about an illegal narcotics operation and didn't report it, that was obstruction of justice, at least. Although any knowledge Nelson Krumfutz had of his wife's variations on Mexican Indian rituals might have kept her from hitting him with a full legal whammy. But why, then, would it not have kept her from hitting him with any whammy at all?

Jim Suter had insisted to me that Mrs. Krumfutz knew nothing of the drug scheme. But now I knew that Suter had lied to me about the origins of the quilt panel—attributing it to the drug gang, even though he knew Carmen LoBello had made off with the Krumfutz campaign-bio manuscript—just as Suter had lied to me about the "zit" on his upper lip, a matter that Timmy had agreed to postpone discussing until the arguably larger questions surrounding an attempted murder and a major drug-smuggling operation had been cleared up.

There was also the puzzling matter of the scandalous goings-on that Jim Suter had alluded to when he'd gotten high with Carmen LoBello. Revelations of a drug gang involving the husband of a Pennsylvania congresswoman would have made headlines certainly, although such news would not, as far as Timmy or I could judge, "rock the nation" or alter the outcome of the 1994 congressional elections. So, I figured, maybe the scandal was something else entirely, or even that it was just some weird type of inside-the-Beltway braggadocio on Suter's part.

Timmy was even more intrigued by the historic-scandal possibilities than I was, for they fit his theory of a large, many-tentacled conspiracy. I had been unable to persuade him that the D.C. police had us under clumsy surveillance simply because they were poorly led and lacked imagination, and that neither hospital personnel nor bagel-shop cashiers were threats to us. I agreed with him that drug gangs were ruthless forces to be reckoned with, but that in Washington, unlike in Tijuana and Mexico City, the gangs' reach did not extend into every facet of official and private life. Timmy told me I was naive and I told him he was paranoid, and for the time being we decided to let it go at that.

I arrived in Log Heaven just after two on Friday afternoon and drove directly to the Krumfutz house on Susquehanna Drive. I saw the Chrysler in the driveway but no sign of the pickup truck with Texas plates. Five days earlier bagged leaves had been piled at the side of the Krumfutz lawn. Now the bags were gone, and the yard needed raking again. I guessed Mrs. Krumfutz had her yard crew in on weekends—both for tidying up outdoors and for heartrending rituals indoors—and since it was Friday afternoon, I wondered if her crew might be showing up soon.

I parked in front of the house, walked up to the front entrance, and pressed the button next to a door with three small stepped windows in it. A face soon appeared at the lowest window, and then the door swung open.

"Oh, for heaven sakes, what are you doing back here? I

thought I was rid of you last—when was it? Sunday? And now here you are deviling me again. Well, you can just tell Nelson that if he sends you down here one more time, he has had it! He's got nothing criminal on me, and I've got the pictures in my scrapbook of him committing a felony, and I'll use them if I have to, believe you me!"

Mrs. Krumfutz stood glaring out at me in her pale pink sweat suit, and while she did not appear Mayan-queen-like at all, she did look as if she might rip my heart out if I said the wrong word.

I said, "Mrs. Krumfutz, I left a wrong impression on Sunday. I don't work for your husband."

"How's that? Come again?"

"I am a private investigator, but I'm actually looking into the danger Jim Suter is in, which I mentioned to you, and into the shooting of a friend of mine in Washington. I'm no threat to you. I have no interest in your personal life. I just need more information about a couple of things. May I come in?"

Looking wary, she said, "Information about what?"

"About what you have on your husband that could send him to prison for life, as you put it to me on Sunday. Whatever you've got seems to be in addition to the campaign finance scam he's already been convicted of. Am I right?"

"You bet. Right as rain."

"Is it that you have evidence of the drug-smuggling operation your husband was running with Hugh Myers?"

She screwed up her face and said, "The *what* operation?"

"Are you going to tell me that you know nothing of an elaborate scheme that your husband and Hugh Myers concocted for smuggling narcotics into Central Pennsylvania from Mexico in the seat backs of the GM cars Myers imports?"

"Are you off your rocker!" Her eyes were bright with anger and her voice rose with indignation. "Why, Hugh Myers was a deacon in the Presbyterian Church! My word, don't be spreading a ridiculous story like that around Log Heaven, especially right now. Poor Hugh passed away this morning. He was hit by a car in front of his house on River Street, and the fool driver never even stopped. It was dreadful, just dreadful."

"I'm sorry to hear that. Were Mr. Myers and your family close?"

"No, not close. We're Methodist, and Nelson always bought Chrysler products. But I've known Hugh and Edna for years, and my heart goes out to that girl. It's a tragedy, just a tragedy. Now, where in the world did you get the idea that Nelson and Hugh were drug traffickers? Hugh would never even have thought to do such a thing, and Nelson couldn't even organize some campaign-fund pilfering and get away with it."

"So if it's not drug dealing that you've got on your husband, what is it?"

She signaled for me to enter the house. I followed her in and she shut the door behind us. The place was hung with Yucatecan landscapes, and the shelves were loaded with Mexican pottery and photographs of Mayan ruins. Chichén Itzá, Cobá, and Uxmal were the ones I recognized. The furniture was old, overstuffed pieces draped with colorful serapes. The picture-window drapes were open, and the view was across the Susquehanna to the autumn hills beyond.

"Make yourself at home," Mrs. Krumfutz said, indicating the couch, and she disappeared down a corridor. I leafed through a magazine called *South of the Border Living,* which was aimed at U.S. retirees who lived or planned on living in Mexico. There were pieces on property ownership, tax dodges, and on keeping the help in line. Nothing on the reenactments of Indian rituals that employed beef hearts from the A & P. Or could Suter have been lying about that, too?

Mrs. Krumfutz returned with a K Mart–style photo album done in pale green artificial leather with golden curlicues in the corners. She sat down beside me and said, "Are you squeamish?"

"Not especially." I hoped she wasn't about to show me her collection of aborted fetuses.

Not yet opening the album, Mrs. Krumfutz said, "I'm going out to the kitchen to make a cup of tea. Look through this, and then just holler when you're through. Or when you've had more than enough. If you need to toss your cookies, the bathroom is down the hall. You wanted to know what I've got on Nelson? Well, this is it." She looked over at me, her face sad and tired.

"Thank you."

"Don't look till I'm in the kitchen."

"All right."

"I'm showing this to you," she said, getting up, "even though I hardly know you from Adam, for the same reason I've started showing it to other people. If anything should happen to me, I want the truth to be known about Nelson. Nelson has treated me no better than a dog, and I want the word out on what a big turd my ex-husband is."

"Why didn't you use what's in this album in Nelson's fraud trial, Mrs. Krumfutz?"

Looking weary and resigned, she said, "Because Nelson has a photo album, too, and I'd be pretty darned embarrassed if it got passed around the district."

"Oh."

"So, in that way, we're stalemated."

"I see. A sort of Mexican standoff." I hadn't meant that as a mean joke, but I realized it was one as soon as it came out. Mrs. Krumfutz forced a thin smile, then turned and left the room.

I opened the album and leafed through it. It contained page after page of color photographs showing a nude, middle-aged man, presumably Nelson Krumfutz, performing a wide variety of sex acts with a nude young woman many years his junior. Nelson was a wiry little man, and the young woman—Tammy Pam Jameson?—was slight also and, in many of the photos—which seemed to have been taken on a number of occasions over a period of years—just barely pubescent.

Nelson had begun to develop a paunch in the later pictures, and the young woman's hair color changed from mousy brown to auburn to blond. If it ever occurred to Nelson that the girl's age might have posed a legal problem for him, surely he erred when the two were photographed with the girl seated on a kitchen counter, grinning toothily, her legs spread, Nelson's head between them, and clearly visible next to the girl, just above a butter-yellow rotary wall phone, was a Hall's Beer Distributor's calendar whose current page located the event in April of 1985. My guess was, Tammy Pam was thirteen or fourteen at the time.

I closed the album and walked into the kitchen, where Mrs. Krumfutz was seated in the breakfast nook perusing the front page of the *Log Heaven Gazette*. "Who took the pictures, Mrs. Krumfutz, and how did you get hold of them?"

She looked up and said, "Tammy Pam's best friend, Kelly Bobst, took the pictures. For several years Kelly dated Floppy O'Toole, who runs O'Toole's camera shop in Engineville. Floppy developed the pictures and then kept the negatives. And when he fell out with Kelly in '93, he sent me these prints and asked me if I'd like to buy the negatives. I said no thanks. Floppy thought I'd like to use the pictures to put the screws to Nelson. But, as I say, I couldn't. What I think is, Floppy then offered the negatives to Nelson, and Nelson bought them and paid a high price, using cash he diverted from the campaign fund. About fifty thousand dollars is still unaccounted for, and my guess is, that's where it went, to Floppy. Though I can't prove it."

The teakettle on Mrs. Krumfutz's electric range began to whistle, and she got up and removed it from the burner. "Care for a cup of tea?"

"Thank you. Have you got coffee?"

"I've got Nescafé."

"I thought you might. I'll have a cup of that, please."

"Why, sure."

As she mixed the coffee crystals and hot water, I said, "I can see why you decided not to remain in Congress. Campaign fraud is one thing—that's as American as cherry pie. But these photo albums—that's something else."

"Yes, if the pictures had started coming out . . . I've got two grown daughters, Terri in Aliquippa and Hilaine in Frackville, and I wouldn't want them to be hurt, or their husbands or their kids. So I threw in the towel, despite my ongoing commitment to the rights of gun owners and the unborn."

Mrs. Krumfutz served my coffee in the breakfast nook and slid in across from me with her cup of tea. I said, "None of this may have anything to do with Jim Suter's current troubles. But it might. Either way, I'd appreciate your telling me what you know about Jim, Mrs. Krumfutz."

Apparently relieved by the change of subject, Mrs. Krumfutz spoke for several minutes about her onetime campaign employee and sometime professional acquaintance and casual friend. She described Suter as a committed conservative and an able writer and political operative. She recited a long list of Suter's successes for a number of conservative causes, most of them election campaigns. Suter had also been involved, she said, in several lobbying operations on the Hill, including the campaign to prevent legalization of gays in the military. "Jim's a pansy," Mrs. Krumfutz said, "but first and foremost he's an American."

I let that go, and she went on to mention Suter's work on behalf of a right-to-life constitutional amendment and his pro-NAFTA organizing efforts with Alan McChesney for her and for her colleague Burton Olds.

I asked Mrs. Krumfutz straight out if she had ever doubted Suter's truthfulness. After a long, thoughtful moment she said, "Not on matters that were all that earthshaking, if that's what you mean. Why do you ask?"

Before I could reply, the telephone twittered, and Mrs. Krumfutz excused herself and went to answer it. As she stood by the kitchen counter, I heard her cry out, "Oh! Oh, my Lord! When?"

Mrs. Krumfutz fell back against the counter and shook her head in anguish. I quickly went to her side, for her face had gone gray and the hand holding the telephone receiver trembled.

Again, she cried, "Oh, no! No! Oh, no!" After a moment, she said, "I've got to hang up and call the girls. I'll call you back."

Shakily, she placed the receiver back in its cradle. She moaned, "Oh, my heavens! Oh, I can't tell the girls!"

"What happened?"

"Nelson is dead!" she cried out, and then she began to weep.

Between sobs, Mrs. Krumfutz told me that the caller had been Engineville police chief Boat Pignatelli. The chief told Mrs. Krumfutz that a few hours earlier an explosion had struck the house occupied by Nelson Krumfutz and Tammy Pam Jameson. Both had died in the fire that quickly engulfed the structure. The cause of the explosion had not yet been determined.

I comforted Mrs. Krumfutz as well as I could as she collected her wits and attempted to make a list on the kitchen blackboard of people whom she would need to notify. I suggested she phone a Log Heaven close friend or relative who could be with her. So before she called her and Nelson's daughters, Mrs. Krumfutz phoned her friend Marion Smith. Mrs. Smith said she would come as soon as she checked up on her dogs. She had only just gotten home, she said, after taking a casserole over to Edna Myers, whose husband had been killed earlier in the day in a hit-and-run accident.

Edna Myers's husband, Hugh, was the Log Heaven car dealer who, according to Jim Suter, had been involved in a drug-smuggling operation with Nelson Krumfutz—although Mrs. Krumfutz had found that accusation preposterous. It now occurred to me that both men had died violently on the same day in separate incidents. And they were the two men who could have confirmed—or denied—Suter's wild tale of drug smuggling in GM-product seat backs. Now, suddenly, both were dead. Had Mrs. Krumfutz not been so distraught, she might have noticed that now my hand was a little unsteady, too, and my need to place a phone call almost as urgent as hers.

# 25

I'm heading back to Washington as soon as I can get out of here," I told Timmy, "and then probably back to the Yucatán. Jim Suter's story about drug smuggling into Central Pennsylvania might be true or might not be true, I just don't know. But if it is true—or something like it, maybe even worse is true—then somehow the Mexican gang found out that Suter blabbed to me about it—maybe Jorge's house is wired—and now they are killing all the witnesses."

Timmy said, "Oh. Oh, no. Oh."

I described to him the mysterious hit-and-run incident that ended the life of the Log Heaven GM dealer that morning and the explosion that killed Nelson Krumfutz and Tammy Pam Jameson a few hours later. "I hate to say it," I added, "but now Jim Suter is probably dead, too, or soon will be."

This was followed by a tense silence at the other end of the line. While Mrs. Krumfutz was off changing her clothes, I had reached Timmy in Maynard's room at GW. I could hear Maynard's voice in the background as he talked about a problematical IV with, I guessed, a nurse. Finally, Timmy said, "If some Mexican drug cartel is eliminating all the people who know about its Pennsylvania operations, where does that leave you? And, for that matter, me?"

"We know Suter's story, but we can't prove anything. If the story is true, the gang might think it has to remove anybody who might be in a position to describe the operation to us or to any authority we reported it to. But I doubt if they'd see any reason to actually eliminate us."

"You doubt it? Oh, good. Then, tell me this, Don. Why did the cartel try to kill Maynard? And why did they wreck his house searching for something? Maynard certainly knew a lot less about all this . . . this whatever it is than we do."

"What you say is true."

"Anyway, Maynard doesn't think it's drugs. He wants to talk to you as soon as you get back here—which, by the way, the sooner the better. I clued Maynard in on Carmen LoBello's story on some would-be-cataclysmic scandal Suter talked to LoBello about when they were high, and Maynard thinks he knows what it has to do with."

"He does? What? He can tell me now."

"Hang on."

Timmy put Maynard on the line. "It's the date." Maynard's voice was weak, but steady and clear. "When Timmy told me that this conversation took place in January of this year, I tried to think of what was going on then that might have involved scandalous secret machinations. I couldn't think of anything that was happening at the White House—a potential Jim Sutergate—or on the Hill that month that might have a potential Mexico connection. Which was a connection I assumed, based on subsequent, especially recent, developments. So I phoned Dana Mosel at the *Post,* and she called up all the paper's front pages and told me what made headlines last January that was Mexico-related. What Dana told me this morning sure was interesting. It had nothing to do with drugs though."

"What was it?"

"Bryant Ulmer's murder."

"Congressman Olds's chief of staff?"

"Yeah."

"What did Ulmer have to do with Mexico?"

"Olds was the nominal head of the GOP pro-NAFTA vote-gathering operation in the House, but it was Ulmer who actually ran it. Working directly with Clinton's people, he and Alan McChesney, who was then Betty Krumfutz's chief of staff, pretty much put together the bipartisan pro-NAFTA coalition in the

House. And a nice job they did, too, for the free-trade-at-any-cost crowd. NAFTA passed the House 234 to 200. I agree with labor that it was a bad treaty. It cost jobs on this side of the border and is at this very moment no doubt poisoning thousands of underpaid workers on the Mexican side. But Clinton was a slick salesman, and NAFTA's most vocal enemies were an off-putting bunch, from Perot to Pat Buchanan. So Ulmer and McChesney were able to pull it off. The whole thing really made Bryant Ulmer's reputation on the Hill, and from that time on he was known as Mr. NAFTA. It's also the reason why his murder made the front page of the papers, not just the metro section."

"Maynard," I said, "are you suggesting there's a connection between the approval of NAFTA and Ulmer's murder more than two years later? Ulmer died in a street robbery—officially, at any rate. What could the connection be?"

"Timmy says your cop friend Chondelle Dolan told you there's always been doubt about Ulmer's homicide having been a simple mugging, on account of the type of weapon used."

"Timmy is right about that."

"But what the connection to NAFTA might be, I don't know. I was just thinking of Carmen LoBello's story about a scandal that would have rocked the country and maybe reversed the Republican congressional landslide in '94 if it had come out. Suter got high and mentioned this awful thing that had been preying on his mind last January. That's when Ulmer was murdered. Then Suter dumped LoBello a few weeks later. Jim always dumped *everybody* a few weeks later. But still, the timing of all that struck me as interesting."

"It is."

"It's too bad you couldn't have asked Jim about it when you were down there."

"I may be heading back to the Yucatán. So I can still ask him. First, Maynard, I may phone Jim, if I can track down his number, which he wouldn't give me. He said if I ever called, Jorge might answer. But now I'm wondering if Jim might not be in immediate danger." I described to Maynard the violent deaths earlier in the day of Hugh Myers, the Log Heaven GM dealer, and Nelson Krumfutz and Tammy Pam Jameson.

"But," Maynard said, "those incidents would seem to buttress Jim's story of a drug-smuggling operation, not a NAFTA connection. Unless, of course, the NAFTA campaign and the drug cartel are somehow interrelated."

"Yeah. Unless that."

I told Maynard I guessed I'd have to speak again with Red Heckinger and Malcolm Sweet, who seemed to be Suter's eyes and ears in Washington, and his main local contacts. "Who are those two goons anyway? I had half a lunch with them the other day, and they're about as subtle as Willard Scott. They seemed to want me to think they were mob-connected, but it was all the worst sort of amateur theater and not convincing."

"They're lobbyists for the Pennsylvania Association of Broadcasters. One of them is originally from Log Heaven—Heckinger, I think. Jim has done some lobbying and PR work for the PAB over the years. In fact, that's how I think he made his first connection with Betty Krumfutz, who always looked out for the PAB's interests. They're a couple, and they've been known to give dinner parties at their place in Georgetown, where, following coffee and after-dinner drinks, the guests have been asked to move into the den and spank each other."

"Somehow I'm not surprised to hear this."

"In fact, Bryant Ulmer was part of that circle, and Alan McChesney, too, and McChesney's boyfriend, Ian Williamson."

"I met McChesney in Burton Olds's office on Tuesday," I said, "and Williamson was there, too. McChesney spoke poorly of Suter—as so many men do—and told the usual story of ecstasy with Jim and then a sudden nothingness. McChesney also said he wouldn't be surprised if Jim was mixed up in a drug operation with Jorge—yet another vote for that scenario."

"I wonder what made Alan think that. Jim was never involved with out-and-out crooks before, that I ever heard. Did

Alan mention that he saw me on Saturday, not long before I got shot?"

"No, your name never came up in our conversation. Following Suter's instructions, I was still being cagey on Tuesday as to what I was investigating and for whom."

"That's funny. I saw Alan at the quilt display near Jim's panel, and he might reasonably have connected any investigation of Jim with me, since Alan knew we were friends, and he would surely have read or heard about my getting shot down on E Street later on Saturday. McChesney must have seen you and Timmy at the quilt, too. I was going to say hi and introduce you, in fact, but Alan was talking to some other people, and then we came to the quilt panel with Jim's name on it, and soon after that he was gone."

At that moment, an idea that had been vague in the back of my mind moved forward and began to take on an actual shape. But I did not yet recognize the exact shape of the idea, and I said only to Maynard, "It is odd that McChesney didn't make the likely connection and maybe even ask me if you were my client. But he didn't."

"McChesney is not famous for being dense."

"What's he famous for? Besides after-dinner spankings?"

"For thoroughness and decisiveness. And, I guess I should add, ruthlessness."

"Oh, ruthlessness, too."

Mrs. Krumfutz had not yet emerged from her bedroom, where she had gone to change clothes, but a knock came at the front door now, probably, I figured, Mrs. Krumfutz's good friend Marion Smith. Before answering the door, I spoke briefly with Timmy again, assuring him that I would soon head back toward Washington. I advised him to remain in Maynard's room with its police guard outside, and without hesitation he said he would.

A small female face was now peering in through the bottom stepped window in the Krumfutz front door. As I moved to open the door for Mrs. Smith, I decided that when I found a pay phone on my way out of Log Heaven, I would not call Heckinger or Sweet or Alan McChesney or even Jim Suter. I would phone the airline and make some necessarily convoluted arrangements for a fast trip back to the Yucatán.

# 26

Just before noon on Saturday, October 19, a week almost to the hour from the time Maynard had stared in amazement at Jim Suter's panel in the AIDS memorial quilt, I pulled off Highway 307 onto the beach road at Los Pájaros.

I had spent the previous evening, on my return from Log Heaven, checking in on Timmy and Maynard at GW, then shaking any tail Ray Craig might have still had on me by slipping on and off a variety of subway trains at D.C. Metro Center and other nearby stations. I ended up at the Farragut West station, near the White House, where I caught a cab to National Airport.

I had booked the first leg of my journey under the name of Cray Mameluke, paid cash for the ticket, and arrived uninterferred-with in Miami soon after midnight. There I reserved a seat on a 7 A.M. flight to Cancún under the name Donald Strachey, the name the airline would see on my passport. If my movements were being monitored, I guessed, this would be done at the Washington end, rather than in Cancún, and surely not in Miami, a mere transit point that was one of several to the Yucatán.

From my hotel near Miami International, I phoned Maynard's hospital room and woke him up so that I could be reassured that he was safe. He was, as was Timmy, asleep on a couch in the nearby visitors' lounge. I also phoned Chondelle Dolan at home, woke her from a sound sleep, too, and described what I had learned over the past four days from Carmen LoBello, Betty Krumfutz, Maynard Sudbury, and—for what it was worth—Jim Suter. I said I might need her advice and help when I got back to Washington, and she said fine.

Dolan told me, "It looks like maybe your boyfriend the conspiracy nut wasn't such a nut after all."

"Could be, but I'm still having a lot of trouble believing that a Catholic schoolboy's lurid fantasies about what makes the world go round might actually exist in modern-day reality. The evidence, however, does seem to keep pointing that way."

Dolan said, "The world we live in isn't the same world it was just ten years ago. Nowadays they don't call these things conspiracies, though. Now it's called synergy."

Dolan soon hung up to resume the night's sleep I'd interrupted, and I, too, caught a few hours of restless semiconsciousness, before heading to the airport and the flight to Cancún, my second in three days.

When I rounded the first bend in the Los Pájaros beach road, I saw not one but three vehicles in the driveway of Jorge Ramos's house. The big mud-spattered Suburban was there, along with a couple of Jeep Cherokees. I drove on, glancing at the house in hope of catching a glimpse of Suter. All the louvered windows were open, but I saw no one inside moving about.

Walking up and boldly knocking on the front door would have been macho in a way that might have been appreciated locally, but it might also have been suicidal. So if Suter was inside the house and still alive, I knew I'd have to get to him in some other way. I turned around at the next driveway, maneuvered my rental car through the mud and potholes back out to the main highway, then drove back up 307 to a hotel near Yalku.

I rented snorkeling equipment, reluctantly leaving my passport as collateral, and returned to the beach road, parking at a closed-up and apparently unoccupied house a third of a mile up the beach from the Ramos house. I changed into my bathing suit, and ten minutes later I was floating twenty yards off the Ramos beach, interested in the gray ray that flopped across the sandy seafloor six or seven feet beneath me, but even more interested in the scene on the Ramos terrace. Two large, muscular, dark-haired men in chinos and polo shirts were seated in the shade of the house, one on a chaise and one in a deck chair, and a third man in a skimpy bathing suit—I recognized him from the now all-too-familiar head of hair—sat stretched out on a chair in the sun.

For fifteen minutes I swam slowly back and forth, like a U-boat off Scotland, hoping the two guards, if that's what they were—was one of them Jorge?—would go inside the house. Finally one of them did get up, but the other one stayed put. The one who went inside, however, returned shortly with a couple of bottles, it looked like, and another object. The second man then joined him at a round table where they both seated themselves and began to do something with the unidentifiable object. A deck of cards? No, the motions were not card-playing motions.

When the two seemed to become more deeply engrossed in their activity, I moved in closer to shore. Suter now seemed to be looking my way, so I lifted my mask, pointed theatrically at my upper lip, then vigorously and repeatedly shot Suter the finger. When I saw him stiffen and continue to stare at me, I pulled my mask back down and resumed an easy breaststroke in a northerly direction.

A moment later, when I glanced his way, Suter stood up, slipped out of his bathing trunks, and headed toward me in a leisurely way. With the sun above him, he was magnificent to behold. But now his beauty kindled not appreciation or desire in me, just sudden anger. What a careless, destructive man he was. And when he reached me and chimed, "Strachey, I thought you'd *never* show up!" it was all I could do to keep from swatting him with my snorkeling mask.

I snarled, "You are getting people killed! Do you know that?"

Startled, Suter said, "Who? Now who's been killed?"

"Why, Nelson Krumfutz and Tammy Pam Jameson and Hugh Myers! Suter, you dumb fuck! What did you tell Jorge that you told me?"

Suter lost his coordination for an instant and nearly slipped under the water. He recovered, gestured urgently toward the north, and as we both began to swim that way, he said breathlessly, "They knew you were here on Wednesday. They asked me what I told you. I told them I made up a story to throw you off." He watched for my reaction as he swam.

"You made up the drug-smuggling story? All of it?"

"The part about Nelson Krumfutz and Hugh Myers, sure. I thought you'd be smart enough to be scared off by the whole drug-gang angle. These are not people you want to want to play with, even a little, and I wanted to impress that on you, Strachey. That's all I meant to do. And the Ramoses do have drug-gang connections. Not in Pennsylvania though. Just in Washington and Alexandria."

I looked back toward the Ramos house. The two men were still seated, absorbed in whatever they were doing. "Well, Jim, you miscalculated. You miscalculated badly."

"They actually *killed* Nelson and Tammy Pam?" Suter said, spitting seawater.

"Well, of course they did! Somebody in Washington was telling them that I was not only competent but dogged, so they couldn't risk Nelson's coming up with a convincing denial. They had to kill Nelson and Hugh Myers, not because they were witnesses to drug smuggling, but because they were witnesses to your lie. And the Ramoses decided that once I uncovered your lie, I would go after the real and even worse crime that the bunch of you were involved in. For Christ's sake, Suter, don't you understand how vicious and remorseless the Ramoses are? You tell me how savage they are, but you don't act like you really understand it. Jesus!"

Suter stopped swimming and looked at me. We were close enough to shore now for our feet to touch bottom. We stood there in the crystalline blue water, the Caribbean sun blazing down on us, and he said, "You know what really happened, don't you?"

"A lot of it, yes. You can fill me in on the rest."

"How did you figure it out?"

"A number of people provided information that I pieced together. That's usually the way an investigation goes—a lot of digging, a certain amount of luck. In my asking around about you, Jim, Carmen LoBello was especially helpful."

Suter actually had the decency to blush. "Carmen's pissed off at me, I suppose."

"You don't suppose it. You know it. And let me tell you something else, Suter. I think I noticed a small sore on my upper lip yesterday. If you gave me herpes, the Ramoses are going to feel like Rosie O'Donnell in your life next to me."

"I seriously doubt that," he said mildly. "Anyway, I wasn't oozing viral fluids on Wednesday, so you're probably safe. Look, Strachey, I've made a decision. It looks like I really have no choice. I'm ready to take you up on your offer. Get me together with some uncorrupted authority, if you can find one—I'll take a chance, I guess, on Janet Reno's Justice Department—and I'll tell what I know in return for a chance just to disappear and start over."

"Oh, you've made that decision, have you? When did you make it?"

"Just now." Suter looked back at the two men bent over the table on the Ramos terrace. "I'd have made the decision an hour ago if I had known you were going to show up and rescue my ass. But I had no way of knowing you were going to find me irresistible a second time. I guess I'm just a lucky so-and-so. Now, how do we get out of here?"

I looked up at the men on the terrace and said, "I don't know. How do we?"

"Is your car nearby?"

"Just up the beach."

"Jaime and Ramon are absorbed in their dominoes. It will be fifteen minutes before they notice that I'm not here. Let's go."

"You're naked."

He shrugged. "Have you got an extra pair of shorts and a T-shirt?"

"Sure. But I don't know about shoes that will fit. And whatever else we'll need to get you on a plane at Cancún. Your passport, for instance."

Suter began to swim again, faster this time, and I swam with him. "We've got one stop to make, where I can pick up clothes and documents. Anyway, we're not going to Cancún. As soon as they realize I'm gone, Jaime and Ramon will notify the Ramoses, and they'll be watching for me at the airports in Cancún and Mérida and probably Chetumal. There's another way out of here that I've been working on since we spoke on Wednesday. It'll take more time than flying to Miami, but it's uncomplicated and I know the people involved—they're actually competitors of the Ramoses—and I know this will work."

I said, "Don't tell me. We're going to be driven for four and a half days in the back of a truck to the outskirts of San Diego, where we'll crawl under a chain-link fence by the light of the moon and hope we're not ripped apart by Border Patrol rottweilers."

Suter looked at me as he swam, his wet locks gleaming in the hot light. "No, what I have in mind is easier than that—and a lot more romantic. We'll be traveling by sea. We can cuddle naked under the stars, Strachey, and make love again."

What a piece of work he was. "Jesus, Suter, do you really call what we did the other night making love?" He seemed to hear what I said, but Suter did not meet my eye and did not reply. "Anyway, I told my boyfriend I wouldn't screw around with you again. So that's that. Forget it. What we can do tonight is have a long, informative talk. With you doing most of the talking and all of the informing."

"I can see that you're going to insist on being in charge. Doesn't your boyfriend get tired of that? It really seems to me, Strachey, that you've got some control issues to work out."

I ignored this drollery—if that's what it was; you never knew with Suter—and soon we came to the deserted house where I had parked my rental car. We walked out of the water and across the beach. A small group of nude sunbathers lay on towels twenty or thirty yards away, some with their heads beneath makeshift palm-frond shelters, but none seemed to show any interest in us.

Suter and I shared the one towel I had with me, then quickly dressed, with Suter slipping into the extra briefs, khakis, and T-shirt I'd brought along. The pants were a little loose around his slim hips, so I gave him my belt to hold his drawers up. Suter crouched in the backseat as we passed the Ramos house. I stopped at the main highway while he hopped into the front seat, and I followed his directions north up Highway 307 toward the resort and retirement town of Playa del Carmen. I made a quick stop to return the snorkeling gear and retrieve my passport, and then—like all the other maniacal drivers on the two-lane highway—we moved fast.

Half an hour later, on the outskirts of Playa del Carmen, Suter returned to the backseat and crouched down again—he said the Ramoses had people working for them everywhere on the Yucatán coast—and directed me down a muddy road with ruts like canyons and into a compound where the road dead-ended.

Suter conversed briefly in Spanish with a middle-aged man in work clothes—something about a boat and a trip and the weather. Suter told me he'd be right back, he had some phone calls to make—it did not reassure me that apparently I was not to overhear these conversations—and then he disappeared into a bright blue, one-story cement house with bars on all the windows.

I climbed out of the sweltering car and stood looking around. There wasn't much to see, just the house and a high cement wall around it with shards of glass embedded on top. The workman stood impassively next to the side door of the house, smoking a cigarette, and, it appeared, waiting for Suter.

I said, *"Buenas tardes."*

*"Buenas tardes,"* the man replied.

I gazed some more at the wall.

Suter returned a few minutes later wearing his own khakis,

T-shirt, and leather sandals and carrying a large black canvas suitcase. He handed me my clothes and said, "Get your stuff out of the car. Manuel will return the Chevy to the rental agency. We're being picked up."

"I believe I have to turn the car in. And under the terms of the rental agreement, I'm the only person authorized to drive it."

Suter smiled. "Just give Manuel the keys. It'll be fine." Suter pulled a roll of U.S. bills out of his pants pocket, peeled off four fifties, and handed them to Manuel.

"The keys are in the ignition," I said. "I guess I'm not the boss after all."

"Sure you are," Suter said, showing me his famous teeth—and cold sore.

Seconds later, a decrepit VW Bug, with one dented gray fender and one dented green one, pulled into the compound. The driver was a slender, tanned bleached blond in scruffy cutoffs. He had a tattoo of three intertwined nasturtiums on his left shoulder. He looked Californian, but Suter greeted the man in Spanish, which, when the blond replied, sounded like his native language.

I rode in the front seat with the driver and Suter slouched in the back, our bags upended on either side of him. After ten minutes of bumping and sliding up and down a series of unpaved back roads north of town, we came to a simple wooden house on the seaside that appeared deserted. We quickly carried our bags around the house, where a small boat was beached. The blond unlocked the beachside door to the small house and soon carried out an outboard motor. After he had resecured the house, we shoved the boat into the water and the blond attached the motor to it. We climbed aboard with our bags. The blond got the motor going and soon we were headed north.

"What's this from?" I asked Suter. *"The Old Man and the Sea? Kon-Tiki?"*

He grinned and said, "It's a Carnival cruise, Strachey. Romance on the high seas. I'll be your Kathie Lee, if you'll let me."

The blond cracked a little smile. I said nothing until we

rounded a palm-lined point, and there looming ahead of us, bobbing on the light swell, was a forty- or fifty-foot cabin cruiser.

"Oh, I see," I said. "That looks comfortable enough."

"It is," Suter said.

"Where are we headed? Key West? Miami?"

"No, we'll soon be on our way to La Coloma."

"Where's that? Florida?"

"Cuba."

All I could think to reply was "None of this would surprise Timothy Callahan."

Suter said, "It's simple. Nobody will be watching for us in Havana. From there we fly to Mexico City—there are several flights a day—and then on to Washington. A piece of cake."

"If you say so, Jim." I wondered again what Timmy would make of this twist out of MacInnes or Ludlum, and what I should make of it.

# 27

"Now tell me the truth. The *whole* truth, if you're capable of it," I said to Suter.

We were stretched out on a couple of chaises under the stars on the foredeck of the cruiser, the *Leona Vicario* from Playa del Carmen, as it headed north-northeast across calm water. We had finished a light supper, as Suter had described it—a loaf of bread, two bottles of beer, and a rubbery object the youngest crewman had found in the sea, hacked up on a board with a machete, and sprinkled with lime juice. Suter had asked me how I thought the fresh conch was, and I said fair.

"I'm capable of telling the truth when it suits my interests," Suter said, "which it frequently does, and which it certainly does now. Most people in Washington would describe me as a truth-teller, in fact. Of course, when it *doesn't* suit my interests to tell the truth . . . well . . . I guess you could say that that means I have some veracity issues to work on."

"That's how you might put it. I'd just say you're a liar."

"Not tonight." Suter waved his beer bottle at the magnificent starry vault above us. "How could anybody be anything but a truth-teller in the face of that?"

"Now there's a good line, Suter. A new one, too, for you."

He grinned.

"So where did you get the money that's in the suitcase? I saw you grab a gob of bills a while ago and pay off the captain of this boat. Is that suitcase you picked up in Playa stuffed entirely with U.S. currency?"

"Yes, it is." He smiled.

"Whose is it?"
"I'd say it's mine."
"Do the Ramoses say it's yours?"
He raised his bottle to the stars. "Fuck the Ramoses."
"Is it drug money?"
"Some of it."
"What's the rest of it?"
"The Ramoses' sources of income are wide-ranging."
"Uh-huh."
Suter added nothing more.
I said, "Won't they soon miss the money?"
"No."
"Why not?"

"Because it's cash Jorge has been skimming off the family operations over the past two years. He had it hidden under the roof of a house he owns in Playa. After I heard that Maynard had been shot and some of the Ramoses were out of control, I took the money and stashed it with some friends of mine in anticipation of what I am doing now—disappearing from the Ramoses radar screen. Jorge will have rushed back from Mérida tonight after hearing that I'm gone. But he won't be able to tell his family that I took three point two million dollars' worth of their money, because then they could say, 'What money, Jorge?' The Ramoses will be scouring eastern Mexico for me, not because I've got their money—which they will never be told about—but because of what I know about them."

"Because, for instance, the Ramoses know that you know that they bought the NAFTA vote."

"You got it."

"These assholes actually changed modern history. Jesus, Suter."

He shrugged. "There's no need to be melodramatic about it, Strachey. NAFTA might have passed anyway. It was close."

"Oh, well, when you put it that way . . ."

"It was a question of switching seventeen votes. Alan McChesney coordinated the campaign. I helped out, and so did a couple of other Hill people with Mexican-government business contacts and experience."

"Was the White House in on this?"

"Those clowns? Don't be silly."

"So the most historic piece of U.S. trade policy of the decade was made not by U.S. or Mexican elected officials, but by—who?"

Suter was staring at me now wide-eyed. "Are you really as naive as you sound?"

"No, I'm not. So who got what in return for their NAFTA votes?"

"The only outright buying of votes," Suter said conversationally, "was in the House. NAFTA pretty much sailed through the Senate. Of the seventeen House votes purchased, six were for vacation houses on the beach at Los Pájaros."

"Congressman Grandchamps, whom we saw on the beach on Wednesday, was one of those?"

"Right. Mexican law forbids outright ownership of beachfront property by foreigners, but there are easy ways around that. Banks hold the titles to property, and North Americans and other non-Mexicans buy long-term leases. So anybody planning on nailing the NAFTA vote-sellers need only follow the paper trail through the Mexican banking system."

"Okay. That's six."

"Another seven voters," Suter said, his curls fluttering in the warm breeze, "simply wanted campaign contributions that were laundered and untraceable. Vacation houses are nice, but for most House members reelection is what they anguish over night and day. They have to. It's how the system is set up. And overall, it works."

"It works for those who can afford to buy into it, yeah. So that's thirteen votes. Four to go."

"Three congressman wanted young women, and one wanted young men. There's nothing complicated about those motives, is there, Strachey?"

I said no.

"Strachey, you look discouraged." Suter shifted in his chaise and flopped a lithe bare leg over the side. "You needn't be. Few congressmen are out-and-out crooks like these seventeen. Most House members are—how to put it?—only as smart as they need to be. But they are, by and large, an honest lot who—even if they pocket wads of campaign cash in return for their votes—only accept cash and favors from those industry and other groups whose positions they honestly agree with. That's not corruption, that's enlightened self-interest."

"How did McChesney identify seventeen congressmen who were buyable on NAFTA? That must have been a project in itself."

Suter grinned. "You'll love this. Alan hired a psychological and public-opinion consulting service—an outfit that does focus groups and whatnot—and had these guys insinuate themselves into the summer party retreats in '93. Newt ran one for the Republicans and the Democrats had theirs—touchy-feely conferences where the participants all bare their ideological souls and plot strategy to save mankind through party-sponsored legislation. The consultants came back with a list of twenty-six names of male and female representatives of both parties who were considered buyable types. We only used seventeen names. The other nine Alan was holding in reserve."

I swigged from my beer. "Fascinating."

"Isn't it?"

"So who shot Maynard? And why?"

Suter said nothing. His bare chest rose and fell in the moonlight. He shifted on his chaise but didn't speak.

"Maynard was your friend," I said. "Once he'd been your lover. Not that that would have singled him out in a crowd."

Suter ignored the slur. After a moment, he said, "When Maynard saw me in Mérida last month, I was afraid something insane like this would happen. I'm just sick over the whole thing, honestly. I thank God Maynard survived the shooting. I just thank God for that."

"So who shot him?"

"According to Jorge, two of the Ramos drug gang in Alexandria shot and meant to kill Maynard. Alan McChesney told them to do it. Alan saw Maynard at the AIDS quilt display reading pages from the Betty Krumfutz campaign bio on the panel with my name on it, and Alan thought *I* had submitted the panel and was sending messages to Maynard and other people about where I was and what I knew about Alan and the Ramoses. Alan had the Ramos goons rip the papers off the panel, shoot Maynard, and search his house for connections with me as well as any incriminating information Maynard had that he might be getting ready to publish. Of course, no such information existed and Maynard had no such plans. Carmen LoBello had submitted the quilt panel to embarrass me, and the whole bloody chain of events started with nothing more than an absurd misunderstanding."

I thought again of Timmy and his feverish conspiracy theories, and I said, "In your letter from Mérida to Maynard warning him away from you and all this crazy crap, you instructed him not to reveal your whereabouts under any circumstances to *(a)* anyone on the Hill or *(b)* anyone in the D.C. Police Department. Why did you tell him that?"

"On the Hill, Alan might have heard about it. Alan knew where I was, of course, but what I was really telling Maynard was 'Don't connect yourself with me. Don't even mention me if you want to be safe from Alan and the Ramoses.' And the Ramos drug-operation people have their own dirty cop high up in the D.C. department. A Captain something-or-other."

"Milton Kingsley?"

"That's it."

So I was the chump, after all: the conspiracy-theory skeptic, the literal-minded (lapsed) Presbyterian, the naive provincial—Rutgers, Southeast Asia, Albany—who believed that individuals, simply being clumsy or neurotic, were behind nearly all major human folly. "My partner, Timothy Callahan—who attended parochial schools as a child—predicted some huge and melodramatic thing like what you have just described to me. I told him he was paranoid."

Suter laughed.

"I told him he'd read too much Sanders and Ambler and Ludlum. I told him the cause of almost all human misery is individual human weakness. I told him conspiracies like the one you just described to me exist only in popular entertainments and that real life is at the same time simpler and a hell of a lot more interesting than big, complicated, secret plots are."

"Sometimes real life is," Suter said, "but less and less so every day. Ludlum and Oliver Stone aren't just melodramatic entertainers. They are prophets, and they are manufacturers of self-fulfilling prophecies. Anyway, in the corporatized global economy, you don't call what happens conspiracies anymore. You call it integrated strategies."

"Someone else said nearly the same thing to me just last night. She called it synergy."

"All those guys on airplanes reading John Grisham might or might not share Grisham's moral disapproval of his worst characters' treacherous behavior. But mostly they read him because he describes the business and government world they know, or that they see coming and that they want a piece of. Human folly is still human folly, Strachey. It's just better organized and more efficient than it used to be."

"So what's the big difference between Big Brother Joe Stalin and Big Brother whatever it is you're endorsing here, Suter?"

"Much higher standard of living. Infinitely more personal freedom. Are you kidding, Strachey? There's no comparison."

"It's still Big Brother—Conglomerates and the Governments They Buy Big Brother—making people's decisions for them about the ways they'll live the only lives they'll ever have."

"Oh? So who's complaining?" Suter said dismissively, and opened another bottle of beer.

I said, "So. Did Alan McChesney have Bryant Ulmer killed?"

Suter nodded once.

"Why?"

"Because Ulmer, a bit of a wuss who couldn't be trusted, wasn't in on the Ramos-McChesney plan to fix NAFTA. And when Ulmer found out—Ian Williamson got drunk one night and let it slip—Bryant went to Burton Olds and threatened to go to the FBI if Burton didn't go himself. That wasn't going to happen, since Olds had been part of the scheme from the beginning and knew where all the bodies were buried. Olds warned Alan that Ulmer was about to stray from the reservation, and Alan had the Ramoses' drug people kill Ulmer on the street and make it look like a mugging."

Suter lay quietly, looking up at the stars. I said, "Did you know this at the time?"

"No. Jorge told me a few days later. It's part of what he had over me." Suter still did not look at me.

"And it was McChesney who ordered the murders of Nelson Krumfutz, Tammy Pam Jameson, and Hugh Myers just so they couldn't tell me that your big, elaborate diversionary tale about drug smuggling in Central Pennsylvania wasn't true?"

"You'll have to ask Jorge—or Alan. But that would be my guess."

I thought about everything Suter had just told me, and of his plans for us to make our way to Havana, and from there by air to Mexico City and on to Washington and directly to the Justice Department.

"Are you certain," I asked Suter, "that when we get back to Washington, you'll be able to make anybody important believe that this bizarre story of yours is true?"

"Oh, sure. Or if I don't, you will." I didn't know at the time what Suter meant by that. I should have asked, but—yet another botched job on my part—I didn't.

# 28

When I went belowdecks at eleven, Suter said he had some more letters to write—to his mother and to a couple other people he said would be concerned about his disappearance—and he said he would come down to his bunk in another hour or two. I had my own small cabin, and with the door securely locked from the inside, I went straight to sleep, body and soul depleted.

I awoke the next morning just after seven with the boat rolling this way and that way, and my stomach trying to keep up. Out my single porthole I could see low clouds and a choppy sea. In the distance, a palmy shoreline was visible, and green hills.

I shaved, washed up, dressed, and went in search of coffee. The galley was deserted—no steak and eggs sizzling on the grill, no conch fritters even—so I guessed Suter was still asleep. Up above, the second-youngest crew member was at the boat's wheel. The captain, seated nearby reading a Spanish-language edition of the *Miami Herald,* looked up impassively and said, *"Buenos días."*

I returned his greeting, and when he went abruptly back to his newspaper, I returned to the galley and found my own Nescafé and a couple of mushy *plátanos.* Nor was I optimistic about stumbling on an IHOP near the harbor in La Coloma.

By eight-thirty, with still no sign of Suter, I went up to the captain, who was back at the wheel as the *Leona Vicario* moved even closer to land. It was now evident, in fact, that a midsize harbor lay dead ahead.

*"¿Dónde está Señor Suter?"* I asked.

*"No hay."*

*"No hay?"*

The captain shook his head and retrieved a business-size envelope, folded in half, from his jacket pocket. He handed it to me and did not react in any way when I muttered, under my breath, "Hell."

I made my way to the aft deck, took a seat, and looked at the front of the envelope, which was addressed to "Married Man Donald Strachey, barricaded in his chambers." I opened the envelope and removed four handwritten, legal-size, yellow sheets of paper, taking care that they did not get away from me in the stiff breeze. The letter from Suter read:

> Dear Strachey,
>
> Sorry, my friend, but the plan I described to you—no can do. Oh, can—but won't. There's a better way for both of us.
>
> You go ahead and round up the bad guys. They're all yours. Be a moral hero—a role I seem destined not to play. I guess I've just got too many "issues"—or whatever you choose to call them.
>
> Enclosed herewith please find a list of the seventeen congressional out-and-out crooks, along with descriptions of their rewards for their NAFTA votes and the means by which these transactions were conducted and concealed by Alan McChesney. I'm not sure how exactly to nail McChesney for Bryant Ulmer's murder. But my guess is, once you nail McChesney on the NAFTA scam and tie him to the Ramoses, he'll go all blubbery and begin to name names—or Ian Williamson will, or better yet Jorge will, in order to strike a deal. Let's just hope that none of them implicates Hillary! Hey, just kidding about that.
>
> As for *moi*—what to do? I have no intention of putting myself at the mercy of pointy-headed bureaucrats, especially Clinton-administration pointy-headed

bureaucrats, who'll want to resettle me as a forest-fire-tower maintenance crew chief in Coeur d'Alene. I like the tropics. Washington? Los Pájaros? Havana? There's not much difference for me. So, by the time you read this, Strachey, I will have been picked up by an associate of Captain Muñoz off Cabo Corrientes and deposited there along with my ample grubstake.

You might reasonably ask, Strachey, why it's going to be socialist Cuba for a capitalist pig—weasel?—such as myself. Because, my friend, Cuba is nothing if not the future of capitalism in the Caribbean. Latin America knows this, and Europe, and Asia—they're all doing deals ten miles a minute with the socialist Cuban officials who will instantly metamorphose, I can assure you, into capitalist Cuban officials mere seconds after Fidel's last cigar finally explodes. Only Jesse Helms–ridden Washington—O! A principled man in the Congress!—is failing to prepare for that delicious, highly remunerative moment when Fidel croaks, and within days a thousand resorts and casinos and sneaker factories blossom!

But I'll be there—have, in fact, already made elaborate arrangements to establish myself quite soon under a new identity, the name on my passport of another country—my flag of convenience, as it were. I can't be the golden boy forever, Strachey, but I can be the man that the other golden boys wish to get to know better. We all do what we must in life, or, failing that, what we can. Am I right? What this all means is, finally I'll have the time and the wherewithal to write my novel.

I am honestly sorry to have fucked you over in this way, Strachey—even though you are, I have to say, one of the smuggest men I have ever known. Talk about *attitude.* And naive? Less so than you were just a week ago, I think. Still, you've got your simple charms. There's a part of me that will always remember fondly our fifteen minutes of love—rather a lengthy commitment, really, for a man as emotionally unreliable as I'm alleged to be by some. And, of course, I'll always grow sentimental whenever I think of the little viral souvenir I may or may not have left on your fetching upper lip.

Captain Muñoz has arranged for another associate of his to drive you the hundred miles from La Coloma to Havana airport, where a seat on a flight to Mexico City has been booked in your name and the ticket paid for. After that you're on your own.

Please extend my regrets once again to Maynard. Tell him I loved him more than any other man in Washington whom I ever made briefly happy. He's a real prize for whoever wins him.

So long, Strachey. Come for a visit in post-Millennium Havana. Bring your wise boyfriend—a man who obviously knows a lot about the nature of human folly, past, present, and future.

Altogether sincerely this time,
Jim Suter

I glanced at the pages with the names and details of the NAFTA scam, then refolded the papers and placed them back in the envelope. This I stuffed deep in my pants pocket as the *Leona Vicario* cruised into the harbor of a port town that looked as if not a single thing in it had changed in thirty-five years.

# 29

Twelve hours later, back in Washington, I found Timmy, as I hoped and expected I would, at Maynard's bedside. Timmy had now been at GW, either in Maynard's room or in the nearby lounge, for over forty-eight hours. Timmy wasn't his freshest. He was rumpled, needed airing, and had a two-day growth of beard. But he was as happy to see me intact as I was to find him safe and unharmed by the Ramos gang.

I ran through the entire story once for Timmy and Maynard. They listened, rapt—all but goggle-eyed—and they rarely interrupted me until I got to the part about my half-day transit through Cuba, about which Maynard wanted to know every last detail.

"I've got to track Jim down," Maynard said. "Jeez, what a story!"

"I think he'll be elusive."

"Oh, I can do it. I'll find him."

Timmy said to me, "So?"

"Uh-huh. I hear what you're thinking."

"Not to rub it in or anything."

"No, it would be unlike you to do that."

"But . . . I guess I was right about the conspiracy. Donald, you did have me wondering a few times if I wasn't just conjuring this stuff up—wild imaginings fed by my early historically suspect religious education. But I wasn't imagining much of it, was I?"

"No, Timothy, you were basically on the mark, conspiracy-theory-wise. I was wrong, and I apologize for . . . for living in the past. The recent past, but still the past. But now, as people keep explaining to me—Chondelle Dolan, then Suter—everything old is new again, in certain depressing ways."

"This plot does sound sixteenth-century Italian," Timmy said, "despite the contemporary terminology. I can almost imagine Machiavelli urging princes to maximize their possibilities for interface."

"So, what," Maynard asked, "are you going to do with the incriminating evidence Suter gave you? Incriminating, that is, if Jim didn't make all that stuff up about McChesney and Burton Olds and the Ramos family. And, of course, incriminating if the people making the big bucks off NAFTA don't immediately hatch an even more insidious plot to cover up the original one, and none of this ever comes out."

"At the airport," I said, "I made photocopies of the documents, as well as Jim's letter to me, minus personal references. I also phoned several interested parties, official and unofficial, and asked them to meet us here in this room at ten o'clock. Since it's a police matter and you're feeling so fit, Maynard, the head nurse said she thought that would be okay. I wasn't able to reach Bud Hively at the *Blade,* but Dana Mosel is coming, Chondelle Dolan, and of course the inevitable Ray Craig."

"Craig isn't a part of the conspiracy?" Timmy asked nervously.

"No, I think he likes to follow us around because he's in love with us. He doesn't know it yet, but it's either that or he's simply incompetent. Anyway, the Ramoses' man in the MPD is this Captain Milton Kingsley."

With that, Craig appeared in the doorway of Maynard's room, reeking, and fifteen minutes early. He must have heard what I said, but he did not react and just flopped onto the empty bed next to Maynard's and glared at me.

Chondelle Dolan soon arrived, then Dana Mosel from the *Post.* They all listened with fierce concentration and copious eyebrow-raising and jaw-dropping as I retold the story of the conspiracy to fix the NAFTA vote and the murders and the attempted murders it had led to directly and indirectly. Mosel took several pages of notes.

After I finished my narrative and passed out copies of Suter's annotated lists, Mosel asked for clarification on a number of points, to which Craig, in a surly tone, objected each time. "This is a matter for law enforcement," he snapped, "not for the media."

I ignored these pro forma protests and said to Mosel, after she'd run out of questions, "I believe, Dana, if I'm not mistaken, that you've got reporters and editors over at the *Post* with long experience in following money and paper trails. True?"

"We sure do."

"Well, I now offer this material from Jim Suter to you and to your paper free of charge."

"We couldn't accept it any other way. Thank you."

"What about the U.S. attorney's office?" Dolan asked. "Shouldn't they get a copy, too? A lot of the violations here are federal."

I asked, "Would you mind, Chondelle, providing copies of these papers to the feds first thing in the morning?"

"I surely will do that," she said.

Craig snorted, "This is not Lieutenant Dolan's case! Lieutenant Dolan has no official connection with this case, and if anybody goes to the U.S. attorney's office tomorrow, *I'll* do it!"

"Will you?" I asked.

"You're goddamn right I will. I'd love to nail Milton Kingsley to the wall. I've never understood how a man on a captain's salary can drive a Ferrari. I've had my suspicions about that man for years. I'll be on the feds' doorstep with this at eight A.M."

Dolan shrugged. "That's okay with me, Lieutenant."

I suggested that Craig might also try to serve as the MPD liaison to the Log Heaven and Engineville, Pennsylvania, police departments, and that way he would get a free trip somewhere nice, too. I didn't offer to accompany Craig to Central Pennsylvania, but I did plan to make one more trip there myself. This was to reassure Betty Krumfutz that whatever front-page news stories included her and her late husband's names in the coming months, none would mention her role-playing variations on Mayan ritual sacrifices. Only I knew about that—now that Nelson Krumfutz's photo album had presumably gone up in flames with his Engineville house—and I planned on 100 percent discretion when it came to certain noncriminal but nonetheless problematical matters that had cropped up inadvertently in recent weeks, including some of my own.

After Mosel left to catch a couple of *Post* editors before they retired for the night, and Dolan went to meet the date she'd left downstairs in the hospital lobby, and Ray Craig went off to arrange for a guard—instead of a tail—so that Timmy and I could safely return to our hotel room for the night, we said so long to Maynard.

"Thanks for clearing all this up, Don," he said, "and for giving me an incentive to go to Cuba. I've been wanting to write about Cuba for years, but I couldn't think of anything to say about it that hasn't already been written. Maybe I'll go down there and the story will turn out to be different—you always have to be ready to let that happen. But it sure sounds as if the Cuban story is, it's the next Cancún."

Timmy said, "Don't eat too many black beans while you're down there," and the two of them yukked it up over that.

We left Maynard for the night, met Craig at the nurses' station, and accompanied him down to his MPD car, parked, naturally, in the fire lane. Timmy and I held hands because we were happy to be reunited, and also because I wanted to show Craig how much we meant to each other, and to let him know that if he was in love with us, he was going to have to quit smoking and have all his clothes dry-cleaned before we would ever consider having him move in with us. I explained this to Timmy after we were back in our hotel room on Capitol Hill, and he said he understood that I was trying to be funny.

I told Timmy again how gratified and relieved I was to be back with him, and to be alone with him for the first time in days. I said I actually liked his two-day growth of beard—I'd never known Timmy to go this long without shaving—and he gave me a funny look and said, "I had a razor with me at the hospital, but I decided not to shave."

"You did? How come?"

"I'm growing a mustache."

"You? A mustache?"

He just kept giving me such an odd look, not entirely friendly either, and I thought, Oh hell.